THE VIOLENT ONES

By
E. HOWARD HUNT

I0616694

ARMCHAIR FICTION
PO Box 4369, Medford, Oregon 97504

INSIDE THE MIND OF A WATERGATE BURGLAR

It was a red fury that drove Paul Cameron to Paris, into a maelstrom of intrigue and violence. In the center of that whirlpool he found a flaming nightclub singer, a fortune in illegal gold—and quick death on every side. Here is a novel that carries you with breathless speed into an exciting adventure that will leave you breathless by story's end.

The author of "The Violent Ones" is Watergate burglar and infamous Nixon "plumber," E. Howard Hunt. Before his deep involvement in politics and national intelligence, Hunt was a mystery and intrigue writer for many years, right up into the 1950s. But it is his involvement with the CIA and the Nixon Administration that he will always be remembered for. Yet, it is clear that Hunt was a very skilled and knowledgeable fiction writer. In reading "The Violent Ones" it is fascinating to examine the fictional machinations of Howard Hunt's mind. Machinations that would eventually carry over into his real life profession as a CIA operative.

FOR A COMPLETE SECOND NOVEL, TURN TO PAGE 143

CAST OF CHARACTERS

PAUL CAMERON
Fresh out of prison, he went back to Paris to aid a friend, only to find the war wasn't really over, and he still couldn't trust anyone.

RUTH
Her virtues had dwindled over the years, so had her marriage to Cameron since she spent a lot of her time in bed with another man.

PHIL THORNE
He was Cameron's longtime friend and war buddy, but now he was in deep trouble. He wanted to live…<u>and</u> keep the bootie!

MARI
This beautiful nightclub singer had been just about everybody's "bed pal" during the war. Had she been too hardened for love?

MARCELLE
She was now playing a deadly game for gold. But she was full of lies and full of secrets—could she be trusted?

COUDET
This fat, balding embezzler should have been killed in the war. But at least he wasn't an outright murderer…or was he?

ASTREL
A "competent" Parisian policeman assigned to a murder case. The trouble was he couldn't—or wouldn't—solve it.

CHAPTER ONE

SEAT 23 on the New York-Paris flight had been empty since Shannon. The man in seat 25 was asleep, his right arm propping his body against the occasional yawing of the Constellation. When the plane banked slightly, the late-afternoon sun shone through the plexiglass window, touching the man's face. The light penetrated his eyelids, creating a changing world of red that hummed and pained until he woke and leaned forward. He put his face in his hands, felt the rasp of his day-old beard.

A stewardess was serving coffee a few seats ahead. When she came to seat 25, she said, "Coffee now, Mr. Cameron?"

He nodded and took the warm plastic cup from her hand.

"Too much sun? Shall I draw the curtain?"

"No. I want to see the coast of France."

She looked at her watch. "Landfall in forty minutes."

"Thanks."

She smiled, then moved aft, prim and poised and very certain of her place in a world ruled by men. When Cameron finished his coffee, he walked forward into the washroom, turned on the electric shaver, and sanded the stubble from his chin.

Washing in the small aluminum basin was not a success, and after he had dried his face he walked down the aisle to his seat. His eyes were still sensitive from sleep when he looked through the bubble window, down at the Irish Sea.

Clouds appeared suddenly, then vanished, leaving the plexiglass smeared with air-blown droplets that shivered past in the slipstream. The sea was calm in the late summer afternoon. Below, to the left, was a fishing smack, its wake a tracery of white from twelve thousand feet. Five miles ahead a tanker bore sluggishly toward Liverpool.

The dying sun gilded the sea, blinding him until he closed his eyes and turned away. Leaning back against the yielding upholstery, he felt the monotonous, boring vibration of the ship's four propellers. Their harmonic drone became a babel of voices that beat against his brain. The beat became a crescendo of pain and remembrance racking his mind until his body was weak, and his hands gripped the seat arms as though to restrain himself from running away.

He opened his hands slowly and looked at them. They were flushing with blood again, blood that surged back into the pallid, drained palms. Palms. Blood on the palms. Palm Sunday. Bloody Sunday, when you smashed the taunting face of a devil you hated—Roy Sprackling, who laughed when you learned about him and your wife. The sneering swine who had hit you first and kicked you when you were down; kicked you until you dragged yourself up and flat-handed the side of his devil's neck, dropping him to the rug, where he lay bloodily hemorrhaging, and you laughed uncontrollably until people took you away...

But even now you remembered the woman you had married. You recalled the lift of her breasts, the rise of her forehead, the slope of her flanks, the small curved gathering of her leg muscles. You remembered those things because over the years they had become part of you like your fingerprints, the color of your eyes, the rhythm of your heartbeat, unidentifiable from yourself. No separate entity, this old well-remembered smoldering coal of your loins. You would always remember, because it was the price you were paying for giving yourself away.

And Ruth would remember too. She had a good memory for faces, a good memory for bodies that had claimed her before yours. She had not forgotten Roy (the smooth-faced sneer, the locker-room laugh, the inflection of interrupted smut, the bravado of a ruttish boar), and she would never forget him now. She could never forget her lover lying on the floor; never forget the limpness of his hands, the twitching of his cheek, and the ashen face of the condemned paralytic. His half-dead, desiccated body was hers now. Hers alone, and forever.

The stewardess tapped his shoulder. He looked up to see her pointing below. "There's France," she said. "Have you seen it before?"

He nodded.

"Did you come over on business?"

"I'm not sure."

Her eyebrows drew together. "You don't know?"

"A friend asked me to come."

"Oh," she said uncertainly. "He must be a very good friend."

"We grew up together," Cameron said. "We were in the war together. As friends go, he's one of the best."

He watched her walk forward to the next seat, a little sorry that he had upset the pat little airlines speech she had been prepared to deliver.

But he had no plans for making a flight reservation west. He was nearing the end of a one-way ticket. Half an hour more and it would be up to Phil to tell him what the plans were. Cameron was glad that Phil Thorne had not been stateside when he was convicted for assault against Sprackling. Phil would have done something if he had been around. It would have been quixotic and unnecessary and would have helped no one at all. And the Foreign Service would not have approved.

The fields and forests below were beginning to purple in the June evening. It was the France that had raised him; the country he had known and loved and fought in and deserted. Now, in the end, he had come back to her, repentant for intervening infidelities. And for him, always, it would be a France of dusty, troop-trodden roads, and liberated *vin rose* and a girl named Marcelle...

The warning panel flashed red, and Cameron reached automatically for his seat belt. He tightened it across his thighs and lifted a battered briefcase to his lap. Looking at its scarred sides, he smiled wryly. It was not what Phil would carry, on an Atlantic crossing. It was not Mark Cross or Brooks. It did not say *Corps Diplomatique* each time you looked at it. Instead, it was old and comfortable and somehow sound, and the students who had watched him carry it to class so many times felt that he was probably a pretty good assistant professor of French.

The plane was west of Paris now, heading south for Orly. Below was Louveciennes, then La Celle St. Cloud; and glittering in the last light of day, Versailles's cross-like Grand Canal. From the air, Paris was an obese body supported by twenty-one spindly legs—routes from the provinces. It was a wax intaglio with careless spidery tendrils, a piece of spined costume jewelry, a diadem, a veined ulcer.

Now, to a rising whine, the flaps began to trail down and out from the long thin wings, slowing the plane like a liner backing its screws. The quick deceleration made Cameron lean forward, and as the plane banked heavily, he could see the runways of Orly, jeweled with lights in the new purple night.

The Constellation dropped like a bloated eagle toward the end of the runway. It settled in a rush of wind and slowing propellers. Cameron tensed himself for the initial wheel contacts, and when they came, concrete tearing the rubber nylon, searing, smoking, skidding, he took them easily, relaxing when the nose wheel touched and the plane was rolling smoothly parallel to the concrete.

It was eight o'clock when his passport had been stamped by the Surete, and he walked to the low customs barrier to claim his baggage. The mustached *douanier* said in English, "You have something to declare?"

In French, Cameron said, "Only the cigarettes."

"Nothing more?" the douanier asked in his native language, as he chalked a cross on Cameron's worn Gladstone.

"Nothing."

"Do you stay long in France, m'sieu?"

"One cannot know."

"You are glad to return to France?"

"Glad and not glad," Cameron said, lifting his bag from the barrier. "I am happy to see Paris again, but I regret the condition in which I will see her."

"Ah," the douanier said gravely. "I understand well. I, too, can manage a little philosophy. For eight hundred francs a day I stand behind this little cage and perform like an animal. I ask questions and I chalk the crosses." He chalked Cameron's brief case. "If you leave France again and return, be sure your valise is seen by me. I cannot ask questions of an American who speaks my tongue as you do; I will only chalk the crosses."

"I will arrange it," Cameron said. He shook hands with the douanier and pushed open the glass door that led to the airdrome's waiting room, looking for Phil as he walked.

A voice crackled over the public-address system, calling his name. There was a message, the voice said, awaiting M. Cameron at the information bureau. Cameron walked past the bureau and continued ahead until he had reached the opposite door. He opened it and walked down the queue of taxis until he found an empty one. The driver started the meter, and while the taxi was pulling out of line, Cameron leaned forward. He said, "Old friend, you appear to be a man of discretion."

The driver did not turn around. "Certainly," he said. "One does not conduct successfully a taxi for thirty-one years without acquiring a mountain of discretion."

"Then stop when we are beyond the lights, return to the waiting room, and claim a message for M. Cameron."

The taxi swayed to a stop. The driver turned around and peered at Cameron in the semidarkness. "You are M. Cameron?"

"It is a matter of concern?"

The driver shook his head. "It makes no difference. But to be certain, I understood you to say the name was Cameron."

"*Vous avez raison.*"

The driver opened the door and walked back along the drive, into the lighted area, and Cameron saw him open the glass doors.

The night, now, was fully dark. The meter glowed a little, and the headlights carved yellow sectors out of the darkness. A Citroen swung past the taxi, then a Renault; later two taxis and a Fiat. Finally Cameron heard the scrape of sole leather against macadam, and saw the drive returning. When he was beside Cameron's window, he reached inside and handed Cameron a small blue envelope. On it Thorne's printing had lettered "M. Paul Cameron."

The driver moved back of the wheel. "Is that what you desired?"

Cameron nodded. "This is it, old friend."

"You are reluctant to be seen?"

"Perhaps." He tore the end from the envelope and pulled out the folded sheet.

"No one saw me receive the message, m'sieu. The affair was managed with discretion."

"All matters should be managed with discretion."

"In France that is so. It is a way of life."

Cameron leaned forward, holding the sheet so that the meter light shone against it.

The driver said, "Where do you wish to go, m'sieu?"

Cameron squinted as he began to read Phil's careful writing. "The way of discretion, old friend. *Allons-y!*"

"Certainly, m'sieu. But with a view to precision, perhaps you will specify our destination."

Still reading, Cameron quoted: "The road of excess is the path to the palace of Wisdom."

"Parfait," the driver said. "And in this case?"

"For the moment, old friend, direct this ancient vehicle toward the Hotel Crillon."

"With pleasure." The driver meshed his gears. "A rendezvous, perhaps? Someone waits?"

"Sure," Cameron said, in English. "Someone always waits." He looked at the message and read it again. It said:

Couldn't break away in time to meet you, so I'll be waiting by the Bois— corner Blvd. Maillot and Blvd, des Sablons. My car will have one headlight burning. Pull up behind it, honk four times, and when I drive off, follow until I stop. Look back from time to time to see if we're being followed.

Cameron took a package of cigarettes from his pocket, struck a match, and lighted one. He leaned back against the torn, bulging upholstery and inhaled deeply. When he had exhaled to breathe again, he held the burning match under the message and watched it curl into ash and drop to the uncarpeted floor. Then he ground the ashes into nothingness with his heel and watched the gray, shadowed walls of the cemetery of Thiais until they were part of the darkness behind.

CHAPTER TWO

THEY HAD reached the Jardin du Luxembourg before Cameron noticed that thin summer rain had begun to fall. It misted the windows, diffusing the lights of Montparnasse, distorting the facade of St. Sulpice, and then a passing truck covered the windows with spray, making it impossible to distinguish the dark outlines along the Boulevard St. Germain. He leaned back and closed his eyes, trying to relax, until he felt the jolting cobbles of the Concorde bridge; then he gripped his brief case involuntarily and leaned forward to see the high, illuminated Obelisk, the dancing colored panaches that swirled over the fountains, and at the Tuileries the feeling came over him powerfully that his journey was at its ending.

At the corner of the Rue de Rivoli the driver turned and said, "I did not think you would choose the Hotel Crillon."

"Why not?"

"You are neither a tourist nor a diplomat."

"I can manage a certain amount of diplomacy," Cameron said. "When I have to."

"*Bien,*" the driver said. "It is a desirable facility when one has need of it."

"I am not well known for diplomatic action," Cameron said. "*Pas bien connu.*"

"Nor are you a type who would inquire of me where in Paris a lonely visitor might meet and enjoy a young girl for an evening."

"No."

"The thought does not interest you?"

"I know a dozen more *maisons de rendezvous* than you, old grandfather of procurers. Ours is a useless exchange of words."

"Not useless," the driver replied. "Futile, perhaps, but not useless."

The taxi slowed as it swung toward the curb in front of the Crillon. The driver bent forward, pulled back the hand brake, and turned to Cameron. "In this brief association," he said, "each of us has learned something of the other. You know that I am old, that I work when I can as a procurer, and that I am discreet."

The Crillon doorman opened the taxi door, and began lifting Cameron's valise. The driver continued, "I know of you that you are secretive, a little of the cynic, and that you have forgotten how to laugh."

Cameron gave him a five-hundred-franc note. "Be contented, old friend," he said. "I haven't heard anything funny since they lynched Mussolini." He got out of the taxi and followed the doorman through the rotating entrance door into the carpeted lobby. The doorman started to walk toward the desk, but Cameron said, "Not now. My room will not be ready, so I ask that you retain my valise until later."

The doorman nodded and Cameron tipped him.

"I understand, m'sieu. You will know how to regain it." He put down the valise and called sharply to a porter. Cameron walked down through the lobby and turned off into the lavatory. He washed his hands, splashed warm water across his face, dried himself, and walked back through the corridor. Before he reached the lobby, he went out the side entrance onto the street, and stood in the dim light looking up at the American Embassy until a cruising taxi pulled over to the curb.

Cameron got inside and closed the door. "Bois de Boulogne," he said. "At the corner of the Boulevard Maillot and the Boulevard des Sablons."

"Entendu," the driver said, touching his cap. He was young, and under the street light his face looked tired. He drove to the Faubourg St. Honore, turned left at the Palais d'Elysee to the Champs Elysees. The thinning rain was bringing people out of the sidewalk cafes, out of Foquets, Marignon; a queue was forming in front of a cinema that featured the Marx Brothers in *Horse Feathers.* Then the Claridge was at the right, and ahead he could see the magnificent bulk of the Arch, illuminated by the glaring brilliance of the Champs at night—the way it had looked before the war, not shadowed and mute as he had seen it last.

There, under the Arch, was the torch of the Unknown Soldier, leaping and flickering, fading and brightening anew in the rain-born wind. A pediment of the Arch obscured the flame as the driver turned into the wide-laned Etoile, and Cameron watched the whirling of the spoke-like avenues until the taxi headed west down the broad Avenue de la Grande Armee to the Porte Maillot; jogging onto the Boulevard Maillot, on past the entrance to the Bois de Boulogne (the wooded highway that led to the Pavilion d'Armenonville of other summers), slowing and hugging the curb behind a stiffly angular Rolls with a masked headlight.

"Voici," the driver said. "And now, m'sieu?"

"Press gently on your horn four times," Cameron said. In the taxi's headlights he could see the Rolls' black-and-white CD emblem, the bronze Embassy marker, and when the taxi's horn had bleated four times, the driver asked, "Like that?"

"Like that. And now let us follow."

The Rolls growled into life and moved ponderously ahead, turning into the Bois and the dark rain-drenched lane of the Route de Madrid. For five minutes Cameron watched the Rolls' tail light wind ahead, and when its brake lights glowed red, he leaned forward, money in hand, and said, "I'll get out here." He gave the driver two hundred francs. When the two cars had stopped, he opened the door and stepped onto moist gravel, blinking in the darkness, feeling the leaf-shed mist on his face, hearing the night sounds of a forest in the rain. The taxi backed, swung out onto the Route, and chugged away toward Longchamps. The Rolls' door opened, and when Cameron reached inside, his hand was gripped. A husky, well-known voice said, "Thank God you came, Paul."

Cameron gripped the hand of his friend. "You asked me at a good time, Phil," he said. "I was available." He sat on the seat and closed the door. There was a double window between the Americans and the chauffeur, but they spoke to each other in English.

Thorne's long, handsome face seemed drawn, his eyes uncertain. He said, "Sorry about the mysterious rendezvous, Cam."

Cameron shrugged. "There must be a reason behind it," he said. "We're getting old for games."

Thorne shook his head. "We're in the middle of one. A big one. When I wired you I knew it would be too big for me. I even thought I might be smothered before you got here."

"And now?"

Thorne's face lightened. "No problem," he said. "We'll have a few laughs and then pull out."

"How do you mean?"

"We'll retire...for life."

"That takes money."

"We've got it."

Cameron tapped his wallet. "My trial cost money; and they don't pay union rates in the pen. I've got less than two hundred dollars to my name."

"How much was your plane ticket?"

"Call it three-fifty."

Thorne took a thick sheaf of thousand-franc notes from an attaché case beside him, and put it on Cameron's lap. "Don't mind traveling, do you?"

Cameron looked at his friend. "I never have." He saw his friend's face soften.

Phil said, "Maybe this will make you forget."

"It could help."

"Want to tell me about it?"

"I sent you the clippings. You know as much as anyone."

Thorne's eyebrows raised. "Did you want to kill him?"

"I nearly did."

"And now?"

"I want to puke when I think about it."

"Why did you ever marry her, Cam?"

"Why does anyone get married? You can tell me as much as I can tell you. I wanted to live normally, have a wife, a home, and a family." He smiled crookedly at Thorne. "All I really got was a second mortgage."

Thorne said, "I met a girl a few months back..." then broke off, and looked at his attaché case. "You said you didn't care if this meant traveling."

"What goes with the ticket?"

"A name," Thorne said. "A name I'll give you later."

"A name and a game," Cameron said, looking at Phil.

"We've known each other for thirty years. Who would have thought we'd find ourselves mixed up in these things?"

Thorne looked away. "It happens," he said. "I'm not defending myself."

"What about your career?"

Thorne snorted. "The promotion's too slow," he said. "The pay's too small."

"You never needed money."

"I need it now. Lots of it." His hands opened and closed. "I've written my last report, kissed the Counselor's ass for the last time. I've wasted my life when I should have been living it."

Cameron put his hand on Phil's shoulder. "I won't ask questions. I won't ask what changed your way of thinking, and I won't try to talk you out of whatever you have in mind. I'm only an ex-con, Phil. What happens to me doesn't matter. If you want to change your mind, don't feel obligated to go through with it on my account."

Thorne looked out into the darkness. "You didn't have to say that, Cam. I know how you feel. The trouble is, you don't know how *I* feel. You don't know how I got into this business. It's out of character for both of us; but I won't be changing my mind."

"Why not?"

"Because I can't."

Cameron lighted a cigarette. He inhaled and exhaled before he spoke. "It would have to be something like that."

"It's why I left a message for you. It's why we're meeting like this...so they'll never find out about you."

"You'll tell me who 'they' are?"

"Not now. We haven't that much time. We'll have to meet later. At my apartment." Thorne took a deep breath and fumbled for a cigarette. "But we can cover part of it now. The part that's easy." He flicked open his lighter. The noise it made was precise, expensive. Its flame showed his face thinner than Cameron remembered it; thinner than in '44.

Thorne said, "Both of us fought here during the war, Cam. You got here the hard way—Utah Beach. I swung in on a chute and spent the next six months running from Krauts."

"That's an oversimplification," Cameron said. "I didn't like parachutes; you didn't like walking."

Thorne managed a smile. "You always built me up, Cam," he said. "Maybe that's what's wrong with me. Anyway, and those months I was back of the lines, working with the Resistance, I learned things that never added up, until a couple of months ago."

"Tell me," Cameron said. "Like what?"

"From the moment I hit French soil. I found out that the Resistance, as such, was a pretty shaky movement. Too many old hatreds for a strong and unified anti-German effort. Too many special interests."

"Like the FTP?"

Thorne nodded. "The Tireurs-et-Partisans had their own plans for France. Their boss, Thorez, was in Moscow getting briefed for his role as commissar. His toadies, Cachin and Casanova, went underground and laid down the line that the FTP would cooperate in a *maquis* with the Armee Secrete only so long as the FTP got what they wanted out of it."

"That's on the record."

"So it turned out that our people in London—politically unsophisticated—dropped arms and gold to the Maquisards without pausing to wonder what would happen to the arms and the gold after the Germans were gone."

"Do you know what happened?"

Thorne inhaled heavily. "I was with the Maquis at Charrou waiting for a big resupply drop. The planes came over the drop zone on time, and I saw the cylinders kicked out. Twelve of them."

"Go on."

"Only three cylinders showed up at our headquarters. Only three, Cam. And the cylinder that held the operational gold was missing."

"Expensive evening."

"Very. Only now I know the other nine cylinders weren't lost. They were located by The Faithful, and hidden. Cached. The FTP branch of our maquis didn't use the arms or the gold against the Germans. The comrades saved them for *la guerre apres la guerre*. The Commies were in the fifth-column business with our help, and they intended to stay in business after we went home and mothballed our uniforms."

"So?"

"In France, gold isn't hard to trace. It's illegal—like in the States. But so long as it's just gold, you can't do much with it. You have to take the metal somewhere and turn it into money."

"Switzerland?"

"That's the obvious place. Macao is another. Certain places in Hong Kong, Canton, and Bangkok will give you dollars or pounds or kronor or francs for gold—and at a damned good rate."

"The question emerges," Cameron said. "Who's got the gold?"

Thorne smiled thinly. "I know."

"How did you find out?"

"First, I agreed to help certain people get the gold out of the country. Then I figured out where the gold would be."

"They've waited this long to move it?"

"The gold disappeared in 1945. Now they have a lead on it, and I'm supposed to be ready to move it for them when it's located."

"Can you do it?"

"I can do it."

"Why would they move it now?"

Thorne ground out his cigarette in an armrest tray. "Two reasons, Cam. They're getting ready for trouble in France, and they've started trouble in Indo-China. Plenty of trouble. The kind that takes money and costs lives."

"To summarize: You've agreed to move gold for them, the location of which they don't know—but you do."

"That's it."

"I suppose it makes sense," Cameron said. "How do I fit in? Am I leaving France right away?"

"I'm not sure," Thorne said. He looked at his wristwatch. "Christ, I've got to run, Cam."

"How soon do we meet?"

"Midnight," Thorne said. "You've got the address—Quatorze Rue Chauveau-Lagarde."

"I take it you aren't working at the Embassy tonight."

"Hardly. I said I'd met a girl."

"You didn't have to tell me," Cameron said, a little irritated. "I figured it all by myself. I know the unimportant things, Phil. We'll have to cover the things that count later."

He felt Thorne's hand on his arm. "I'm sorry, Cam," Thorne said. "I'm a long way from myself. I'll try to catch up by midnight." Thorne opened the glass partition and spoke to the chauffeur. The Rolls engine boomed into life, and the heavy chassis lurched onto the lane again. When they were near the Cascade, the Rolls stopped and Cameron got out. The Rolls drove off, up the Allee de Longchamps toward Paris, and Cameron stood near a streetlight in the wind-borne mist until a cruising taxi stopped. He slammed the door, wiped the rain from his face, and said, "Hotel Crillon."

CHAPTER THREE

THE Crillon doorman said, "Ah, m'sieu, perhaps now your chambers will be prepared."

Cameron tipped him again and took the Gladstone and brief case. "Perhaps," he said. "However, my plans have changed. The climate does not appeal to me. I fly to Besancon."

"A formidable season," the doorman agreed. "Concurrent with the *grandes vacances—la cloture annuelle.*" He walked to the curb with Cameron and opened a taxi door. "Next week I entrain for Le Croisic. Perhaps you know Le Croisic, near the mouth of the Loire?"

"I have heard much good of it," Cameron said. He got inside the taxi, the door closed, and the taxi chugged away.

"Your destination?" the driver inquired.

"A hotel," Cameron said. "Near the Madeleine. Someplace inexpensive."

"Entendu," the driver said. "La Vaison, on the Rue de Seze."

"Allons," Cameron said. *"Allons-y."*

The Hotel Vaison had a one-eyed concierge, a cramped, dusty lobby with a cracked marble floor, and a lingering odor of meals prepared and eaten in antiquity. The open elevator rattled shakily against its metal guides as it bore Cameron to the fourth floor. Before he reached his room, he had decided that while the Vaison was better than a Montmartre hotel, within six months it would have to be rebuilt upward from the street, or razed from the top down.

He unpacked his Gladstone, hung two suits in the closet, examined the collars of his shirts for dust and frayage, put them in the armoire with his underwear, and lighted a cigarette. For a while he stood in front of the window, looking out over the roofs toward the Madeleine, silhouetted against the skyline. Then he wound his wristwatch.

He had been back in France a little over two hours.

Later, when he had shaved and changed his shirt, he rode the lift down to the lobby and hailed a taxi. Thorne's apartment was only five blocks away, but he was not due there until midnight. It was hard now to remember the places he had known before the war. Some of them would be closed now, out of business. Others would have been changed by the war; the owners dead or vanished, no longer on the scene to welcome their favorites. Instead, usurpers would be in charge, their followers changing the surroundings, the spirit and *ambiance* of the cafes he had known before. But after you were a certain age, you should stop reaching back; you should remain satisfied with your memories—the hazier, the better. Like the way he remembered the Cafe Adour, a few steps off the Quai on the Rue du Bac.

Cameron leaned forward and spoke to the driver. "Do you know the Cafe Adour?"

"Adour...Adour?" The driver scratched his head. "In Montparnasse?"

"No. Cross the Seine at the Pont Royal. Rue du Bac."

The driver nodded and swung south toward the Louvre. Now that the rain had stopped, traffic moved faster. Fiats and Simcas scuttled across intersections, dodging busses, policemen, and pedestrians. Cameron felt his body begin to charge with currents of anticipation. He trembled a little. It was as though fresh water were beginning to flood long unused conduits. His blood warmed and surged...

What you had gone through was like a long deadening torture that had in the end immunized you to pain and emotion. You had channeled your reactions so that now what you did, what you saw could not cake old wounds with salt. It had been a long, enforced anesthesia, blanketing you from the pain of the moment. The depths of suffering had of themselves produced opiates, and now that they were draining away, your flesh could glow, your mind could function, your thoughts could find expression...only not too much at once, he warned himself. Slowly, easily at first, until a wholeness exists. To rush, to exult would be to strain and rupture. Your mind would bleed again, slowly and sickeningly, like the oozing of mortal blood...

Past the Tuileries now, wet and glistening in the reflection of the streetlights. Then the taxi bucked upward to climb the arc of the bridge. Over the Seine, the Gare d'Orsay to the right, ending where the gray facade or apartments began along the Quai d'Orsay.

The driver slowed at the end of the bridge and said, "Where to, m'sieu?"

"Straight ahead," Cameron replied. "A few doors on the left."

He sat forward, leaning to one side so that he could look at the entrances on the Rue du Bac. One, two, three...then he saw the familiar hand-painted sign. He said, "Stop," sharply, involuntarily, and the taxi groaned to a stop. Cameron paid the driver and slammed the door behind him.

He looked at the nonprofessional lettering on the sign, "Cafe Adour," and thought that at least the sign was unchanged, as he remembered it. Music came from inside the cafe, its unfamiliar sound startling him. He had never before heard music at the Cafe Adour. There had been the harmony of good conversation, laughter, and women's voices; the aroma of *fines cafes* and the jingle of francs in Robert's cash drawer. But no instruments, no singing.

As he stepped down from the street, he told himself; Don't let this become a *recherche du temps perdu.* You'll stay here an hour, two hours, and you'll hate the changes you've found, you'll pay your bill and leave. Then you'll meet Phil and get back to the business at hand. You didn't come to France to rack yourself with memories. Prison ended everything. Phil offered a chance to crowd the past from your mind. Only don't romanticize an ordinary situation. Open the door, have your drink, and walk out.

He turned the tarnished brass handle and stepped into the cafe. Warmth surrounded him, the sound of a woman's singing filled the room, and while he stood uncertainly, a man in a dark business suit came toward him.

"A table, m'sieu?"

Cameron nodded and took off his coat. He carried it on his arm as he followed the man to a table near the end of the room. As he walked his eyes took in the changes: new tables, freshly painted walls, ceiling lights, a parquet dance floor, uniformed waiters, and a small dance band playing softly behind the spotlighted singer. Folding his coat over his chair, Cameron sat down and took a wine card from the man.

"Some wine, perhaps?" the man said in English.

"Some wine." He looked at the man. *"Une coupe de champagne."*

"T'ris bie," the man said, and folded the wine card. Cameron said, in French, "Also, for the sake of God, something to eat."

The man turned. "You surprise me, m'sieu," he said. "It does not seem possible that an American can speak like one of my countrymen."

"It is entirely possible," Cameron said. "What is there to eat?"

"For you," the man said, "a beefsteak. *A point?*"

"No. *Saignant.*"

"Hardly warmed," the man agreed. He scribbled the order on a pad, tore it off, and handed it to a waiter. He came closer to Cameron and asked, "This is your first visit to the Cafe Adour?"

"My first to *this* Cafe Adour."

The man shook his head. "You remember," he said sadly. "You are the first this month who knew it as I did."

"I came here often," Cameron said. "Not with these people, but with others. Here are only strangers."

"This new world is filled with strangers. The faces are new, but the ideas are old. Every day the ideas grow older. They hang in dark cellars and stink like rotten meat."

"I once knew a man named Robert," Cameron said, motioning the man to sit beside him. "But that was years ago."

"He was my brother," the man said. "I am Vincent."

"And Robert—is he dead?"

"In 1944," the brother replied. "There was little money and many bills. I remade the Adour. It was necessary to survive."

"I knew your brother well," Cameron said. "My father knew him, too."

The waiter came with a split of champagne and two glasses.

Vincent poured the champagne and raised his glass. "You were a friend of the old Adour," he said. "Let me hope that you will also be a friend of the new."

The cold, clear wine cut the tired thickness in Cameron's mouth. He drank deeply, and saw that the singer was about to begin a new song. As she started the first notes, he noticed that her voice was rich and moving, the accent strangely foreign. Her face was young and symmetrical. The nose was tilted slightly, the lips filled with motion. Her hair was very light, parted in the middle, and fluffed out so that the curls fell seemingly naturally in a crowning oval.

Vincent said, "You like the girl?"

"I haven't really listened," Cameron said.

"I think my patrons come here for Mari," Vincent said. "Truly, my wine is no better than that of a thousand other *boites* in Paris. My food is good, but as you will learn, not exceptional." He twirled the glass between his fingers. "Mari...it would be hard to find another such as she."

"What is her country?"

"Hungary."

"When did she come to France?"

Vincent shrugged expressively. "How is one to know? Mari has a dozen stories—a hundred. Sometime during the occupation, I think. Perhaps with a Boche. Who can say?"

"She is young."

Vincent nodded. "So she has many admirers—even some of influence."

"A protector?"

"I do not know. If so, it is of her choosing."

The waiter brought food for Cameron, who turned away from the singer. As he began to eat, her song ended and applause broke around his ears. He saw Vincent motion briefly, and in a moment heard beside him the rustle of silk and felt Mari's presence. He turned and rose as Vincent said, "Our guest was a friend of Robert."

Mari looked at him coldly. In French, she said to Vincent, "This pig eats when I sing. Must I sit with this American bag of stupidities and listen to his belching?"

In French, Cameron said, "I am enchanted to meet you, mademoiselle. If you will join us I will attempt to guard my stomach."

He heard the quick intake of her breath, saw the scarlet flush across her cheeks. Her eyes moved quickly from his. She stamped her foot at Vincent. "You make a fool of me," she said, and took

Cameron's champagne glass from the table. She emptied it quickly and threw it at Vincent. The glass shattered on the table and people turned to watch. Before she could turn away, Cameron caught her wrist and drew her toward a chair. He twisted her wrist lightly, and with a little cry she sat down in the chair beside Cameron.

Vincent said, "Little fool, you have made a spectacle of us; you with your tongue and your sudden angers."

A waiter quickly brought three fresh glasses and another split of champagne. Cameron felt Mari's eyes smoldering. He said, "The boss told me you brought business. Is this how you do it?"

She tossed her head and looked at Vincent.

Cameron picked up his knife and fork and cut a slice from his steak. He said, "I was at fault. One used to come to the Cafe Adour only to eat and drink. Now one comes only to listen." He swallowed some steak. "I did not know."

Vincent cleared his throat quickly and said to Cameron, "How long have you been back, m'sieu?"

Cameron drank a sip of champagne. "Since nightfall," he said.

Mari's eyes opened. "From America?"

Cameron nodded. "Why?"

She looked away. Her shoulders were round and molded, creamlike in their texture. Jeweled pendants hung from her ears. "I ask out of politeness," she said. "To show an American that we French have not forgotten our manners."

Cameron touched the rim of his glass. "Of the three of us," he said, "only one is French. *N'est-ce pas?*"

Mari said, "If I am not a citizen, this is my country of choice."

"Or opportunity," Cameron said. "I know your story, *cherie:* landed acres outside Budapest, titled ancestors; then the war and destitution. Suddenly a kind officer befriends you, takes you with him to Prague, Stuttgart, and finally Paris. That's fine, it's good fun—only the kind Colonel wears *feldwebel* gray and a monocle, and after D-Day you can't find him any more so you bleach your hair and start warbling scales."

Mari was rising slowly to her feet.

"Don't feel lonely," Cameron said. "It's not an unusual story. There are many like you in France: beautiful, burnished, and bought. If the Armee Secrete had found you in '45, they'd have shaved your head—if you'd been lucky!"

The blow was lightning fast, and it hurt. Her hand caught him just below the eye and rocked him in his chair. He saw her gather her skirts quickly and run toward the dressing-room door, heard the choking beginning of sobs.

He rubbed his cheek dazedly and looked at Vincent. Vincent said, "Perhaps you are right, m'sieu." He spread his hands. "But the war is over. The issue has been decided. We of the Adour try to forget." He stood up, wet a napkin in champagne, and handed it to Cameron to hold against his bruised cheek.

Cameron said, "I went too far. I didn't think she'd care."

"One cannot always be right," Vincent said. "Perhaps this time you were wrong." He moved toward Cameron. "Come back to the Adour," he said. "Come back when you can forget."

"I'll be back," Cameron said. He took away the napkin and felt his swelling cheek. "I'm not ready to say I was wrong...but maybe she really can sing."

"You will hear," Vincent said, "and now you will excuse me?"

"Certainement."

Vincent walked toward the entrance, and when his back was turned, Cameron rose and went quickly through the backstage door. The passage was narrow, and a woman's sobbing led him to a dressing room.

He stood for a moment, deciding what he would do, and then he pushed open the door. Mari was sitting in front of a dressing table, her head buried in her arms.

Her body shook as she cried.

Cameron walked to her and said, "I passed it out pretty freely back here. I didn't think it would make any difference." He kept talking as she turned to look up at him. "Maybe I was right, maybe I wasn't. That's not the point. The point is that I had no business opening up on you the way I did. You've got a right to put the past behind you. So have I."

She wiped tears from her eyes with the hem of her dress. Cameron felt himself beginning to relax. This was better. He could talk to the kid. He said, "If you say so, Mari, you're

French—born in Paris if you want—and with a hell of a Resistance record."

The girl said steadily, "Why do you come here now?"

"I told you," Cameron said. "I behaved badly. Unnecessarily so. I'm a little ashamed."

"You do not have to apologize," she said. "You are a patron. It is my job to entertain all who come to the, Cafe Adour."

"You don't have to entertain drunks or boors," Cameron said. "You're not a Montmartre *poule.*"

Mari stood up and righted a fallen slipper with her toe. "You know nothing of me, m'sieu—no more than I know of you. So do not decide what I am." She put her hands on his shoulders. "What would you say if I told you that until last week I lived in an apartment over the Quai—that an Englishman provided the apartment? That and much more?"

Cameron looked at her small hands with their fine surface veins. "I'd say it was your affair."

"You would not ask why I sent him away?"

"If I'm supposed to." He took her wrists in his hands. "Why did you send him away?"

"Because he talked of his wife. Always of the cold English marble. This man, he wanted to talk of his wife when he was with me, and feel shame." Her hands moved toward his neck. "What would an American talk about?"

"Not about his wife," Cameron said. He did not want to kiss the full lips so close to his, but suddenly the space between them vanished, and her lips were on his, her teeth hurting him. He released her wrists and held her hips. Her body seemed to mold itself against his and he could feel its beating pulse. His left hand cupped the hollow of her neck.

There was a knock on the door. *"Encore, Mademoiselle Mari,"* the callboy's voice said. Her body stiffened. She moved away and quickly began brushing her hair. *"Merci,"* she called. *"Immediatement."*

Cameron walked to the door. He opened it, and she said, "You will hear my songs?"

"Not tonight."

"You will come back again?"

"If you wish."

She turned and faced him angrily. "We would not have embraced if I had not liked you."

"Oh?" he said. "I hadn't realized it was anything personal. I said to myself. She's just a girl who's naturally friendly."

He closed the door and her hairbrush struck the place where his head had been. He went back to his table, paid his bill, and looked for Vincent before he left. While he was walking up the stone steps to the street he could hear Mari's voice singing in the café behind him.

CHAPTER FOUR

IN THE *conciergerie* of Phil's apartment building, Cameron pressed the lift button and waited until the cage settled and stopped at the ground floor. It took him slowly to the fifth floor, and as he closed the guard door, the hands of his wrist watch lay at midnight.

The hallway carpet felt over-thick, as though for tenants who wanted to keep secret their arrivals and departures. An engraved card on the third door carried Phil's name. Cameron rang the bell.

He listened for Phil's approaching steps, and not hearing them, started to reach again for the button. But the door opened quickly and he saw Phil, collar open, hair disheveled, motioning him inside. When the door closed Cameron saw that it was thick enough to make the apartment almost soundproof. He took off his trench coat and offered Thorne a cigarette. Then he realized that Thorne was not entirely sober.

Phil said, "Always be punctual, Cam. Always do things on time." He swayed a little as he walked into the study. Cameron followed him and said, "Something wrong with punctuality?"

"No," Thorne said. He sat in a chair behind a large carved desk. "Points up sense of responsibility. Responsibility among thieves. Like dressing for dinner in the jungle." He licked the cigarette in his hand and lighted it. The wavering flame blackened the white tube to his fingers. Thorne cursed softly and shook his hand.

Cameron sat in an overstuffed chair and said, "You're over your ears in sauce, Phil. We'll talk tomorrow."

"Can't wait," Thorne said. "Got too much to say. Plans to make." He looked at Cameron, and his eyes wavered. The fine, thoroughbred face was hazy in the weak light of the desk lamp. The eyes were sunken.

Cameron said, "You're tired, Phil. We'll let this wait."

Thorne shook his head. He ran his fingers through his hair and made an effort to concentrate. "Shouldn't have got you into this," he said. "Too much to ask."

"Your face has the pleasant color of a slug's belly," Cameron said. "I'm putting you to bed."

"No," Thorne said. "No time for that. I'm not sick. Just had too much brandy."

"You were never a guy for the sauce," Cameron said. "What happened to you?"

"Good question." Thorne's elbows were on the desk, his hands supporting his head. "Pertinent question. What happened to Thorne?"

Cameron lighted a cigarette. He looked for physical evidence of drinking, but saw none. Thorne said, "I never missed Sunday school, never cut a class in college. Always on time at the Embassy. Great future...great future." His face relaxed, his gaze became piercing. "Only there's no future left for either of us."

Cameron leaned forward and put his hands on the edge of the desk. "I didn't fly across the Atlantic to have you tell me there's no future ahead—nothing worth living for. I could figure that out in prison. If you're willing to lie down and be walked on, you'll do it alone." He stood up, and saw Phil's eyes rise in alarm.

"Don't go, Cam," Phil's voice pleaded. The slackness was gone from it. "I'm indulging myself too much. Feeling sorry, telling myself I'm not to blame."

Cameron sat down. "Tell me about it," he said. "Give me the picture now. The details can wait."

Thorne exhaled, then stubbed out the cigarette on an Italian ceramic tile. He sat upright, brushed back his hair, and began. "I took a few days' leave last spring," he said. "I'd been working hard—felt played out. Went to Cannes, but the weather was bad. I'd driven down, so I kept driving. Nice first, then Monaco. Finally Menton."

"Why Menton?"

Thorne shrugged. "Less French than the others. More Italian. I stayed at Menton."

"What kept you?"

"A wheel," Thorne said. "A wheel and an ivory ball."

Cameron nodded. "I can take it from there," he said. "You won, then lost; then you won again, and when you lost a good deal, you plunged."

"I'd been overworked and I wanted excitement." Thorne smiled crookedly. "I got it."

"How much did you lose?"

"Over a million francs. Close to fifty thousand dollars."

"So you wrote a check."

Thorne nodded. "It was the only thing I could do. The woman who owned the casino agreed to hold it for a year—with interest."

"How generous," Cameron said. He sat back and looked up at the dim ceiling. "But in a few weeks she got in touch with you. Said she'd suffered reverses, needed the money. If you didn't redeem the check she'd turn it over to the Embassy."

"She said that and more," Thorne said. "It wasn't very original and it wasn't very subtle. She knew damned well I couldn't possibly get the money. And she knew the Foreign Service doesn't like its officers writing bad checks."

"So you came to an agreement with her," Cameron said. "What was her proposition?"

"The gold," Thorne said. "Getting the gold out of France. Getting it to Saigon."

"Can you do it?"

Thorne nodded.

"And how do I fit in?"

"You'll be waiting for it," Thorne said. "They'll have a man ready to receive it, but you'll get it."

"And what happens to you?"

"I'll be on my way to meet you."

Cameron looked at his dying cigarette. "You said they weren't sure they had the gold. Do you have it?"

"Not yet."

"But you know where it is."

"I can touch it whenever I want to."

"Then why don't we hijack it, buy back your check, and call the thing square?"

"If they were just hoods it might work," Thorne said, "but they're more than criminals. They're fanatics—dedicated to world revolution. You can't buy them off. You can't make peace with them." He wiped his forehead. "We could never come back to France again. We'll have to start life somewhere else."

"I'm looking forward to that," Cameron said. "And just in passing, whose gold is it?"

"It came from Fort Knox," Thorne said. "It was a wartime operational expenditure, like a tank or a plane. The French government claims it; our military attaché has orders about it. The Armee Secrete alumni and the FTP comrades would like it. Everybody wants a private army," he said. "The guy with the gold can be general."

Cameron leaned forward and offered Thorne another cigarette. Light from the desk lamp fell across his face. Thorne touched his cheek. "What happened, Cam? You've got a hell of a bruise there."

"I went back to the Cafe Adour," Cameron said. "I preferred eating to listening, and the singer resented it."

"Mari?"

Cameron nodded. "You know her?"

"Everyone does."

"Not much of a recommendation."

"She's not a girl I'd recommend."

"Because she's kept?"

Thorne laughed. "Hell, no. That would disqualify most of the women in Paris. Mari knows too many people, hears too much, plays too hard." He looked at Cameron. "She's not the kind you'd want to bring home to Mother."

"I haven't thought about Mother all day," Cameron said. "Mari knows what she is, and she's honest enough to admit it."

"That's part of her charm," Thorne said. "But she's still a whore."

The word slapped Cameron. He felt his lips contract, tasted hers again, felt the pressure of her body. Almost unconsciously he wiped his lips with the back of his hand. He said, "Is she Hungarian?"

"She's just a good diplomatic lay," Thorne answered. "Nonpartisan. She'll go with the Russian consul one night and attend a Croix de Feu meeting the next."

The telephone jangled suddenly and Thorne answered it. He spoke in monosyllables, quietly at first, then animatedly. When he replaced the receiver, he stood up. "I've got to go," he said. "Meeting someone."

"A woman?"

Thorne buttoned his collar. He nodded.

"Mari?"

"Hell, no. Why?"

"You know so much about her."

Thorne picked up his tie from the desk and tied it. "I know what everyone else knows," he said. "Forget her."

"Where are you going?"

"I'll be back," Thorne said. "Wait here for me."

Cameron stood up and stretched. "Give me a few names to think about," he said, "unless you've got a collection of feelthy postcards."

Thorne scribbled on a pad. He tore off a sheet of paper and handed it to Cameron. "Think about these until I get back."

Cameron looked at the three written names. "Victor Coudet," he said.

Thorne put on his coat. "Chief of a wartime Gaullist maquis," he said. "I knew him well during the Resistance days. He's looking for the gold."

"Georges Venat."

"The FTP commissar of our maquis. Georges was headed high if the Russians had reached Brest. Right now he's in disfavor with the Party. Figures he can square himself if he pulls this coup with the gold."

"Claude Astrel."

"A Surete inspector. Claude wants to claim the gold for France—he says."

"All honorable men, I'm sure," Cameron said. He walked to the door with Thorne. "Going far?"

"Not far. And not for long. A *bistro* down Malesherbes."

"So long."

Cameron saw Thorne walk toward the lift, then closed the door. He came back into the study, turned on the big Dutch-made radio, and listened to a record program from Luxembourg. When he tried to light a cigarette, his lighter sparked dryly, and he went to Thorne's desk for a match. Striking one against its box, he noticed a picture under the glass desktop. He caught his breath and forgot the burning match in his hand. He looked at the girl's face, at her eyes, her forehead, her hair, until suddenly his fingers pained and he dropped the charring match.

He put the cigarette in his mouth and looked at the door. Was Phil with her now? Was he meeting Marcelle somewhere for a drink, arranging another rendezvous? And how had their paths crossed? She must be the girl Phil had mentioned in the car. And presumably Phil did not know that he had known Marcelle or that she had known Cameron—that he had seen her last on the road to Rouen, almost four years ago.

He felt sweat stand out on his forehead. He sat down in Phil's chair and took the cigarette from his mouth. Unconsciously his fingers shredded the rolled tobacco, letting it drop onto the rug. Then he looked away from the light and dropped his head to his arm. Blood pumped through his brain, making his bruised cheek throb. The radio blared the end of a French jazz record.

It was, the announcer said, half an hour after midnight.

His mouth felt as though it were coated with shellac. The glass desk cover was sticky with spilled cognac. A brandy glass lay on its side, the rim chipped in falling. Cameron touched it with his finger; it rolled in a circle, back to his finger. The radio made staccato testing sounds. The room was damp; he felt suddenly cold.

Wiping his lips on the back of his hand, he sat up, eyes avoiding the light. The room was empty. Phil had probably come in and gone to bed. Cameron looked at his watch: nearly four o'clock. He turned, rose, and went to the window. Parting the curtain, he looked down into the street. Streetlights flickered through a suspension of fog. Somewhere in the neighborhood an automobile horn bleated. No one walked the street below; there was no sound of life.

Turning from the window, Cameron fumbled for a cigarette and lighted it, his hands feeling as though they wore gloves. He walked to the radio and turned it off. Funny Phil hadn't done that when he came back. There on the desk was the paper on which Phil had written the three names. Cameron took it in his fingers, creased it slowly, and stuck it into a coat pocket. His knees were beginning to ache; he had been drunk. He had looked at a picture and folded. Now he knew he must see her again. Phil would know how to reach her. Phil would tell, or by God... He found himself walking quickly down the corridor toward the bedroom. The door was open and Cameron flicked on the light. He took a deep breath and leaned against the wall. The bed was untouched.

Cameron looked into the bathroom, the kitchen, and out into the hall. Only emptiness. A strange feeling of loneliness came over him. What had happened since midnight, while his brain was sodden, his body numb?

And then, as his senses cleared, as his conscious self regained control of his reasoning, a question forced its way into his mind, shaking him as it emerged: Where, exactly, was Phil Thorne?

In the bathroom, while water plunged into the bowl, Cameron looked at his face in the mirror. His eyes were puffy and bloodshot, his cheek still discolored from Mari's blow. He soaked a bath towel in cold water and scrubbed his face with it. Then he threw it into the tub, turned off the water, and went back to the study. He wrote a note for Thorne: "Waited until four-thirty. Call you tomorrow."

Then he took his trench coat and hat from the hall chair and went out into the corridor, locking the door behind him. He did not wait for the elevator, but went quickly down the five flights of carpeted stairs into the dark conciergerie. He opened and closed the glass door quietly, and as he buttoned his coat against the penetrating fog, gray light from the street outlined something lying on the marble at his feet.

Bending over, he touched the object's bulk, and knew that it was human. His eyes saw a hat lying nearby. The body wore a light topcoat; it lay limply, like a broken marionette. Cameron's fingers could find no pulse. His right hand turned the head upward, the neck swiveling unresistingly.

Striking a match, he shielded it and looked down; then he blew out the flame and got quickly to his feet. Even with the staring, inverted eyes, the lips contorted in the grin of death, the body was Phil Thorne.

His neck, Cameron knew, had been broken.

Everything that had happened since his return to France swept over him in a hideous cacophony of voices, sounds, and sensations. He walked away from the body, into the darkness of the conciergerie. Leaning against the wall, he threw up. When his stomach had emptied itself, he forced himself to breathe deeply, regularly, and then he went back to the corpse. Now he would have to go back to Phil's apartment to destroy the note he had left.

Methodically, he began searching the corpse's pockets for a key.

CHAPTER FIVE

HE CARRIED Phil's body into the conciergerie on his back, grasping the stiffening wrists with his hands, and began the long climb upward, leaning forward to balance the body's weight. By the time he had reached the apartment, his heart was pounding insanely and his eyes felt as though his brain were pushing them out of their sockets. In front of the door, he lowered the body until he could turn the key in the lock. Then he trundled the cold, dead weight inside and locked the door.

Cameron went into the study, poured brandy into a glass, and drank it down. Then he carried the body into the bedroom and rolled it onto the bed. By now his strength had almost failed. He sat beside Phil's body, shaking, and emptied the pockets onto the bed. There was a bundle of francs, several identification cards, ration coupons, an address book, four telephone tokens, and a Beretta 9-mm automatic pistol.

The pistol's magazine was full; it had not been fired. Cameron put the pistol in a pocket of his trench coat, looked at the identification cards, and returned them to the beautifully tooled billfold. He kept all but thirty-five hundred francs, pocketed the address book, and went out of the bedroom. In the bathroom he retrieved the soggy towel he had used, and went over the apartment trying to remember where he might have left fingerprints. He washed his brandy glass and replaced it on the shelf with the others. He wiped the cognac bottle, then took it into the bedroom and pressed it against Phil's hands.

In the study he raised the glass desk cover, took out Marcelle's picture, and wiped the glass clean. He burnished the faucets and the radio dials, then he turned off the study light and looked down at the street. There were no policemen below. The Rue Chauveau-Lagarde was empty.

Going down the stairs, he made himself analyze the situation that faced him: Phil's body would be found within two days at the most. If Cameron reported the murder he would be placed under suspicion (no alibi, bruised face), and if the Surete didn't find Phil's murderer, they'd put the arm on Cameron. They'd learn about Marcelle, about Ruth, about the trial.

When he reached the conciergerie, he stepped around the place where Thorne's body had lain. His stomach began to turn over again, but the cognac had given him a false, momentary strength. As he turned onto the sidewalk, the Beretta slapped his thigh reassuringly.

Cameron did not go directly to the Rue de Seze; he avoided the open Place de la Madeleine by turning down the Rue de l'Arcade and cutting through the Cite Berryer to the Rue Tronchet, and finally down Rue Vignon to the Hotel Vaison.

The Vaison's night concierge snored, his head leaning against a defaced mailbox. His thick lips fell away from the gums, revealing tobacco-blackened teeth. His adenoidal breathing covered the sound of Cameron's climbing footsteps.

In five minutes Cameron had packed. He must leave now, unobtrusively; wait someplace where he would be inconspicuous until he could take a train from Paris. Where he went was unimportant; what was important was to stay out of jail until the killer was caught, or until Cameron could piece things together from the few clues Phil had left behind. If he went to a small city, he would be noticed; Dijon, Lyon, Avignon were out. Brussels was too expensive; Holland, too remote.

Spain? No, he had no visa. Getting one would take a couple of days. He could be traced in Spain; extradited. Then why not Italy? No visa necessary. Naples, Bologna, Rome. One more American would not be noticed in the flood of summer tourists. He took the Beretta from his trench coat, forced back the slide, and ejected a cartridge. The pistol was in excellent condition. He returned the cartridge to the magazine, slid it inside the grip, and put the pistol into his trouser pocket.

In the bathroom, Cameron saw that his beard had darkened his face, but the bruise stood out, red and blue from subcutaneous hemorrhage. It pained when he touched it. He decided to shave before leaving the hotel.

While he was taking his shaving articles from the Gladstone, he looked again at Phil's address book. Scrawled inside the front cover was the name Verlalx; inside the back: Monceau. The names could mean anything, anybody. He closed the address book, put it in his shaving kit, and went into the bathroom.

He had finished shaving and was rinsing his face when there was a knock at the door. Probably the waiter to ask what he wanted for breakfast. Yet it was not even six o'clock. He draped the towel over his neck and opened the door.

A woman pushed the door toward him, came into the room, and closed the door behind her. She said, "Where is he?"

Cameron walked back toward the bathroom. "I'm not a tourist," he said, "and it's too early for commercial pleasure. Or too late. Try me again, about noon. He took his shirt from the doorknob and began putting it on.

"Where is M. Thorne?"

Deliberately, he said, "Why would I know?"

She walked toward him, into the light from the door. She was young and small and her face looked very tired. She looked older than the last time he had seen her—older, even, than the picture he had taken from Phil's desk. His heart began to pound, and he said, "Why do you care where he is, Marcelle?"

She stiffened at the sound of her name. "He was to meet me last night." She turned and looked at the Gladstone lying on the bed. "When did you return to France?"

"Last night," he said. His hands were beginning to shake. He had difficulty buttoning his shirt. "How did you know I was here?"

"Philip told me."

"You lie," he said. "He told no one." Cameron walked into the bedroom, taking his tie from the bed. "You told him you knew me?"

"Never."

"Why not?"

"It did not seem necessary. He fell in love with me. You were in America. Not even a letter…"

He took her wrists roughly. "When did you meet him?"

"In April."

"Where?"

"At a resort."

"For what reason did you meet him?"

She twisted out of his grasp. "I was ordered," she said. Her lips were defiant. "I owe nothing to anyone. Nothing at all to you."

"You didn't know I was in France. Someone followed me. Then you came to inquire." He tied his tie. "Why?"

"Because I fear for Philip."

He laughed shortly. "You're a little late, Marcelle," he said. He took a key from his pocket and held it between his fingers. "If you want him, you'll need this. He doesn't open doors anymore."

She gasped, her face whitened. "Dead?"

"Murdered," Cameron said. "They broke his neck like a chicken's." He caught her wrists again. "I think you knew about it all the time. Whose side were you working for, Marcelle?" He reached toward the telephone.

"What are you going to do?"

"I'm going to conduct a speed test," he said. "We'll see how fast the police can get up here. I want to learn how long it takes them to make a woman talk."

She screamed piercingly, but his hand covered her mouth, cutting it off. When she bit his hand he struck her mouth. Blood began to flow. Tears flooded her eyes, her shoulders shook rackingly. He drew her roughly to him, his mind beginning to spin. He said, "A man's dead. Maybe you helped kill him."

"No," she said, sobbingly. "No, *no!*"

"I didn't think you'd say you had." He held her face between his hands. "Who did it?"

"I don't know."

He struck her. As her head snapped back, he struck it again. Blood trickled from the corners of her mouth; her face was marked with streaks of red and white. He brought her to him again, and drew her lips to his. They were hard, compressed. He forced them apart and tasted blood. Her body went limp. Cameron pushed her down on the bed. "I dreamed of kissing you again," he said, and wiped his lips on his wrist. "Only it wasn't like this in my dream."

She sat crying on the bed, while he put on his coat. She said, "Why don't you telephone?"

"I'd rather take you there," he said. "I wouldn't like to explain how you happened to be here."

Behind him a man's voice said, "Just how *would* you explain it, m'sieu?"

Marcelle said, "Victor!"

Cameron turned slowly. *"Alors,"* he said. "The jackals gather. Welcome, M. Coudet."

The man was nearly as tall as Cameron. He was middle-aged, balding, and he held a pistol in his hand. He came toward Marcelle and helped her from the bed. His left hand touched her face, and he said, "My dear, did he kill our Philip?"

Marcelle shook her head. The man began searching the Gladstone.

Cameron laughed. "Let's call the police," he suggested. "Let's turn over our problem to them."

Coudet shook his head. "We are not quite ready to admit the problem is that complicated." He moved away from the Gladstone.

Cameron looked at Coudet's hands. "You couldn't have broken his neck," he said. "Not alone. Not unless someone held him for you."

The pistol moved quickly. "Woman-beater," Coudet spat. "I should shoot you now."

"Make awfully sure," Cameron said. "If you don't kill me with the first shot, I'll beat you to death with your own gun."

Coudet began backing from the room, talking in a low voice to Marcelle. Cameron felt cold sweat in his palms; he wanted to rush Coudet, kick his stomach, see the gun fly upward, then choke him to death. Coudet opened the door, and Cameron said to Marcelle, "Hurry back, sweetheart. We've got memories to relive; explanations to make." The door closed and he was alone.

Sitting on the edge of the bed, Cameron felt the old weakness come over him. This time it came as a compound of fatigue, fear, and shock. There was a knock at the door, and Cameron rose wearily to answer it.

A porter said, "Are you ill, m'sieu? We have heard sounds…"

"Bring me a brandy," Cameron said.

"But, m'sieu, it is not yet permitted. In a few hours."

"Now," Cameron said. "Bring it." He closed the door and walked back to the bed. He straightened his disarranged clothing, repacked his bag, and when the brandy came, he drank it, paid the man, and put on his trench coat and hat.

After he had paid his night's bill at the desk, he carried his brief case and Gladstone as far as the Place de la Madeleine and hailed a passing taxi.

The driver said, "Gare St. Lazare?"

"No. Rue du Bac."

"What number?"

"Cafe Adour."

As the taxi moved through the almost vacant streets, Cameron watched charwomen walking to work in the early dawn; bicyclists with handlebar baskets of bread sticks careening rapidly down the Rue Cambon. Newsvendors were opening up their kiosks. At the Rue Castiglione, Cameron had the driver stop. He motioned to a man lounging beside a newsstand, and bought a copy of each morning paper on sale.

By the time the taxi had reached the Pont Royal, he had read their front pages. Phil's body had not yet been found. Leaving the papers on the taxi's seat, Cameron got out at the Cafe Adour. He paid the driver and went down the steps to the closed door. It was locked, and he could see no one inside. He walked up to the pavement and stood, wondering what he could do next, when an old woman, shabbily dressed, walked past him and down the steps.

He heard the grating of a key in a lock, and turned quickly. "Madame," he said, "perhaps you will allow me a favor."

"Of what nature, m'sieu?" she asked disinterestedly. The door swung open.

"I need a small amount of information," he said.

She looked at him from head to foot. "If you want to know about Mari, I will tell you that you do not have money enough for her."

"I am her cousin," he said. "Her Hungarian cousin." He took two one-thousand-franc notes from his pocket and handed them down to her.

The old lady stuffed the paper money into the folds of her dress. "Welcome to Paris, Hungarian cousin," she said. "Mari lives nearby." She pointed toward the Quai. "Five entrances to the left, then to the third floor."

"A thousand thanks," Cameron said. "I have come far to see her."

The charwoman snorted. "If you are fortunate, a bed will be waiting." The door closed loudly.

Cameron picked up his luggage and walked toward the Quai.

He stood in a hallway outside a door. A plate of polished silver was set into a dark oak panel. A name was engraved on the silver. The name was Mari.

Cameron rang the chimes and listened to their echoes die away down the corridor. He looked out of the hall window and saw the Louvre, gray and cold and formal, on the other bank of the Seine. A few cars moved over the Pont du Carrousel; a skiff cast off into the Seine's slow current. A few early risers walked rapidly in the cool summer morning.

He listened, then pushed the chime button again. He looked at his wristwatch until two minutes had passed. Then he turned his back to the doorway and leaned on the button. The chimes began a repetitive, echoing fusion of sounds that mounted in volume until, suddenly, the door opened, and he turned to see Mari.

"Are you alone?" he asked, picking up his luggage.

"Why?"

"I need a few hours' sleep."

"Where were you last night?"

"I talk better inside."

"No." She started to close the door.

Cameron swung the Gladstone against the door panel. Its impetus opened the door, pushed Mari aside. Cameron stepped in and closed the door behind him.

"What do you want?" Her face was expressionless.

"A little sympathy." Cameron began walking toward the rear of the apartment.

Mari followed him, her arms clasped in front of her, hugging the thin, peach-colored negligee to her body. She said, "How long do you want to stay?"

"Expecting somebody?"

"Only for dinner."

"I'll eat in my room."

"You'll be gone."

Cameron laughed. She said, "I can call the police."

He had reached an open door. Inside was an unused bed. He motioned toward it and she nodded.

He said, "In the next few days you may hear a lot about me, but you won't believe it."

"Why won't I?"

He sat on the edge of the bed, took off his coat, and unlaced his shoes. He straightened up and undid his tie. "You won't want to believe it."

She pushed aside his brief case with the tip of her satin mule, touched her cheeks with her palms. "So now it begins again for me," she said wearily. "Now you come into my life to change it again, twist it, shake it beyond recognition."

"It doesn't have to be that way."

She touched his forehead with the tips of her fingers. They felt cool, steady, relaxing. She said, "You are married."

He pulled his shirt over his head. "Not now."

Cameron reached for her hand and pulled her down beside him. "Listen," he said. "A man was killed last night."

"Who?"

"A friend."

"I am sorry. One has many enemies; so few friends."

He nodded. "I started to leave Paris, but I was seen. Now I must stay."

"What can I do?"

"Say I'm your cousin. From Debrecen." He stood up and went to the bureau. He opened a drawer.

"What are you looking for?"

"Pajamas. I thought the Englishman might have left a pair."

"You bastard," she said thickly. "What an animal you are to remind me of him!"

Cameron closed the drawer and went back to the bed, conscious that her eyes were on his. He sat down and fatigue engulfed him; his eyes pained. He reached back to uncover the pillows, and felt her move into his arms. The negligee parted.

He told himself that he did not want to make love now, that he could not do justice to the challenge. He did not want to look bad in comparison to the others. Leaning back, he pulled her to him, feeling her full breasts against his body, the warmth of her thighs on his.

Slowly she said, "You will hurt me, *mon cher.*"

"No."

"You would not intend to, but you will." She put a finger to his lips. "Some men are like that. I see it in you."

He shook his head, but her lips were on his, seeking him eagerly, painfully, relentlessly. He turned on his side so it would be easier for both of them.

CHAPTER SIX

WHEN he woke, Mari was gone and he had no idea what time it was. He bathed, shaved, dressed, and walked out of the room into the connecting corridor. He called, "Mari...Mari," then waited for her footsteps.

Behind him, a voice said, "You are hungry, m'sieu?"

He turned quickly, but saw only a uniformed maid. He said, "I am hungry."

"A place is set for you in the dining room."

"*Merci.* And where is Madame?"

"I don't know, m'sieu. She said only that her cousin had arrived this morning, and that he would be hungry."

Cameron nodded, and walked into the dining room. "What time is it?"

"Almost three, m'sieu."

Not a long rest, he thought, only a displaced sleep. He remembered Mari and wondered when she would return. The maid brought calf's liver and a rasher of bacon; *haricots verts, pommes frites*, a light cheese soufflé, and coffee. He ate quickly, and left the apartment.

At the Pont de Solferino he crossed the Seine mingling with the mid-afternoon crowds. He walked to the Orangerie and took a taxi to the Trocadero. There was a *brasserie* he remembered at the Place d'Iena. Sitting at a sidewalk table, he sipped a vermouth-cassis and read the Paris newspapers. So far, there was nothing about Phil. He looked up at the Tour Eiffel, remembering the first time he had gone there with his father. It had been then, as today, warm and pleasant. His father had bought him a balloon, and while he had been eating mint ice on the open terrace, the string had slipped from his hand, and the orange balloon had risen swiftly, like a frightened bird, until it had topped the Tricolor at the apex of the tower. Even now, Cameron could remember leaning against the railing, looking upward until the balloon was lost in the clear blue sky.

For a while your life could be controlled, then one day something slipped and you lost control. After that you were a creature of chance, rising or falling with the currents of existence, but always aware of the ultimate rendezvous.

Through chance he had rediscovered Marcelle; through chance he had met Mari. For an hour, he had known her incredible, demanding passion; he had experienced Marcelle's love for weeks. What was she doing with Coudet? What was her relationship to this countryman of hers? What had she been to Phil?

He thought of his friend's body, cold and contracted, lying in a darkened room, oblivious to the sounds of life from the street below. But Phil was not lying there. Phil had laughed and left the room last night, promising to return. He had not returned. What Cameron had stumbled over on the dark paving was not Phil. The clothing was the same, so were the hair and eyes, but the limp weight he had carried upstairs was not the Phil he had known, not the guy he had grown up with.

Cameron tried to think of Phil at something he liked doing: racing an MG or a Lancia from Narbonne to Hyeres; following the Tour de France; walking in the Bois de Vincennes...

That was how you had to think of someone who was gone. *Dead.* It was a word you read in the newspapers; death was something that happened to someone else far away. Yet it had come to Philip Thorne, leaving behind a gray white corpse that was probably beginning to smell up an otherwise tasteful room. Because you could think objectively of death did not mean less regard for your friend, less respect for death. It meant, instead, that where there had been two, there was now only one—and but for chance, again, the survivor would have been out of France by several hours.

Thorne had not wanted to die. He had not expected death in the darkness when the killer broke his neck. Maybe he was knocked out first, so the murderer could make certain of the job. In any event, you owed Phil a try at the one who did him in. You had fought his battles before; another one would be no novelty. So that brought it back to you—to you and the man somewhere in Paris who had closed your friend's eyes, stopped his heart from beating, his ears from hearing, his body from feeling... The issue was clear.

Cameron got up, walked inside the brasserie, and began looking through a telephone directory, searching the A's. The name was easy to find: Astrel, Claude.

A woman's voice answered the telephone. *"Qui?"*

"M. Astrel, please."

"He is not here. At four o'clock he is in his office."

"Thank you," Cameron said. "Unfortunately I have forgotten M. Astrel's number."

"Ministere de l'Interieur."

"Of course," Cameron said. He went back to his table, paid for his vermouth-cassis, and caught a taxi to the Place Beauvau.

Troisieme Inspecteur Claude Astrel sat behind a scarred antique desk in a dark, high-ceilinged room. The carpet was worn, the thick green curtain moth-eaten. Afternoon sunlight filtered through a grilled window, mottling Astrel's fat, oval face. Two staring eyes protruded from his shaven, Ottoman skull. Astrel ejected a butt from his gold cigarette holder. He pushed Cameron's passport back across the oiled tabletop. "You have an interesting history, m'sieu."

"Have I?"

The bald head nodded slowly. The protuberant eyes watched sausage-like fingers insert a dark Oriental cigarette into the burnished gold tube. A match ignited the cigarette. A cloud of heavily aromatic smoke issued from the blubber lips. They said, "An interesting history—none of which is reflected in your passport."

Astrel pushed a buzzer, and in a moment a uniformed man entered, carrying a dossier. "When you, an American, request an appointment—in excellent French—I am moved to inquire concerning your history." He looked at the dossier on the desk, but did not open it. "You are a man of violence, m'sieu," he said. He smiled. The lips drew back over thick, white teeth.

"Of violence?"

"Yes. I think so." He opened the dossier and ran his finger down a page. "With little provocation you attempted to kill a man." He looked up at Cameron.

"He was my wife's lover," Cameron said. "What would you do? Give him a house in the country so they could meet more privately?"

Laughter began somewhere deep inside the dark blue uniform. It shook the wattles under Astrel's chin, contorted his puffy cheeks, compressed his eyes. Finally it stopped.

Cameron said, "I served time for what I did."

Astrel nodded. He closed the folder. "Nevertheless, a man lies paralyzed. Never to move again, never to know the ecstasy of passion, never again to possess a woman."

"He found ecstasy with the wrong woman," Cameron said. "I imagine he finds time now for memories."

Astrel exhaled a cloud of smoke. "One must tire of looking at the ceiling. The creature would be better if he were dead."

"Perhaps," Cameron said. "I'll let this be a lesson to me."

Astrel looked at him quickly. Too quickly, Cameron thought. The American said, "One of my friends is missing."

"M. Thorne?"

"Yes."

Astrel extended a little finger, drew a writing pad under his palm. "How many days?"

"I don't know. He was to meet me last night at Orly. He never appeared."

"How disquieting. Perhaps he drank too much and sought solace with a poule."

"If he'd drunk too much he'd have more sense than to go with a woman."

"You know him very well?"

"We were like brothers," Cameron said. "We grew up together."

Astrel nodded. "Your father once was consul at Lyon."

"Phil's father was consul general."

"And now the son is lost. Have you any thought where he might be?"

"None," Cameron said. (Did the thick lips droop disappointedly?)

"Who are his friends in Paris?"

"I don't know. He wrote of friends, but the letters are destroyed."

"Yet you remembered my name."

"He wrote it recently."

"What did he say about me?"

"Very little," Cameron said. "He wrote that you were an important member of the Surete and that he had occasion to see you on certain matters."

The eyes stared fixedly at Cameron. "You do not recall the matters of which he wrote?"

"He did not specify."

Astrel inhaled deeply, pushed his chair a few inches from the desk. Cameron could see his belly now, but it was not fat in the sense that Goring had been fat. It was part of his contour, of the man's gross solidity. Astrel said, "I will confide in you, m'sieu. M. Thorne and I have a mutual interest. It is an affair of gold."

"Gold?"

"M. Thorne desires to claim it for his government; I, for mine." He looked at Cameron and his eyelids seemed to flicker. "Before the gold may be claimed, it must be found."

"*D'accord.*"

Astrel laid down his cigarette holder. He leaned toward Cameron. "And why did you come to France, m'sieu?"

"I needed a holiday."

Astrel shook his head. "We have a copy of the cable sent you by M. Thorne. He requested your presence in France." He blinked at Cameron. "What assistance did he ask you to render?"

"He hasn't asked me," Cameron said. "Maybe he will when he sees me."

Astrel smiled. "We will exert every effort to discover your friend. The case is close to me, for M. Thorne is my friend, too."

Cameron rose.

"You have not inquired of your Embassy?"

"Not yet."

"Then I will inquire for you," Astrel said. He did not rise. Cameron picked up his passport, put it inside his coat pocket. His fingertips touched the smooth side of Phil's Beretta.

"Where may one reach you, M. Cameron?"

"Cafe Adour. Vincent will know."

"A convenient address," Astrel said. He waved his hand toward the door, and Cameron walked away from the desk. At the door Cameron heard his thick voice say, "Let us hope our friend is found very soon."

Cameron said, "Do you think he is dead?"

"I did not say so."

"It was your implication."

Astrel stood up. "Do *you* think he is dead?" Cameron closed the door.

He walked the four blocks to the American Embassy in the warm afternoon sunlight. Music came from a children's carrousel in a small tree-shaded park; candy butchers, ice-cream vendors, and balloon salesmen added their colors, noise, and odors to the quiet Paris air. He was sorry when he reached the quiet, tree-shaded Avenue Gabriel, leaving behind him the sunshine, the vivid scenes of life, and the good memories that had touched him for a few minutes.

Turning in the front gate, he walked across the cobbled courtyard toward the Embassy entrance, then changed his mind and walked back to the Avenue Gabriel. He stood at the corner of the Place de la Concorde, looking across the gray-white expanse at the Obelisk, the fountains, the bridge, the facade of government buildings across the Seine, and then he stopped a taxi.

Riding across the Seine, he told himself that he would go back to the Embassy tomorrow; talk with Phil's secretary when there was more time. Maybe she would know other names; maybe she could supply some of the missing pieces. Someone would have to.

He got out of the taxi at the Cafe Adour and went down the steps and through the open door. Someone said, "The cafe is not yet open, m'sieu."

A woman was singing in the dimness at the far end.

Cameron said to the waiter, "I'm not hungry," walked past him, and sat at a table beside the dance floor. Mari had not yet seen him. Her face was hidden behind a song sheet. She sang:

"Il fait nuit dans man coeur,
Plus un reve a l'horizon,
Plus une lueur..."

until she had seen him. Then she lowered the music and sang to him, without faltering, until the song was finished. Then she nodded toward him and the accompanist began another song.

Cameron motioned toward the waiter. *"Vermouth a la glace* for me; champagne for Mlle. Mari."

She smiled when she saw him order, and when the song was over she said something to her accompanist, put her music on the piano top, and came to Cameron's table.

She sat and said, "What made you willing to hear me sing?"

"Circumstances."

"Because we were together this morning?"

"No." He gave her a cigarette, lighted it.

"*Alors?*"

"I wasn't happy at what I've been doing. I wanted to find you."

"Did you sleep late?"

"Nearly three." The waiter arrived with their drinks.

Mari sipped the champagne. "Are you staying with me tonight?"

He shrugged his shoulders.

Her brows furrowed angrily. "Is the service not satisfactory?"

"Hardly that. I don't know where I'll be from one minute to the next." He finished his vermouth quickly. "Can we go?"

"Why not? It cannot matter greatly to you whether my songs are sung perfectly or whether I require more practice."

He took her arm tightly. "You worry too much about yourself," he said. "You should be worrying about me."

They walked to the apartment, and when they were inside he drew her to him with a quickness and a desire that shamed him. Wanting to be with her, he knew, was an escape from the reality of the Rue Chauveau-Lagarde. He could find forgetfulness in their emotional maelstrom—forgetfulness of the staring-eyed corpse, of the bloated Astrel, of Marcelle, whom he'd never possessed... He said, "I want you, Mari."

"Later." She began to draw away.

"No. Now."

"Here?"

He nodded and kissed her again. Her blouse fell to the floor; her shoes tumbled against a leg of the divan. He could feel her nails cutting into his naked shoulders.

When he woke, he was in his bedroom. The window was dark. He turned on the light, and raised himself to his elbows. The time was after nine.

He heard Mari's steps coming toward the door, and called, "I'm awake."

The door opened and she stood there perfectly gowned, beautifully coiffeured, newly made-up, her lips looking as though they had never been touched. She said, "This paper is for you." She unrolled a copy of *Ce Soir* that she had been carrying in her hand. The black streamer said, CORPSE OF AMERICAN DIPLOMAT FOUND. A lead flared: NECK BRUTALLY BROKEN.

Cameron put down the paper. "Well," he said, "now you know."

"Are you in danger?"

"Probably."

"You must leave France."

"Not yet. Not until I know who killed him."

He heard her catch her breath. "You did not kill this man?"

"You think I did?"

Her face flushed. "It does not matter."

"I didn't kill him." He put his hands around his neck. "But I'm just guillotine size." He got out of bed and held her from behind, so that he would not crush her flowers, so that he would not be tempted to kiss her again. "You've got a boarder, cherie. Worried?"

She said nothing for a moment. Then she turned and kissed him lightly. "I don't want you to go," she said. "Not just yet. Not while you need me."

CHAPTER SEVEN

THAT NIGHT he did not leave Mari's apartment; nor the next day, nor that night. Why return to the reality of the police, of Astrel, when there was food and drink and Mari in the dark quietness of a bedroom over the Quai?

Then, on the third day, while Mari was at the cafe running through some new songs from the *Gaie Paix Ou?* score, Cameron began drinking black coffee and thumbing through Phil's address book. Beside one of the names was a penciled notation: "Fridays."

Nothing more.

The name was Barjeval. Mme. Pierre Barjeval. The address was an apartment somewhere toward Courbevoie, near the Ile de la Grande Jatte. The Rue Perronet.

Cameron thought of calling her, and looked through the telephone directory. The 1947 directory did not carry the name of

Pierre Barjeval. Cameron wondered who she was. Someone Phil had admired, probably. Cocktails with her every Friday. If she saw Phil that frequently, she could know who his friends were; perhaps even his enemies.

Cameron shaved, splashed cold water over his face, and stood on the Quai waiting for a taxi. The day was damp and drizzling. A gray fog rose from the Seine, hiding even the opposite banks. Finally an ancient Renault, plowing through puddles, its headlights glowing, stopped and took him a board.

Traffic was almost at a standstill, and after half an hour they had only reached the Porte des Ternes. It reminded him of other gray afternoons he had known in France; as a schoolboy confined to his home; as a dogface slogging down the rutted road between Marie-du-Mont and Carentan the summer of Marcelle. Cameron remembered how he had met her, the way he had fallen in love, and the memories spun around and around until he realized that the driver was shouting at him, and that the taxi had stopped on the Rue Perronet.

A cardboard sign propped against the lift housing said that it was not running because of the rationing of electricity. Cameron learned from the concierge that Mme. Barjeval lived on the second floor, that she was an elderly lady whose husband had died during the war.

He rang the bell and waited until he heard the soft, measured tread of a woman's feet. The door opened and the woman said, "I am Mme. Barjeval. Do you wish to speak with me?"

"My name is Cameron—a friend of Philip Thorne."

The door opened wider. The lady stood aside so that Cameron could enter. She was tall and her hair was quite gray. Her face was lined, but Cameron could see that the features were fine and that once she had been beautiful. Although her dress was old and stained, her manner was patrician. Probably eccentric.

The apartment was almost completely dark. Cameron struck a match to find a chair. Mme. Barjeval said, "Forgive me m'sieu I will turn on the lights." She touched a hall switch and there was light in the room. She moved gracefully toward Cameron and said, "I had not planned to see anyone for another hour. That is why you find me in darkness." She sat in a chair a few feet from

Cameron, and as she turned toward him, he realized that she was blind. The discovery chilled him, and he found himself gripping the arms of his chair. He said, "You were expecting M. Thorne?"

"It is Friday," she said simply. "Philip calls each Friday at five." She smiled a little. "But if you are his friend you would know that."

"I know that," Cameron said. "I didn't realize it was Friday."

"Then you will stay until Philip comes?"

The words were out before he could stop them: "He's dead, Mme. Barjeval."

Her body stiffened, her face froze—all but the corners of her mouth. They were working rapidly, the taut muscles straining against collapse.

Cameron said, "I'm sorry I said it so brutally, Mme. Barjeval, but he was killed."

He waited then until she spoke. Her breath came gaspingly, forcing out the words: "Someone from the Maquis?"

The question surprised him. It had not occurred to him that she would know that phase of Phil's life. He said, "I don't know. The murderer hasn't been found."

"When did it happen?"

"Three nights ago." He told her briefly why he had come to France, what had happened since then, and why he had decided to seek her out.

She said, "You must wonder why he bothered with an old woman like me."

Cameron started to reply, but she continued: "We were comrades during the war. This apartment you are in was a safe house used by the Armee Secrete. Many Allied flyers rested here until they could be taken to the Channel. I was, as I am now, blind. So the Germans, and the *milice*, did not think I could aid my country."

"They couldn't afford a mistake like that."

"You are generous." She sat more erectly, more stiffly, as though to stress the militancy of her courage. "One day a man of importance was brought here—I will not trouble you with his name—and his escort was Philip. Someone informed the *milice*. The search was close—up and down the Rue Peronnet—but we were not discovered. It was then that Philip promised he would come back to see me—I, an old, forgotten woman." She paused and touched the corners of her eyes with a white lace handkerchief. "He kept his promise. Hundreds of hours we have talked here, sitting where you and I sit now. He had become my only channel to the outside world—my eyes..." She began to cry noiselessly. Cameron went to the old walnut sideboard, poured a small glass of cognac, and brought it back to her.

"You are kind to an old woman," she said. "I am grateful." She rose. "If you will trust my slight ability, I will prepare coffee for us."

"Of course." He rose, and followed her into the kitchen. He could see that although there might be dust in the corners of the room, Mme. Barjeval had scrubbed shining each pot and each pan. She went unhesitatingly to a cupboard, opened it, and brought out a can of American coffee. She held it toward Cameron and said, "Philip brought this to me. There are so many things one cannot find any more." She moved from the sink to the stove, measuring the coffee and water, lighting the stove's feeble gas flame, and finally, when there was coffee steaming and black, Cameron carried their cups into the salon.

He said, "Philip was in trouble, Mme. Barjeval. Did he speak of it to you?"

She shook her head slowly. "He did not have to tell me, M. Cameron. His voice told me. After he returned from Menton the change occurred."

"Yes."

"Did he tell you what had happened?"

"No," Cameron lied. "He was killed before he had time." He looked out of the windows at the darkening buildings across the street. "Did he mention any names to you?"

"A few. One Mme. du Casse, who owns the gambling casino at Menton."

"Good," Cameron said. "Astrel?"

She nodded. "One of our wartime associates."

"Verrat?"

"Another."

"Anyone named Monceau?"

"No."

"Then what places might be named Monceau?"

"There is a street, a park, a square, and a villa. Is that enough?"

"Too many," Cameron said. "How about the name Verlaix?"

"There were two of them in the Maquis," she said. "They were brothers; a foundry worker and a juggler. The *milice* killed one. The other was reported to have fled from France."

"Which one escaped?"

"The juggler."

"Where would he be?"

She shrugged her shoulders. "Even for a very good juggler life would now be quite hard. Perhaps he is in Belgium, or Spain, or Switzerland. Even South America."

Cameron shook his head—always too much or not enough. He asked, "Did you ever hear him mention a girl named Marcelle?"

"Many times, m'sieu. She has even been here with Philip. For coffee."

"How recently?"

"Three Fridays ago. I was given to understand that they were in love. Did they plan to marry?"

"I wasn't told," Cameron said evenly. His stomach began to tighten again. He felt hollow suddenly. "Do you know where she lived?" He hoped that Mme. Barjeval would not know, so that he could forget Marcelle. But the old lady said, "Marcelle called to thank me for her visit and left her address. Rue Dunois, number eighty-five."

"You have a remarkable memory," Cameron said. His mouth was unpleasantly dry. He finished his coffee.

Mme. Barjeval heard the sound of his cup on the saucer. She said, "Is there some way in which I may help?"

"Only one," he said. "If the police ask for me, I must trust your discretion."

"I am asked many questions," she said. "I answer only those I choose." She rose steadily, tautly, and extended her hand. "May I hope that you will sometime return here, m'sieu? My weeks will be long, now that Friday has lost its significance."

"Of course I'll come."

"If you have lost a brother, I have lost a son." Two tears appeared under her eyes, rolled downward, and dropped.

Cameron said, "Phil was fortunate to have known you, Mme. Barjeval. I know that I am fortunate, too."

"*Au revoir,*" she said. "I will pray for Philip—and for you."

"When the man is found, you will be the first to know." He went out of the door and walked down the stairs, through the conciergerie and onto the street. The rain had stopped, but the fog was as dense as before. Darkness would come early to Paris tonight. A cold wind from the Seine brushed his face, chilling him as he walked four blocks to the Partes des Ternes. He bought a third-class Metro ticket to the Madeleine, changed at the Etoile, and when he climbed up the steps at the exit, he saw that darkness had finally come.

Cameron walked three blocks to Phil's apartment building, mingling with the early evening crowd that jammed the narrow sidewalks. There was a key in his pocket, and as he touched it, it seemed to chill his fingers. He could think of no reason to return. Unless the apartment had been rented or placed under Embassy seal, it would be vacant, empty of everything but memories of a white, tortured face, of a stiffening body facing the ceiling—of the death of a man who had been his closest friend...

He turned into the doorway, took the lift to the floor above Phil's, and stood at the head of the stairs listening.

No sounds came from the floor below.

As he walked quietly down, he could hear children's voices, food frying on a stove. From somewhere across the Rue Chauveau-Lagarde a piano echoed hollowly. Outside the door he listened again; listened for footsteps or the sound of drawers being opened. Then he took a deep breath, turned the key in the lock, and went in. The apartment was dark; the blinds were closed. He walked toward the study desk and turned on the lamp. As he raised his head he caught sight of a man's face: thin, crooked lips, colorless eyes, an arm descending on his head. Something hit his skull, blinding him with pain. Then he felt himself fall against the desk and the pain drifted away, taking him into a soundless labyrinth where he held his breath and waited in the dark for the Minotaur...

His face was being slapped. Hard. Stingingly. He raised his hands to protect his eyes and a voice said, "Good evening, M. Cameron."

He opened his eyes and blinked. Light hurt his pupils. He looked away, at his legs lying before him, oddly crumpled and relaxed. He tried to move them and saw them bend. Hands helped him to his feet, pushed him into a chair. He put his elbows on the desk, held his face with his hands. The voice said, "you are not badly hurt, m'sieu. There was no blood."

"Fine," he said, and turned to see Claude Astrel's bloated face looking down at him. "Fine. There's no blood, so I'm perfectly O.K. Is that the way the Surete figures it?"

"In your case it suffices."

He touched the back of his head. A monstrous boil had ripened on his skull. He drew away his fingers. If he touched it again it would burst. He closed his eyelids and said, "Who hit me?"

"What were you doing here?"

"Who hit me?" He heard the scratch of a match. A cigarette was lighted. Smoke seemed to billow in front of his face. The harsh smell nauseated him. He coughed and staggered from the desk, sat down in an upholstered chair. Pain beat through him like a metronome.

Astrel said, "You are more fortunate than your friend; your neck is entirely whole."

"I'm lucky." He got up, went to the cabinet, and drank a double shot of cognac. He leaned against the cabinet and said, "I asked you who hit me."

"A man named Verrat."

"Oh." He looked at the empty glass and filled it again with cognac.

"You have heard of Verrat?"

"No," he lied. "Who is he?"

"Nobody...now. But he was an important man once. If the Russians were to occupy France, he would be important again."

"A Communist."

Astrel inclined his head.

"How do you happen to be here?"

"We have been watching M. Verrat. He entered the apartment; you followed. I heard you fall, but by the time I reached you he had gone."

"How?"

Astrel gestured casually. "The kitchen window. The fire escape."

"Why didn't you go after him?"

Astrel chuckled. "For what reason? If he had killed you we would have found him by tomorrow. Unless you want it known that you entered this apartment illegally—as you have done—there is nothing to do."

"Thanks," Cameron said dryly. "I'll remember that." He drank the cognac, moved away from the wall, walked into the bathroom, and turned on the cold water. When the bowl was filled, he sat on a stool and soaked his face. Then he wet a towel and held it on top of his head. The coldness seemed to isolate the pain, drawing it from his arms, his legs, and his lungs.

Astrel came into the bathroom and sat on the edge of the tub. He ejected a cigarette butt into the toilet, put a fresh one into his gold cigarette holder. Cameron dried his face and combed his hair gently. He asked, "Why were you watching this—Verrat?"

"Because he is one who must be watched. He, too, seeks the gold—for purposes hostile to France." Astrel reached into his pocket, took out a key. "You entered with this, M. Cameron. If you did not see M. Thorne, how did you acquire it?"

"He mailed it to me."

Astrel handed the key to Cameron. "I return it to you." Cameron said, "How do I find M. Verrat?"

"In the Thirteenth Arrondissement—Rue du Tage." Astrel walked into the corridor; Cameron followed. Astrel said, "I would not seek him alone, or after dark." He stopped at the door. "There is not yet any need for you to talk with M. Verrat. If you are as enthusiastic as you seem, let me suggest that you converse with Mme. du Casse."

"Where is she?"

"Menton. She is the proprietor of a gambling casino."

"Did Thorne know her?"

Astrel drew on his gloves. "Why not ask her yourself?" he said. "M. Thorne knew many people." He eased his bulk into the hall. "Let me suggest that you advise me of future moves. You have learned a painful lesson by acting alone. My resources are not without value."

"I gathered that," Cameron said. He closed the door and went back to the study. He picked up his hat from the floor, and saw the disarrayed blind behind which his attacker had hidden.

Turning out the lights, he wondered if a man like Verrat would have broken Phil's neck, then used only a pistol butt on Cameron. The disparity in technique bothered him. And had Astrel really had Verrat under surveillance, or had he been following Cameron? Was it even Verrat who had struck him down? He opened the door, looked down the darkened hallway, and walked to the lift.

The cobbled street glistened under the flickering street light. He adjusted his hat painfully and took the Metro to the Quai.

CHAPTER EIGHT

MARI said, "You must be more careful, my dear. You were unwise to return to his apartment."

Cameron's fingers touched her neck. He had been sleeping and she had wakened him. Dawn was only an hour away. He said, "I didn't get anywhere. I don't even know why I went back."

"The other man must have had a reason for being there."

"I'll never know what it was."

She leaned on one side and took his face between her hands. "When you find what you look for, you will leave."

"Yes."

She kissed him and in her mouth was the taste of mint. He said, "I don't know what I'm doing any more. When I came back to France I hoped to find something that would give me direction." He looked up at her, seeing the full outline of her breasts, the hollow of her throat. "I didn't find it."

Mari ran her fingers through her hair. "Sometimes life provides compensations."

He felt suddenly guilty, ungrateful. "Meeting you was more than I deserved."

She looked away from him, at the gray window over the Seine. "Who can say what one deserves, or does not deserve?" She rose and stepped out of her shoes. Her fingers did something to the waist of her dress, and it parted and fell away from her body. She turned off the light over the bed and he could hear the soft rustle of silk-enclosed elastic slipping down over smooth skin. He pulled aside the covers and then she was beside him. Her arms went around his neck, pressing her body against him. His body warmed to the fire of hers. But when he kissed her cheek, he could taste the salt of her tears.

He left the apartment before noon, ate at Le Bossu, and while he was sipping coffee, made a list of theatrical agents from the telephone directory.

The first one had an office on the fourth floor of an old building on the Rue Tiquet. He had never heard of a juggler named Verlaix, adding that it was hard enough to get bookings for talented clients without being plagued by such buffoons as jugglers.

The second, on the Boulevard des Italiens, had known Verlaix, but that was before the war. The agent had been, at the time, in a juggling act, playing the same music hall as Verlaix. According to him, the juggler was an ordinary-appearing fellow, neither tall nor short. *Tiens*, a man could change in ten years...perhaps now he was bald, or wore a mustache, or had become corpulent.

Cameron said, "If you played the same place, perhaps you had the same agent."

"No. Regrettably, no."

Cameron tried number three. Rue Reamur. M. Jacques Lussac.

M. Lussac wore a stained hound's-tooth suit, a lint-ridden beret, and a cheap watch on his lapel. Clients were waiting, he said; his time was valuable. Cameron gave him five hundred francs.

Said M. Lussac, "You have come to the man with the best memory in Paris."

"Show me."

Lussac rose majestically, opened a scarred filing case, and drew out a cheaply bound volume. It was a theatrical yearbook, the kind that blackmails entertainers into buying advertising space. Lussac leafed through it, stopping at a page that listed sword-swallowers, acrobats, and animal acts. His grit-lined thumbnail indicated a badly lighted photograph. "Verlaix," he said. "Is it not he?"

Cameron looked at the face. "It could be anybody," he said. The face was a model of anonymity. Draw a box mustache on the upper lip and it was Hitler. Or circle the eyes with glasses and you had Hirohito. Sketch in a full beard and you had one of the Twelve Apostles. Cameron said, "I'll take the picture."

M. Lussac's face fell into lines of sadness. "You ask a great deal, m'sieu," he said. "This volume is no longer obtainable. For me it contains many poignant memories. Some of those who were my friends are dead. I cannot …"

Cameron gave him another five-hundred-franc note. "Have a few drinks," he said. "With a belly full of Chablis you'll enjoy thinking of your friends." He ripped the page from the book, folded it, and walked to the door. "If you learn where I can reach Verlaix, tell me at the Cafe Adour."

M. Lussac bowed dramatically. "*Entendu,*" he said. "*Bien entendu, m'sieu.*"

Cameron went down to the street and walked a block to the office of the next agent. He was climbing the stairs when he looked up and saw a woman leave the agent's office. She did not see Cameron until he stood in front of her blocking the stairs.

It was Marcelle.

He said, "Everyone's going professional these days." He took her wrist, pulled her toward him, and made her walk back down the stairs beside him. She struggled to free herself, but he bent her palm toward her forearm, making her moan.

She said, "I can call a policeman."

"So can I. And whom do the flies want to see? Your bald-headed pal or me?" He drew her into an alcove under the stairs. They could not be seen from the street.

"Victor is…"

"…a guy with a gun who shows up at the wrong places at the wrong times." He put his arm around her. "Like you."

Her eyebrows lifted in surprise. "Why do you say that?"

He drew out a pack of cigarettes, lighted two, and gave her one. "You've just come from an office where you were asking questions." He held her chin so that she could not look away. "What kind of questions?"

She said, "I…I wanted a job."

"What kind of job?"

"Dancing."

Cameron laughed mirthlessly. "You never owned a pair of shoes until you were eighteen. You may be able to dance, but not for money. Not as an entertainer." He exhaled toward her face, and took his hand from her chin. She did not turn from him. He said, "If you think I don't know, I'll tell you why you were there."

"Tell me."

"You're looking for a man named Verlaix."

The quick intake of her breath gratified him. He said, "Jugglers are popular this year. Last month they'd work for coffee and croissants. Now everyone wants jugglers." He flicked ash from his cigarette. "Or is it only the jugglers named Verlaix?"

"Go away," she said. Her voice was tired, defeated. "Go now while you can."

"Why do you think I've stayed?"

Her eyes lifted a little. She threw away her cigarette. "Not because of me."

The words cut him. He felt his face twitch. He said, "No. Not because of you, Marcelle. Because of someone I knew even before you. Because of Phil." A policeman passed the doorway and he stiffened. Then he said, "Does it surprise you that I'm mixing in something I don't know anything about, just because a friend was killed?"

She lowered her eyes. "Nothing you do surprises me."

"Maybe Baldy did it; maybe Verlaix, or Astrel, or Verrat." He drew her face to his. "Even you might have done it, beautiful. You learned things like that in the Resistance. You could break a man's neck…"

Then her arms were around his shoulders, her face against his chest. Her sobs shook him. His blood began to pound, making his head ache brutally.

She said, "Why did you leave me? Why did you have to go?"

He held her gently, bitterness gone from him. He said, "I left you because I was married—and because the fighting had not stopped. It would have been better if I'd never left France, but I had no choice." He touched the side of her face. "I was obligated."

Her cheeks were streaked with tears. She said, "Even as I am obligated to Victor."

When he finally spoke, he said, "We've got another chance now. Somehow we've collided with each other once more, and it's up to us what we make of it." He kissed her slowly. "Any suggestions?"

She returned his embrace warmly, eagerly. Her breath quickened and she pressed his hand to the small of her back. "Leave Paris while you can," she said, "Go now."

"Give up?"

She shook her head. "No. Forget this—this trying to live another's life. Live your own. You have wasted so much of it already."

"Where would I go?" he said. "What would I do?"

"The world is open to you," she said. "Go anywhere, anywhere." Tears reappeared in her eyes. She brushed them away with the back of her hand.

"Not alone," he said. "I'd rather be in prison. I'll go if you'll go with me."

She looked up suddenly, her eyes wide with surprise. "Go with you?" She looked away and shook her head. "It is not possible. Besides, I would be followed."

"Victor?"

She nodded. "He would not want me to leave. His life is based on finding what Philip discovered."

"If he follows I'll kill him."

"Truly?"

"Truly."

"He will try to kill you," she said, and looked over her shoulder toward the sidewalk. "He sent me here today. He will begin to look for me if I do not telephone him now."

Cameron took her elbow in his hand, moving her away from the stairs. "Let's find a telephone," he said. "I'll even pay for the call."

Sometimes you start to do a thing, and after you do as well as you can with it you give it up because it has become too much, or because something else materializes to which you shift your allegiance. Because you do so, you are neither a coward nor a quitter. You are simply a man who realizes how little he can do in a given case, and because you are practical (because you have been made practical) you withdraw.

Instead of hiding in the sanctuary overlooking the Quai, you have had courage enough to leave; courage enough to break the bond of physical attraction that kept you near Mari. Instead of drinking for oblivion, you sit in a cafe, high above the lights of Paris, on the Place du Tertre, pouring wine for Marcelle, and listening to the music, the laughter of old Montmartre...

He said, "We'll have to leave soon. How do you feel?"

She looked at him across the table. "I feel as though you never were gone from me."

From their outdoor table they could see the huge illuminated dome of Sacre Coeur, looming above them on the hill of Montmartre. Lights were strung around the Place du Tertre, swaying and sparkling in the night wind. Behind them, in the Cafe Tabourin, there was music—a crippled violinist and a grotesquely fat woman pianist. The violinist played off-key and the piano was badly tuned. You did not think of those things, though. You thought of the baggage checked at the Gare de Lyon, waiting until you boarded the night train for Nice—the Sud-Est Express. You thought of the years without Marcelle and the death of a friend and sorrow and the sick hollowness of failure, and you tried to put it out of your mind and concentrate on the girl so near you and the days and months ahead.

She said, "I hope you will never regret what we are doing."

"No."

"Ever."

"No," he said. The violinist limped toward him, leaned on their table. "A special selection, perhaps?"

Cameron looked at Marcelle. She shook her head. "No," he said. "Play anything you like." He tipped the violinist, then tensed as the pianist began one of Mari's songs. Before he thought, he said, "Not that one…" and saw Marcelle looking at him curiously. The music stopped. The pianist began an unfamiliar tune.

Marcelle said softly, "Why not that song?"

He lighted a cigarette, his hand shaking. "I don't like it."

Slowly she said, "It surprises me that you have even heard it. The song is new in Paris."

He said, "Don't ask me to explain. I haven't asked you for explanations. If we start explaining to each other now, we might just as well forget we ever met."

She lowered her eyes. "Perhaps it would have been better to ask and answer before we made our decision."

"Perhaps," he said irritably. He finished his wine and motioned to the waitress. *"L'addition;"* he said. *"Partons."*

Marcelle drew her coat around her shoulders. "So soon?"

He nodded, paid the bill, and stood up. "We've both spent evenings in Montmartre before. Tonight we've got a train to catch."

"It does not leave for an hour."

"It's Saturday night. Traffic is heavy." He held back her chair and she stood up beside him.

She walked away from the table, and he followed her. Neither of them spoke until they reached the Rue des Saules, and when a taxi stopped for them, they kissed wordlessly in the dark. As the taxi rolled down toward the heart of Paris, the sweet-sad music of Montmartre faded into the distance behind them.

Sitting beside her in the *wagon-lit,* he opened a split of champagne and filled two glasses. There was a tension between them of his own making. He felt that he must break it or leave the compartment; get off the train. He said, "I've made a bad start for us. Can we forget it and let everything begin from this moment on?" He handed her a glass, and watched the droplets of condensation roll down the thin stem until she answered him. He had to bend toward her to hear what she was saying: "…never go back to what we used to be. Never."

"No," he said. "But we can take out the good and forget the bad. If we live hard enough for each other, we can forget the past."

The fingers of her hand smoothed back his hair. The train lurched suddenly, spilling champagne on his shirt. She said, "We talk too much. And sometimes talking is not good for love."

He brought her to him, and she said, "Do you love me again?"

He nodded, brushing her cheek with his.

"The way we loved in the beginning?"

"I can't tell. That's how I want it."

She kissed him slowly, with increasing passion. "Then this is the first time," she said huskily. "And everything must be as it was then. I've always needed you. I need you now."

His hand pushed the compartment light switch and there was darkness and the sound of rushing rails. He tried to put his glass in the washbowl but it toppled and smashed. The locomotive whistle blew high and piercingly as the train rounded a bend.

CHAPTER NINE

THEY sat together at a small table under an awning that faced the Promenade des Anglais. Beyond the retaining wall the Mediterranean flashed silkily under the afternoon sun. They had been drinking gin *a citron*, iced, and when the waiter came to refill their empty glasses, he said, "You must return for the Carnival of Nice."

Cameron said, "The Carnival is seven months away."

The waiter nodded. He removed a droplet from the stem of Marcelle's glass with his forefinger. "Surely you will want to return." He looked at Cameron. "You and Madame."

"Surely," Cameron said. He lighted a cigarette and watched a group of children clambering over inflated rubber rafts in the water.

The waiter said, "For myself, I have devised a formidable costume. I will appear in the disguise of a frog."

"A frog?" Marcelle said. "Why a frog?"

"It is so seldom accomplished," the waiter said. He put the empty glasses down on the metal tabletop and leaned on it with his hands. "To remain in character will necessitate locomoting on all fours the entire length of Avenue de la Victoire." He inhaled deeply and touched his diaphragm. "The impersonation requires an excellent constitution. I propose to begin training in October."

"On all fours?" Cameron asked.

"On all fours."

Cameron held up his cigarette and blew away the ash. "You should enter the Tour de France," he said. "The challenge is greater."

The waiter shook his head. "The whole world can bicycle," he said. "It is a rarer accomplishment to impersonate correctly a frog."

Marcelle turned toward Cameron. "Perhaps we will return for the event."

The waiter's face brightened. "I will be pleased to have your opinion of my performance." He swept up the glasses, polished the table top, and walked back into the cafe.

Cameron looked at Marcelle's face, profiled against the blue of the sea. She was tanned now from two weeks on the sand, her hair had lightened, her face was relaxed. She was very beautiful, but Cameron did not think he was in love with her.

She turned to him and said, "Can you smell the mimosa?"

"Yes."

"My sister, who came to the Cote d'Azur on her honeymoon, told me she would always remember the mimosa."

"Did she always remember?"

"She said she would. I have not seen her in two years."

Cameron watched a gull glide by, parallel to the sea wall. He said, "I was sentenced to two years. But for my parole I would still be in prison."

She said, "You could have let me know."

"What good would it have done? As it was, too many people were involved."

She touched the back of his hand with her fingers. "I believe you must have loved her very much."

"My wife?" Cameron shrugged. "I thought so for a while."

"But not now?"

"Not now," Cameron said. "After six months in prison, I discovered it was only a matter of pride."

The waiter returned with two fresh drinks. He put them on the table and the lemon slices bounced against the rims. He said, "It is a source of sorrow to me that you persist in drinking this lemon gin."

Cameron said, "How can it obliquely concern you?"

"Because I am *Niçois,*" the waiter said. "Were we at Antibes I should feel obliged to recommend an infusion of *seiche.*"

Marcelle asked, "What is seiche?"

"A distillation of cuttlefish," the waiter said. "There are those who prefer to follow it with *pastis.*"

"Are you an admirer of seiche?" Cameron asked.

"Profoundly," the waiter said. He shaded his eyes with one hand and looked at the sea. "To the extent that I have caught several dozen cuttlefish at my own instance." He pointed to the east. "A few kilometers toward Monaco there is a shallow cove where the cuttlefish hide. At low tide one may enter the caves." He made a stabbing gesture. "A trident quickly dispatches them."

Cameron sipped his drink. The waiter was a welcome relief from incipient boredom. He said, "At Antibes we will not neglect to sample seiche."

The waiter bowed broadly. "It will be an occasion to hold in memory." He backed away toward the cafe.

Marcelle laughed. "Shall we go to Antibes?"

"No," Cameron said. "I understand that Menton is amusing." He looked at the girl beside him. "Let's drive there this evening."

Something had happened to her face. It was rigid, but the lips said, "Why Menton? Why not Monte Carlo?"

"I've been to Monte Carlo."

"There is nothing at Menton."

Cameron stubbed out his cigarette. "I hear differently," he said.

"From whom?" The eyes were guarded.

"M. Thorne," he said. "My late friend."

Marcelle's hands twisted at her dress. "I thought we came here to forget," she said. "You do not forget easily."

"Not easily."

She leaned forward, her breasts pressing the top of her low-cut blouse. "What do you want at Menton?"

Cameron took out a cigarette and lighted it. He gave it to her, and lighted another for himself. "Conversation," he said. "Conversation with a woman named Du Casse."

"Why?"

"Phil owed her some money. A lot of money."

"Yes."

Cameron leaned back and looked at the sea. The children were dragging their rubber rafts ashore. "She might know why Phil was killed," he said. "At least I could ask her."

Her hand tightened over his wrist. "Don't go to Menton," she said. "It will only mean trouble."

Cameron looked at her. "If Madame du Casse did not have him killed, she has only to say so."

"You would believe her?"

"I might."

"Then believe me. She had nothing to do with it."

Cameron shook his head. "She was in on the beginning. Perhaps she had reasons."

"She had no reason to wish him dead," Marcelle said rapidly. "Only alive was he valuable to her."

"You're probably right," Cameron said. He drank deeply from his glass. "It's a pleasant drive to Menton. We'll go there."

Marcelle turned away from him and put her forehead against her clenched fist. "There is something between us," she said. "At first I thought it was only because we had been separated, but now it is more than just that. I feel that you watch me, listen to me, and say things so that you can pick apart my answers." Her voice tightened. "I hoped that here we could get away from our yesterdays, but you won't let me escape. You'll go on digging and prying until you find out what you want to know." She raised a tearstained face suddenly and looked at him. "Is that what you want? Is that what stands between us?"

Cameron did not answer.

"What if I won't go with you to Menton?"

"You'll go," Cameron said levelly. "Don't think you won't."

Desperately she said, "But you will find nothing there. This Du Casse woman is clever—cleverer than any man. After Menton you will always be in danger."

"It frightens me," Cameron said dryly. "You've got me all scared and shivery." He pushed her glass toward her hand. "Have a drink," he said. "Don't worry about it."

She dried her eyes with a handkerchief. She said, "I hardly know you. You are not the Paul of 1944."

"I'm an ex-convict," he said. "In prison, men change."

"But to what extent," she asked, "and for what necessity?"

He shrugged. "Who can say?" He laid money for the drinks on the table and stood up. "I didn't stay long enough to get that many answers."

You walk past the three-franc chairs on the Promenade des Anglais, under the mop-headed palms, shielding your eyes from the afternoon glare, feeling the tenseness within you binding your insides like a ball of twine, and you know that what you hoped for has not come to pass. The escape has failed. The smell of the sea burns your nostrils, the knowledge of what you must do pounds at your brain. A memory returns fleetingly: a woman singing to a smoke-filled room; a gray dawn over the Quai. Beside you, staring toward the sea, walks a woman almost a stranger.

In their room at the Hotel Marbot, Cameron opened the window toward the sea and partly drew the blinds. That way the breeze filled the room, while the curtains kept out the sun. Looking down at the Promenade, he could see children riding in carts pulled by white-harnessed donkeys. He took off his shirt and flexed the muscles of his arms. Marcelle was sitting on the bed behind him. She said, "Do you hate me?"

He turned and dropped his shirt on a chair. "I don't hate you. Why should I?"

"Because I've disappointed you," she said. "Because you thought you'd find me the same girl you left four years ago."

"Did I expect that?"

"Men do," she said. "If you remembered me at all, you remembered only a girl..."

"I remembered you," he said. "Do you doubt it?"

She ignored the question. "...but you found me a woman." The tracery of a smile moved her lips. "Nothing more—nothing less."

"A woman," he said, and stepped out of his sandals.

"Yes," she said. "But you expected to find someone young and pure. Like your wife."

"My wife?" He laughed bitterly. "No one's accusing her of purity."

"No," she said. "Not the wife you went back to after the war—the girl you married. Don't you remember her?"

He took her wrist, pulled her to her feet. "No," he said cruelly. "I don't remember anyone like that. I don't remember anyone at all."

She tried to push away from him, but he brought her body next to his and kissed her. Gradually she relaxed, and her voice said, "Love me again, Paul. Love me the way I love you."

He closed her lips with his, crushing them until she cried out in pain. Then there were only two of them, wanting and desiring, giving and receiving, and through the quiet room drifted the scent of mimosa in the wind from the sea.

You lie in half-sleep beside the sleeping body of a woman who is a stranger except for shared intimacy. Your thoughts move sluggishly, beyond the event, past the circumstance of your being there, and the satisfaction of detachment grows and isolates you from the spent passion of room 411 in the Hotel Marbot. You notice the way the dying sunlight shines against a straight-backed chair, reminding you of your last class on Friday afternoons, years before, when you would stand before a blackboard and write repetitively: *que je finisse, que je finisse, que j'aie fini, que j'eusse fini,* hearing the rustle of the classroom behind you, the shuffle of your students' notebooks, the scrape of a heel across the worn oak flooring. You looked quickly at your wrist watch to see that the week was almost *fini,* and at exactly five-forty-eight you would walk into your house and Ruth would be in the kitchen cooking filet of sole, and you would mix a shaker of Martinis and thumb through the stack of exam booklets, knowing that Miss Saunders would have missed the meaning of *d'arrache-pied,* and Mr. Bolton would have failed utterly to distinguish between *avoir soin de* and *avoir besoin de*, and then you would drop the booklets beside the chair and sip your drink and look at the woman you had married. Those were always the not-too-bad memories—the ones you could handle, the ones that reminded you only of a channeled and unimaginative life with its once-a-month faculty receptions, standing beside Ruth while she served ugly glass cups of grapefruit-juice punch and talked with your students. What had become of them in the years between, in the centuries while you worked a drill press in the prison machine shop? Had Miss Saunders married the boy with the premature mustache? Did Mr. Bolton lose his tendency to blink when confused?

There were times, periods beyond which nothing of value occurred, when it was better to erase everything the way you could erase the past participle of *conclure*, so that only a black-and-white blur remained to indicate that anything had been there at all.

Detached now from past and present, you saw yourself a refugee from the reality of an empty apartment on the Rue Chauveau-Lagarde. Beside you lay the well-formed body of a woman you had known some eons before, and when you had left her things had disintegrated and reformed in a montage of iron bars imbedded in concrete, wire-mesh cages, the thick oily stench of the machine shop (whirr of the drill presses, grinding of the lathes), and the gray formless mass of numbered and numbed men who shuffled through the wall-enclosed yard. You could find excuses for looking at the sky and thinking of France, thinking of Marcelle, letting your memory take advantage of your mind, until she became a symbol of desire and contentment and the freedom of days long past. And in your mind she had not changed or aged, and the *idee fixe* lasted until a few days ago, when you finally came to realize that in your life there had been two Marcelles, and the one you loved wasn't the one lying beside you.

Cameron turned his head and his cheek brushed the tips of Marcelle's fingers. She stirred in her sleep and her hand pushed back a strand of hair that lay across her forehead. Now her face had relaxed; the little lines at the corners of her eyes had smoothed and vanished. The muscles of her throat lay soft and full above the turn of her shoulders. The breasts that sprang forward when her body was vertical had telescoped and merged into the belt of pectoral muscles, making her torso look almost boyish. He saw the twin aureoles, darkened in womanhood, come from the pink strawberry freshness he had come to imagine in prison. His hand rested on the hollow of her chest, feeling the rhythmic rise and fall of her breathing. He moved closer to her lips, and as he touched them he closed his eyes, and tried to think only of the Marcelle he had forgotten...

CHAPTER TEN

Now, in the early evening, they drove eastward along the Cote d'Azur. Their car was a Maserati, rented from a place near the Marbot. To their right was the blue-black sea, to the left, the rocky slopes of the Alpes-Maritimes with their olive trees, eucalyptus, and twisted Aleppo pines. There was too much darkness now to distinguish the daylight green and red porphyry of the mountains; too dark to see the shadings of the sea as it rolled into the occasional coves below the highway. But the smell of the sea and the cool of the coming night were on them, and Marcelle pulled her kerchief tighter about her hair against the wind that breached the open car.

Thirty-six kilometers to Menton took only forty minutes, and when they reached the town, night had fallen. Slowing the car, Cameron asked, "Which way to the Casino?"

"We are very near," Marcelle said. "Continue on the main road until it begins to rise, then at a fork turn toward the sea, and you will see a sign."

"What will the sign say?"

"It will point toward the Casino."

At the fork, the surface of the road roughened, and beyond a rim of palms Cameron could see the Casino. Its outline above the promontory was low and squat, like an octopus clinging to a rock.

Marcelle said, "We have arrived."

"How do you feel?"

She turned to him and said, "You must know how I feel. I love you, and yet I must watch you balancing on the edge of a precipice."

Cameron chuckled. He turned the long sleek body of the Maserati into the porte-cochere, and a white-uniformed doorman stepped toward them. He opened Marcelle's door and said to Cameron, "You are early for the games, m'sieu. The tables do not open until nine."

Cameron stepped out of the car and took Marcelle's arm. "We're dining," he said. "Don't let the car get lost."

They walked up the inlaid steps to the foyer, and were shown to the bar. Sipping champagne, they watched the dinner crowd arrive, the women furred, the men white-coated. Below them was the sound of waves breaking in the distance lights flashed from fishing boats and buoys. Cameron said, "What do you know of Mme. du Casse?"

Marcelle leaned forward quickly and touched a finger to her lips. "Softly," she said. "Softly, if I am to tell you."

Cameron looked at the bar patrons. He said, "I take it she owns this place."

Marcelle nodded.

"How?"

Marcelle shrugged. "It is a mystery. Some say she won it from the previous owner. Others believe she arranged to have him disappear."

"But not before he gave her the place."

Marcelle sipped her champagne. When she put the glass back on the green onyx table she said, "It is so reported."

Cameron lighted a cigarette for Marcelle, another for himself. "Where is she from?"

"She comes from Nouvelle Caledonie," Marcelle said.

"As to what kind of woman she is, you will be able to decide when you have talked with her."

"There used to be a penal colony in New Caledonia," Cameron said. "Is there any connection?"

"Renee du Casse has native blood in her veins," Marcelle said. "If her father was imprisoned in the colony, he might have married and stayed there."

"He could do that," Cameron said. "How old is she?"

"Thirty," Marcelle said. "Or sixty."

"Good-looking?"

"Not beautiful," Marcelle said. "Striking. Her skin is smooth as a serpent's. She has raven's eyes."

Cameron finished his first glass of champagne. "I can't wait to meet her," he said. "And while we're on the subject, just how did you happen to meet her?"

Marcelle lowered her eyes. "She had known Victor."

Cameron leaned back in his chair. "Ah, yes," he said. "Victor. How are the pure in heart on a night like this?"

"Don't," Marcelle said suddenly.

It was the first time they had referred to Victor Coudet.

Cameron looked at the ash on his cigarette. He said slowly, "You came here before with Victor?"

"Yes."

"You should have told me."

"I find it difficult to tell you anything," she said. "Anything at all."

Cameron refilled their glasses. "I'm not hard to talk to," he said. "It depends upon the subject."

Marcelle lifted her glass and looked out of the wide window at the blackness of the sea. "We were speaking of Victor."

"So we were," Cameron said. "Let's not speak of Victor anymore."

He heard a little laugh in her throat. Her voice asked, "You are ashamed to speak of him?"

"Ashamed?" Cameron said angrily. "That's a strange word, coming from you."

"You mean I should be ashamed."

Cameron said slowly, "Aren't you?"

Marcelle did not look at him. The smoke of her cigarette spiraled upward. In the background a man laughed. "I'm ashamed," she said, "if it gives you pleasure to hear me say it. I'm ashamed each time you look at me; each time you touch me. You treat me like a poule you've patronized for years, and then you ask if I feel shame."

Cameron stubbed out his cigarette. "You owed something to me, Marcelle," he said. "I've wrung it out of you. It hasn't been pleasant for either of us, but now I think we're even."

"Do you?" she asked softly. "And what about Victor?"

Cameron added more champagne to their glasses. "His timing was bad. Victor should have met you next month or not at all."

Her head shook slowly. Her lips said, "Victor is not a young man, like you. And unlike you, he loves me."

"I loved you," Cameron said quickly. "I never loved anyone as much."

"Even yourself?"

He turned away from her. "Even myself."

Her hand covered his wrist. "Philip loved me, too. But I owed him nothing—even less than I owed you. It was your decision to go back to your wife, Paul. I didn't insist that we marry. You could have stayed with me from that time on."

"That's not the issue," he said. "I was married then; you weren't."

"Is it then so different for a man?" she asked scornfully. "Does it..." Then her hand tightened around his wrist, and she whispered, "Renee du Casse."

"Where?" he asked without moving.

"Behind you. She just came in."

"Will you introduce me now?"

"Not now," Marcelle said. "After dinner. She will be in her office. We can talk without interruption."

"Good," Cameron said. He felt his spine prickle and he had to force himself not to turn around to look at the woman he had come to see. His hand shook as he picked up his glass, and as he drank, he saw a woman walking near them, smiling and nodding at the patrons. Marcelle's fingers told him that it was Renee du Casse, but still he did not turn. He waited until she had brushed past their table, and then he saw her small lithe body, her profile, smooth and seemingly featureless from the tight-drawn skin of her cheekbones. Cameron could visualize her darker in color, barefoot, wearing a sarong, a pie-plate straw hat, hair oily black—a woman of the Sunda Islands. Undoubtedly her mother had been a small-boned Melanesian. Renee du Casse turned and looked for a moment at Marcelle. Then her gaze flickered and she passed on, walking the length of the sea window, until they could no longer see her.

Marcelle said, "She is somewhat...distinctive, no?"

"Yes."

"Even so, she is jealous of me."

"Victor?"

Marcelle nodded. "She has wanted him for many years. They were together when Victor met me."

"During the war?"

"Yes. The Casino was a Resistance house. The Germans came here to drink and gamble, while in the cellar lay airmen of England and America."

"Did she know Phil during the war?"

"No. Phil did not come to Menton until last spring." She looked at Cameron. "We met here, at the games."

"I see," Cameron said. "And when he went broke you took him to Du Casse."

Marcelle picked up her glass and drank. "Philip was desperate," she said. "Mine was a gesture of assistance."

Cameron snorted. "I can imagine," he said. "And your cut came from the house." He looked at Marcelle's eyes in the dimly lighted room. "I used to wonder what would happen to the poules in Paris when the houses were closed. Now I find they came to Menton to work for Du Casse."

The crack of her palm against his cheek ripped through the barroom. Patrons at the bar stopped talking and looked down at them curiously. Cameron said deliberately, "Thank you," and rose from the table. He stood behind Marcelle's chair and said, "Get up."

"No."

He dug his thumbs into the muscle that ridged her shoulders. She cried out in pain and stood up quickly.

Cameron took her arm, locked it against his, and walked her out of the barroom. "So you're the sensitive type," he said. "I wouldn't have believed it."

A white-tied maitre came toward them, a large glossy menu in his hand. He said, "Would you care for a table now?"

"Certainly," Cameron said. "We need a little nourishment."

They followed him into the dining room.

Cameron finished his *fine café* and looked at his watch. Nine-seventeen. He looked at Marcelle and saw that her eyes were staring at the dining-room entrance. He said, "Expecting someone?"

Without turning, she said, "Why not? Renee has seen me. Anything could happen. Anyone might come in."

Cameron felt for his wallet. "Anyone but Phil," he said.

Marcelle turned her head slowly. "He knew what he was doing, Paul," she said tensely. "Stop blaming me. I didn't send him to his death."

"We won't argue about it," Cameron said. He put six thousand-franc notes on the bill and pushed back his chair. "Will Renee be in her office now?"

"Probably."

"I can see her myself if you don't want to."

"No. I'll go with you. What difference does it make? She saw me in the bar."

Cameron stood up and drew back Marcelle's chair. As they left the dining room, he gave the maitre a thousand-franc note. To the right, beyond thick glass doors, was the gaming room with its layouts, wheels, tables, and birdcage. So far, the play was light. After midnight more of the Monaco crowd would stop by, hoping new wheels would change their luck.

Marcelle said, "Through the door."

Cameron nodded, and as they approached the glass panels, an electric eye moved them inward. The room was soundproofed and modern. Impressionistic statuary stood among the tables; a late-period Degas hung near the window that overlooked the sea. Somewhere in the background was the sound of string music, muted and unobtrusive. Cameron followed Marcelle between the tables until they were at the far end of the room. She stopped in front of a blond-oak panel and said, "Renee will be inside."

"Thanks," Cameron said. "I'll take it from here."

Marcelle shrugged. "As you wish." She knocked on the panel and in a moment it opened. She spoke into the office. "Renee, an American named Cameron wants to speak to you."

Cameron heard a voice answering, smooth and even, but with a vague accent. It said, "Please come in." He moved forward, and as he passed Marcelle, her hands held him for a moment and she whispered, "Good luck, my Paul."

Inside, the lighting was dim, the air cool. The room was long, at the end a massive desk. Behind it sat a woman in evening clothes. She said, "Please close the door, M. Cameron." She spoke in French, and Cameron closed the door, without realizing for a moment that the woman knew he spoke French.

Mme. du Casse did not move. She said, "And Marcelle?"

"I wanted to see you alone." Cameron walked toward the desk.

"I am honored, m'sieu." The face was immobile; the slightly slanted eyes did not waver. Her hand indicated a chair. She said, "It was not necessary to have Marcelle gain entry for you. Your name would have been sufficient."

"Ah," Cameron said, "I had not realized my name was known in Menton."

"It is known to Renee du Casse."

Cameron crossed his legs and lighted a cigarette. Mme. du Casse said, "You were a friend of Philip Thorne."

"Yes."

"You think I may have been instrumental in his death."

"Yes."

The perfectly shaped, symmetrical lips smiled. "Would you believe me if I said his death was as much a surprise to me as it was to you?"

"I might."

"Then you may consider that I have said it."

Cameron nodded slowly. "Phil was going to do a job for you. I came from America to help him."

"Such was my understanding."

Cameron looked at the violet eyes, the smoothly drawn facial skin, the unwrinkled throat. He said, "You have something Phil gave you. I'd like to have it."

The woman inclined her head. "You would not care to make a purchase?"

Cameron shrugged. "I am without funds."

"How unusual for an American." She opened a drawer of the desk, took out an envelope, thumbed through the contents, and selected a check. "I retained this as a hostage," she said. "I am sure you will understand."

Cameron nodded. "I'm sure I will." He leaned toward her and reached for the check, but she held it just beyond his outstretched fingers. She said, "Now that M. Thorne cannot pay his debts, perhaps his friend M. Cameron would be interested in an arrangement."

"First, the check."

Mme. du Casse placed it in his hand. Cameron looked at it, saw the promised sum over Phil's signature, and took out his lighter. He held the burning check over a jade ashtray and watched it twist and crumple into ashes. His fingers broke the ashes into black powder, and then he sat back in the chair. "What kind of arrangement did you have in mind?"

"It has to do with gold," she said. "The subject, I am sure, is not novel to you."

"Hardly," Cameron said. "Do you have the gold?"

"Not yet," Renee said. "However, that detail does not concern me. The mode of its transportation, however, is a matter of importance."

"I don't have diplomatic immunity," Cameron said. "Anything I send out of France is subject to customs search."

"You have met Claude Astrel?"

Cameron nodded.

"He is not without resource. I recommend that you hold further discussions with him."

Cameron said, "I don't like him. He looks like a grease-covered Buddha."

Renee's laughter was light and brief. She rose from the desk and said, "Will you join me in a *digestif?*"

"Not now," Cameron said. "Marcelle is waiting."

The woman took a crystal decanter from a concealed cabinet and filled a thimble-size jade liqueur container.

She walked to Cameron and leaned against the desk. He could smell a heavy, cloying perfume that was not French but Eastern. Her body was almost childlike. Cameron began to feel a perverse attraction for her. He started to rise, but she pushed him back easily and said, "Do not concern yourself about Marcelle. In things like these she is only an amateur."

Cameron eyed the woman standing before him. "I recognize the professional touch," he said levelly.

"We might do well together," Mme. du Casse said. "It suits me to have you divert Marcelle."

"Because of Coudet."

She sipped the liqueur. "Yes. Because of Victor. Victor, who loved me until he became infatuated with that child Marcelle."

"It happens," Cameron said. He stood beside Renee and stubbed out his cigarette. She straightened, almost as though she was uncoiling, her body brushed against his. "You will return?" she asked. "Now that we know each other?"

"I'll be back," Cameron said. "For details." He turned to leave.

Renee said, "Not that way. The garden exit." She pointed to a door beside a window, and with a small key she opened it. The night air blew in on them. She touched the back of his neck with her hand and kissed him. Her lips were cold and enveloping. He wanted to grip her suddenly, to break this doll woman, but instead he turned his head aside.

Tautly, she said, "I could make you forget your Marcelle—and the blonde one who sings at the Cafe Adour." She stepped back, and as Cameron moved into the doorway he said, "If we're in business, let's keep it that way. Otherwise it gets too involved." He saw Renee smile thinly. She said, "You will do, M. Cameron. Provided you take care of yourself."

He went out of the door and stepped onto soft grass. The door closed behind him, and he saw that he was on a kind of artificial parapet that overlooked the sea. He walked toward a low wall and looked down at phosphorescent waves. The rising moon silhouetted grotesque trees against the horizon. He watched for a moment, breathed deeply to clear his nostrils of Renee's perfume, and began to walk around the side of the Casino, toward the entrance. Marcelle would probably be waiting in the foyer.

He passed a tall growth of foliage that hugged the wall of the building, and as he turned into the farther shadows a force clipped the back of his legs, buckling the knees. As he fell forward, covering his face with his hands, something whished against the side of his head, but his wrist caught the blow, which numbed the forearm. He hit the ground on his right side and doubled his knees against his belly to protect it from the kicks of the two men who were cursing him. Cameron snared an ankle with his hand and jerked the leg toward him. A body fell beside him heavily and Cameron drove his fist into the man's groin. He jumped up, but before he could run, the other man was on top of him, striking his head, his shoulders with the thing in his hand, and when he fell the final time, he could hear behind him the sound of a woman's laughter.

CHAPTER ELEVEN

HE WAS whirling back to earth, rotating painfully, like a spent pinwheel. His body was chilled and rigid. His fingers had turned to ice, but as he revolved, centrifugal force broke the ice jam in his arteries, and blood began to flow into his head. It pounded and throbbed and began to thaw, and in his mind he began to realize that somehow the whole thing had been craftily synchronized so that he would not reach the earth until he was alive again. He flexed his warming fingers and felt them brush something solid. He was conscious now of his breath coming heavily, jerkily. He held his breath a moment, then he filled his lungs again—this time with the heavy air of the earth—and opened his eyes.

The timing was perfect. He was alive, on earth, and in his room at the Hotel Marbot. His hands lay outside the covers. His chest was naked. He looked toward the window and saw a man watching him. Cameron sat up and tried to lurch toward the man. This was the bastard who tried to beat his brains out last night, Cameron thought. He would have fallen out of bed, but the man stood quickly and pushed him back onto the bed.

Cameron cursed him.

The man put on a pair of spectacles, looked at his wristwatch, and took Cameron's pulse. Then he pulled his cuff back over his wristwatch and stuck a thermometer under Cameron's tongue. While Cameron watched, he washed his hands at the washstand and opened a scuffed black hag. He took out some gauze and a roll of adhesive tape. He walked back to the bed, took out the thermometer, looked at it, and put it in a vest pocket.

Cameron said, "I feel terrible."

The doctor shook his head. "Each year more thieves come to the Cote d'Azur."

"Was I robbed?"

"No, they were frightened away."

"Who frightened them?"

"A Swedish gentleman and his wife chose to stroll outside the Casino in the moonlight." The doctor took a straight razor from his pocket, cut some hair from the side of Cameron's head, and applied a bandage. "Your blood clots well," he said. "You have nothing to fear."

"How did I get here?"

"The young lady drove you."

Cameron looked around the room for evidence of Marcelle. He said, "Where is she?"

The doctor shrugged. "Wherever she is, m'sieu, she did not choose to stay. I promised her that I would wait until you wakened and do for you what I could."

"Can I get out of bed?"

"Wait until tomorrow."

"But it won't hurt me."

"Decide for yourself." The doctor put his things in the black bag and said, "Three thousand francs, please."

Cameron pointed at his wallet on the bureau.

The doctor wrote out a receipt. "It is my recommendation that you consult a masseur for the alleviation of your contusions."

"Close the door," Cameron said. "Quietly."

The door clicked fast.

Cameron pushed aside the blanket and looked at his body. It was a mass of green, yellow, and blue marks. His thighs were the worst—the bastards must have worn pointed shoes.

It was agony to get out of bed. He looked in the mirror at his bruised face, at the strip of tape that ran from his temple over his ear. He cursed the men who had worked him over.

Opening a drawer, he looked for Marcelle's clothes. The drawer was empty.

He staggered to the closet and looked for her dresses. One of his suits hung there, beside a torn, dirty dinner jacket.

Nothing else.

The fact that he had been assaulted did not surprise him; not even the fact that Marcelle was gone surprised him. The only thing he found unusual was the fact that he was still alive.

His swimming trunks hung in the bathroom. He got into them, keeping his head up, found beach clogs and a towel, and went into the hall. Halfway to the stairs he felt nauseated. He stepped into the mop closet and threw up. After a while he steadied himself and walked down the stairs to the lobby and across the road to the beach. The midmorning sun blinded him.

He stepped out of the wooden dogs, dropped his towel, and walked into the water. Only when he was swimming face down, breathing deeply, letting the current massage his aching muscles, did his body relax into the racking sobs of frustration.

Wearing a basque shirt and slacks, Cameron drove back to Menton in the afternoon. Renee's house was built on the promontory beside the Casino, and when he found her she was lying on a fiber mat sunning herself. Her entire bathing suit could have fitted inside his shirt pocket. Her body was like a young girl's and if he had not recognized her hair, he would have walked to the house instead of to the mat.

When she heard his footsteps, she turned to look at him. She touched her dark harlequin glasses and sat up. She said, "Oh."

Cameron sat down beside her. "Surprised to see me, honey?"

She drew up her legs, bending them at the knees. "You said you would come back. You keep your promises."

Cameron laughed shortly. "Offer me a drink," he said. "Make friends with me. Pretend you didn't have the boys try to toss me over the cliff."

Her fingers touched the bandage on his head. "You are hurt," she said silkily. "I am so sorry."

"Nuts," Cameron said. "They tried to kill me—or did they just want to find out how much pushing around I could take?"

Renee pushed up her sunglasses and let them rest on her forehead. "How much can you take?"

"I'm alive," Cameron said. He lighted a cigarette and I leaned back on the thick matting.

Renee looked around at the car. "I do not see Marcelle."

"Neither do I."

"She has gone?"

"So it seems," Cameron said.

"You do not care?"

Cameron closed his eyes. "I can survive it." He breathed deeply, and in a moment her hand was stroking his forehead. He let her do it for a moment before he said, "Is that supposed to fix everything Renee?"

"Not everything."

He turned on his side so that he could see her. The weight on his thigh pained him. He said, "Your two gorillas knew their business. They could have jumped Phil and broken his neck."

"They did not. I swear it."

Cameron threw away his cigarette, took her wrists in his hands, and turned them inward. He watched her face. The cords of her forearms tightened, stood out from the small bones, but her face was impassive. Cameron increased the pressure. The heels of her hands were almost vertical, twisted back against their wrists. Turn them another half inch and her wrists would tear.

Her eyes watched him steadily. Perspiration had formed on her upper lips. Moisture stood out on the taut skin below her eyes. He felt like dropping her arms and strangling her. When, at last, she did not speak or cry out, he said, "Nuts" again, and released her wrists.

Calmly she said, "You are strong, Paul Cameron." She looked down at her wrists. Blood was returning to them, and Cameron could see the imprint of his fingers.

She stroked the back of one wrist and said, "Is there anything else you wish to do?"

Cameron rolled over on his back. "I'll listen to your proposition."

"You have imagination," she said. "Do we need to discuss details?"

"Details?" Cameron said. "Oh, hell, no. Why bother with details? I'll pick up a crate for you, tuck it under my arm, and sprint over the Swiss Alps. It's as easy as that."

Renee leaned over him and touched his lips with her fingers. "It should not be difficult," she said. "Perhaps you learned the technique in prison."

"Perhaps." He held her body in his hands. Everything was junior size on this baby. Everything except brains. He said, "How far will the job take me? Geneva?"

She shook her head. "Not Geneva. The French are watching Switzerland for the gold."

"Macao?"

"No. Hanoi."

He lowered her against his chest. "Quite a trip," he said. "Can you trust me that far away?"

She laughed lightly. "Probably not. But you will be watched by men I can trust."

Cameron sat up and looked at the Mediterranean. Then he turned and looked at the Casino. "You've got a good deal here," he said. "You aren't starving. What's the angle? Why does a woman like you mix up in smuggling and politics and violence?"

Renee shrugged. "Perhaps because I am that kind of woman. Because I saw women raised and treated as slaves; because my mother was a woman of color in a land where the whites were rulers."

"New Caledonia?"

Renee nodded. "I was raised in a penal colony. My father was a convicted felon, but because my mother's skin was brown, in the eyes of other whites, she was less, even, than he."

"I thought it would be something like that."

"You are American," she said slowly. "I am surprised you can understand."

"We won't argue the point," Cameron said. "So now you're sending gold to your second cousins so that in Indo-China the Little Brown Man can come into his own."

Her face colored slightly. "It is inevitable," she said. "Nothing can stop us."

"The Workers of the World?" he asked sardonically. "The Enslaved Masses?"

"Nothing can withstand us."

"And what will you be, Comrade du Casse? Commissar of Laos and Upper Cambodia?"

"I will be..." she began, then stopped and turned away from him. "It makes no difference what plans the Party may have for me. I will do what I can until my work passes to other hands."

Cameron laughed nastily. "Say it again," he said. "Say it as though you believed it."

"I *do* believe it. It has been my life. It will always be my life."

Cameron shook his head. "You're too smart to be really convinced," he said. "If you hadn't lived in France, you'd be a better Communist. If you came from the Balkans you might even have turned out to be another Ana Pauker." He spat against the grass. "Instead, you'll let the Party use you until your usefulness is over, and then some night when you hear a knock on your door about three o'clock, you'll know they've come for you." He stood up and flexed his arms painfully. "I'd like to know what'll go through your mind then, Renee. I'd even stay around to find out."

She looked up at him, thin-lipped, baited, but she controlled herself and said, "You are typical of your race—of your class. But even you are not unwilling to be hired for the people's work."

"Certainly not," Cameron said. "Who has more gold than people?" He lighted a cigarette, shielding the flame against the rising sea breeze. He looked down at her and said, "What do you want me to do?"

"Go back to Paris."

"And wait?"

She turned her head. "Someone will come to you."

"Verrat?"

She looked up quickly. "Perhaps Verrat. Why?"

"I'm anxious to meet him," Cameron said. "Someplace where the light's a little better than last time."

"Ah, yes. I remember."

"Where shall I stay?"

"Wherever you choose."

"And you won't lose track of me?"

There was a faint smile on her lips. "We never do."

Cameron said, "Suppose I said I know how to find the gold."

"I would say that you lie."

"Don't be too sure. I had plenty of time to ask questions in Paris, Renee. And the people I talked with weren't afraid to answer." He saw her hand clench the matting.

She said, "Only fools would talk to an American."

Cameron ignored her. "I heard about a man named Verlaix."

"He is dead."

Cameron shook his head. "His brother is dead. Do you know where the juggler is?"

"He is a traitor to the Party. He fled France before he could be brought to trial."

"Then he was smarter than the rest of you," Cameron said. "Mind if I look for him?"

She shook her head. "A search has been made. You will not find him."

"Good," he said. "The Party says he cannot be found. *Ergo,* no one can find him." He looked out over the sea and saw whitecaps beginning to form. "Tell your boys I'm through with moonlight walks, and they'll find my door locked. And windows."

Cameron turned and walked toward the black Maserati. He did not look back until he had turned in the driveway, and then he saw the girl-like woman standing alone on the tan matting. He drove out of the Casino grounds, down to the sea highway again, heading for Nice.

He passed groups of bicyclists, hikers, picnic groups with lunches spread under the branches of cork trees, and high-powered, custom-built Autobineaus, Saoutchiks, and Guillores. This was the season of the *grandes vacances,* but for him it was ending almost before it had begun. He drove at an even speed, feeling his muscles stiffen from staying so long in one position, and the thought of a *wagon-lit* berth to Paris made him wince.

He had tried to run away from an obligation that had come with Phil's death. With Marcelle he had tried to relive a part of the past that was gone. In the attempt, he had lost her, and now there was for him only the reality of what lay ahead, of what he must do.

He pressed the accelerator toward the floorboard and threw the heavy car into the banking of a curve.

CHAPTER TWELVE

INSPECTOR Claude Astrel said, "Each time I see you, M. Cameron, your appearance has deteriorated. Am I to gather that your sojourn on the Cote was not a complete success?"

Cameron nodded. He looked out of Astrel's office window at the tree-lined street beyond. The morning was clear and pleasant. He said, "The trip was entirely unsuccessful."

"And so you come to me for advice?"

"I come to you so that we may discuss a matter of mutual concern."

"Ah," Astrel exhaled. "The gold?"

"Philip Thorne."

Astrel inserted a cigarette into his holder and lighted it. "Unfortunately there have been no new developments."

"I hardly thought there would be," Cameron said. He stood up.

Astrel looked up at him. "You are in a hurry?"

"Only to discover who killed my friend."

Astrel looked at the glowing end of his cigarette. "A laudable purpose," he said. "However, be assured that the entire criminal investigative facilities of the French police are at work on the case."

"When I lived in France," Cameron said, "the police had a reputation for speed. It's three weeks now, and you can't even make a guess."

Astrel shrugged. "Your impatience is understandable. But your attitude is subjective. In the course of a year literally hundreds of similar cases come to my attention. A tragedy occurs—bereft ones seek to discover the guilty."

Cameron felt anger rise. "Then the case of M. Thorne has no novel aspects."

Astrel's eyes flickered. He bent toward Cameron. "Perhaps not. But we are unable to establish his having seen anyone other than you on that fatal evening."

"Try harder," Cameron said.

"You were not entirely successful in removing your fingerprints from glass surfaces in M. Thorne's apartment."

Cameron felt his muscles tense. "Let's say my fingerprints derived from the occasion on which you found me there. My assailant, in eradicating his fingerprints, unknowingly removed mine."

Astrel's jowls shook in silent laughter. He wiped his face with a linen handkerchief and said, "A plausible theory, my friend. But it lacks one element."

"Which one?"

"The detectable presence of additional prints."

"I don't believe it."

"For what reason?"

"He had a housekeeper. Did she wear mittens?"

Astrel pondered the question, then dismissed it with a wave of his gold cigarette holder. "You possess a certain admirable ingenuity, M. Cameron. Attempt to contain it within the bounds of the probable."

Cameron felt his face whiten in anger. His voice edged harshly. "Listen, *flic*," he said, "you're paid to catch killers, not to philosophize about what a hell of a hard job you had. I ask you a few questions about Thorne's killer, and you get nasty. If you think I broke Phil's neck, put me in prison and try to prove it."

Astrel's hand rose pacifyingly. "No accusations have been made, although I confess that the possibility of your guilt was inescapable."

Cameron's fist hit the desk in front of Astrel. "What motive?" he asked. "Why should I want to kill my friend?"

Astrel looked at him steadily. "For a woman," he said. "For a woman named Marcelle."

Cameron sat back in his chair. He forced his voice to remain even. "Phil never knew I had known her."

"Why should I believe that?"

"Because I believe it."

"The woman told you?"

Cameron nodded.

"And you would take her word?"

"She said that Phil never knew. I believe her."

Astrel brushed aside a smoke ring. "Your capacity for belief is refreshing."

"Why should she lie?"

Astrel shrugged. "Why do women lie? To rid themselves of that which they no longer want—to obtain that which they do not have. A lie is easy. With many women it is a way of life."

Cameron felt his throat constrict. He said, "Why should she have wanted me?"

"Because you were a man who walked out on her. She was young then, and she idealized you. In your return she saw an opportunity to attain the unattainable. Thorne was getting ready to leave France—his part was almost over."

Cameron stood up. "We don't think alike," he said. "While you're sitting here trying to pin it on me, I'll be finding the killer."

Astrel ejected the cigarette stub from his holder. *"Bonne chance,"* he said. "May vengeance be yours."

Cameron felt the weight of Phil's Beretta in his jacket pocket. He thought of sticking it into Astrel's paunch. "You're a slimy bastard," he said. "And Du Casse wants me to do business with you."

Astrel's eyes blinked upward. They were shiny as fake opals. "I shall remember your words, M. Cameron. Whatever you do, be sure you do it with extreme care."

"I've been in prison before, gendarme. It was a good classroom." He turned away, then looked back at Astrel. "A man owes me something," he said. "Where can I find him?"

"What man?"

"Verrat."

Astrel's lips curled. "Verrat—and others like him—may be found each night at Le Carrousel."

"Where does he live?"

Astrel adjusted a new cigarette into the holder. "Where do rats live? The alleys, the sewers, the shadows of the Quai. This Verrat skulks sometimes in a den on the Rue du Tage."

"I'll find him." Cameron said.

"If you have difficulty in recognizing the one you seek, inquire for La Puce."

"I'll remember. His *nom de guerret.*"

Astrel laughed until perspiration rolled down his cheeks. He blotted them with his handkerchief. "No," he said. "A *nom d'amour.*"

Cameron walked out of the office and down onto the street.

It was too early for lunch. He walked through the midmorning crowds to Rond Point, took the Metro to Trocadero, and crossed the Pont d'Iena to the base of the Tour Eiffel. Vendors sold hot salted nuts, balloons, and ice cream; a guided group of American college girls giggled past. Tonight they would be chaperoned through a wicked evening at the Casino de Paris ending with cassis at the Lapin Agile. He heard one of them say, "I saw him this morning. He cooked breakfast for himself on the steps of the Palais de Chaillot and shook out his sleeping bag." The girl giggled nervously. "And the guards only looked at him as though he were mad. He's sort of funny looking, I guess, but he's just dreamy. And he has so many ideas..." The girls passed on, beyond earshot. Cameron thought. To hell with guys who flake out on the steps of the UN. To hell with international guilt complexes. He bought a ride to the top of the Tour Eiffel and sat in the sun until noon.

When he came down, he ate garlic snails at a small restaurant on the Rue Camou.

Not until you had checked your hat and coat with a handsome boy and walked down a winding, carmine-carpeted stairway past four, powdered seventeenth century footman wearing codpieces did you realize you were in a fag joint.

Le Carrousel, though, was hardly a joint. The broad stairway ended in a foyer that opened onto a large, deep room that was luxuriously decorated. The crowd was far from shabby. Mixed couples and foursomes sat at tables, and the number of champagne coolers was formidable. A good rumba band played and the dancers swayed, packed together on the dance floor.

Cameron stood at the bar and ordered a split of champagne. From where he stood he could see the entrance and the entire room. Here, the fag influence was hardly noticeable. There were no shabby groupings of fat older men and rouged youngsters; no secluded tables for hard-faced dikes. In fact, if you had not come through the entrance, you would never have noticed the carvings that topped the floor-to-ceiling columns: classical representations of androgynes. But now, as the orchestra stopped playing and the bandstand began to revolve, the facade of normalcy began to lift, and the heavy, clogging sensation of inversion settled over the room like a poisonous cloud.

Cameron sipped his champagne and watched the new string orchestra swing into position. Then the lights dimmed, a spotlight stabbed into the dance floor, and a man stepped from the wings. He adjusted a microphone that descended from the starlit ceiling, and announced a ballet performance by Mlle. Fayette.

Colored lights sprang into life, the orchestra began playing, and a heavy-bodied ballerina pirouetted out onto the floor. Cameron was unprepared for the thunderous applause that greeted the appearance. The ballerina bowed, spreading the puffy ballet skirt, and Cameron noticed the chalk-white face, the muscular arms, the thick, ungraceful legs. Then as the ballerina commenced a *pas seul,* awkwardly, angularly, with steel-cold eyes piercing the crowd, Cameron knew what was off-key.

Mlle. Fayette was a man.

The realization jolted him, and he finished his champagne quickly. As the performance continued, Cameron turned to watch the audience. Their faces were avid, and to Cameron, their anticipation was that of gourmets promised a feast of high meat. Never before had he encountered perversion in such epicurean surroundings.

He had always thought that faggots were gray-bearded old men who whispered in urinals and scratched smut on the walls of latrines. They were young, lipsticked weaklings who talked Picasso and Kafka and rented weekend cabins together on Cape Cod. To Cameron, Le Carrousel presented an entirely new facet of deviation. It catered to the percentage of homosexuality and voyeurism in the makeup of every human being; it glorified abnormality and perversion.

Cameron turned away from what he had seen, but the bar mirror reflected the unnatural performance, and its hypnotic effect over the patrons of Le Carrousel.

Perhaps La Puce was one of the watchers.

Cameron ordered another split of champagne, and while the bartender was filling his glass he asked, "Is Verrat here tonight?"

The bartender looked up quickly. "Never heard of him."

"La Puce?"

The bartender wiped perspiration from the side of the bottle. "He doesn't usually come in until about ten."

He understood now what Astrel had meant when he said that La Puce was Verrat's *nom d'amour*. The half-world of homosexuals had pseudonyms by which each pervert was known; this third sex used its own language in separating its devotees from the currents of normal life.

"I'm looking for him," Cameron said. "I'll appreciate your pointing him out when he arrives." He gave the bartender a thousand-franc note. The bartender smiled with the condescension of a practiced pimp. He said, "You didn't look like a *tapette* to me. Sure, I'll point him out."

"You never can tell," Cameron said. He turned from the bartender and watched Mlle. Fayette bowing off the floor. The orchestra began a tango and a pair of dancers costumed as Argentineans glided into the spotlight. There was only one thing wrong with their dancing, Cameron thought. The one wearing the shawl had been born male.

In the States there had been jokes about transvestites, about trouble at Penn and Harvard getting the Mask & Wig and Hasty Pudding ballerinas to take off their costumes when the show was over. Now he was able to understand the basis for the jokes. The thing with the shawl wore falsies and phony eyelashes, and its back was not supple enough to bend gracefully in the dance routine. To Cameron it was grotesque, but he could not dismiss it because the concentration of three hundred minds acted as an almost tangible force against his own. If you saw it at a carnival, you'd laugh it out of town, but here it was different. Here, jaded Frenchmen and tourists, their wives and mistresses took it seriously, even a little eagerly.

The shawl bent backward until it touched the polished flooring. The dance had ended.

Cameron felt as though he needed a breath of outside air. He turned from the bar, put some franc notes beside his unfinished champagne, and started to leave. The master of ceremonies was saying something suggestive into the microphone; the crowd was laughing. The bartender said, "There's La Puce." He pointed at a small man who had glided into the entrance and was talking with the *maitre d'hotel*. The man's face was thin, rat-like. His hair was peaked, his temples extraordinarily high. Cameron could see Verrat's eyes darting quickly over the crowd. Was he hunting tonight? Cameron wondered. Or was there an old rendezvous to be kept?

His fists tightened, his heart pounded. Was this the intelligence that had trapped Phil and killed him? Was Verrat the final answer?

The bartender said, "Want me to call him over here?"

"No. He's not the one I wanted," Cameron waited until Verrat was shown a table and seated. Then he walked into the foyer, took his hat and coat, and walked up the stairs past the immobile, pompadoured footman, and out to the street.

He breathed deeply, feeling the lingering ache of his ribs. The night was cool and a light rain had begun. Cameron walked across the street to an awninged *brasserie*. He ordered *fine cafe,* and sat at a sidewalk table where he could watch Le Carrousel's entrance. He lighted a cigarette and shielded it from the wind. Listening to the sounds of the nearby Champs Elysees, he sat smoking and sipping coffee and cognac until the other lights along the street went out, leaving only the Geissler-tube sign over Le Carrousel's doorway. He looked at it until it seemed to flicker beckoningly, obscenely, then turned away to rest his eyes on the darkness farther down the street.

Drops of moisture had collected on the sleeve of his trench coat. The Beretta lay cold against his thigh. A mile or so away a girl named Mari would be standing beside a piano singing to the patrons of the Cafe Adour. Cameron's hand brushed his forehead. The days and nights he had spent with her seemed as far away, as vague as a half-remembered dream. The forces that had motivated his leaving were dispelled now; he could hardly understand how they had existed at all.

He had thrown a cigarette butt into the gutter, and was reaching for a fresh cigarette when the lighted doorway opened. A mixed couple stepped out and signaled a taxi, and then two men came out. The men walked down the street into the darkness. Cameron lighted the cigarette, then shoved it into the dregs of his coffee. Verrat was coming out. Cameron recognized the high, peaked skull, the distinctive hairline. Verrat stood impatiently for a moment, looking for a taxi, then turned and began walking away from Le Carrousel. Cameron rose quickly, put his hand in his pocket, and crossed the street.

By now Verrat was almost lost in the darkness, but Cameron could hear the grating of his heels on the cobbles ahead. He gripped the Beretta with his right hand, bent slightly forward, and began to walk rapidly after the man ahead.

CHAPTER THIRTEEN

NOW THAT his eyes were adjusting to the darkness, Cameron could see Verrat's outline ahead. Once. Verrat looked back, quickly, and Cameron flattened against the nearby wall. Verrat seemed to be walking faster now, and Cameron knew that he must close the distance between them before Verrat could reach the Faubourg St. Honore.

There was an alley ahead. He stepped half into it and called, "La Puce."

Verrat stopped, turned, peering back toward the sound.

Cameron said, "You walk too fast."

Verrat took a few steps toward him. His voice said, "You would speak with me? Who are you?"

"An admirer, who saw you at Le Carrousel. I hesitated to make myself known in public."

Verrat's footsteps were rhythmic now, only a few feet away. Cameron kept his head down and said, "The alley is less public."

"Much less," Verrat said.

Cameron turned into the alley, took three steps, and rammed the Beretta into Verrat's skinny belly. He pushed back his hat and said, "My name is Cameron. Does it mean anything to you?" He heard a startled gasp. Verrat turned to run.

Cameron stuck out his foot and tripped him. La Puce lay belly down on the cobbles of the alley. Cameron laughed. "How strong is your neck, Comrade Verrat?"

Verrat's voice raised in a cry for help. Cameron kicked his face viciously. The man's hands clasped it, the body contorted in spasms of pain. Cameron reached down, dug his left hand under Verrat's collar, and pulled the body into the darkness of the alley. Verrat whimpered in pain.

Cameron pulled Verrat's coat down over the arms, binding them to the body. He knelt beside Verrat and said, "We're all alone, Comrade. No one will hear us."

Verrat gasped sobbingly. "What are you going to do?"

"Kill you."

"No! You must not kill me."

"Why not? You killed Thorne."

Verrat tried to sit up. "It was not I."

Cameron pushed him flat against the wet stone. "Who was it?"

"Coudet." His voice hissed the name.

Cameron caught his breath. "Why Coudet?"

"Because of the girl. Because of the gold."

Cameron put the Beretta back in his pocket. He said, "If I killed you the police would thank me. Particularly Astrel."

Verrat screamed and tried to wriggle away. Cameron pulled him back. He said, "I could break your nose now, tear off your ears, kick your stomach until your intestines burst." He bent over Verrat and whispered soothingly, "Who has the gold?"

"Believe me, I do not know." There was despair in the voice.

"Who had it last?"

Verrat did not answer. Cameron put his forearm across Verrat's windpipe and leaned on it lightly. The open mouth fought for air, then the body relaxed. Cameron slapped Verrat's face until blood trickled from the mouth. Verrat's eyes opened and he began breathing again. His face held an expression of horror.

Cameron said, "Once more, who had the gold before it disappeared?"

"Verlaix," the voice gasped. "Verlaix had it."

"Which Verlaix?"

"He is dead," Verrat said. "He was killed and the gold vanished."

"Does Renee du Casse know where the gold is?"

"I do not know."

Cameron pulled out the Beretta and laid it against Verrat's cheek. "Think."

"I swear I do not know!"

Cameron traced a pattern across Verrar's face with the muzzle of the pistol. He said, "I have some advice for you."

"I will follow it. Whatever it is."

"Leave France," Cameron said. "If I see you again I'll kill you." He pushed Verrat's head to one side, chopped the inverted pistol barrel at the temple. The gun sight sank into the thin, covering flesh, leaving a jagged gash. Blood began to flow down over the white, high forehead. The body was limp—as limp as Phil's had been—but with the difference that it still breathed. Cameron felt for Verrat's heart, found it beating regularly, and stood up. He wiped the pistol's wet muzzle on Verrat's coat.

He walked away through the darkness toward the Faubourg St. Honore. At the corner of the Rue de Berri he found a taxi. The driver was sleeping, but Cameron shook him awake and said, "Rue du Bac. Before dawn."

He sat at a corner table in the Cafe Adour, drinking cognac and Vittel. The small orchestra played unobtrusively, and Cameron wondered whether Mari would see him when she came out to sing. His corner was dark, and she would be facing a spotlight. No, she would not be able to see him.

By now Verrat should have picked himself up from the cobbles of the alley and found a physician. It would probably have been better for all concerned—and for France—if Verrat's life had ended back there in the darkness. Cameron felt a surge of satisfaction. Tomorrow night he would arrange to see Coudet.

Someone touched his shoulder, and he turned to see Vincent standing behind him. Cameron said, "I've been asking for you."

Vincent sat down and took a proffered cigarette. He said, "I wondered when you would return."

"How is Mari?"

Vincent shrugged. "Outwardly the same. Do you care?"

Cameron nodded.

"Then go away. You were bad for her, m'sieu. Very bad. But now she is recovering."

"How?"

"Her voice is less heavy; she laughs a little. From time to time she smiles."

"I'll go away," Cameron said. "She'll never see me again."

"Good." Vincent stood lip.

"Do not say I was here."

"Rely upon me." He started to walk away.

Cameron said, "Does she see others now?"

"Others?"

"Men. You know what I mean."

Vincent smiled slightly. "Mari's life is private. I endeavor to keep it that way. Perhaps I would tell you if you would not enlarge it into a triumph."

"Tell me."

"She sees no one, m'sieu. Only myself and my wife."

"That's what I wanted to hear," Cameron said. "I'll go now." He stood up from the table and walked toward the entrance with Vincent.

A waiter came toward them quickly and stopped in front of Cameron. "M. Cameron?" he inquired.

"Yes."

"I have something for you. It was left a week ago." He took a slip of paper from an inside pocket and gave it to Cameron. Cameron tipped him and held the paper under a dim wall light. Perhaps Mari had written. Perhaps she was waiting for him now...

But the paper said, "I have discovered a matter of interest to you." It was signed "Lussac."

Vincent said, "From Mari?"

"No." Cameron walked away from him to the telephone. He thumbed through the directory, looking for Lussac's home address, wondering if a booking agent would be home at one-thirty in the morning.

The listing was easy to find: Rue Fremicourt. Cameron came out from behind the bar and put on his hat and coat. As he left the Cafe Adour, the orchestra began to play Mari's introduction. The closing door cut off the burst of applause.

He stood in the bedroom of a frightened man.

M. Lussac said, "Could not this business have waited until tomorrow?"

"No."

The booking agent got out of bed, stepped into his slippers and put on a dressing robe. His bare legs, his fat, unshaven face looked ludicrous. Cameron followed him into another room, a room that smelled of cabbage.

M. Lussac ran his hand through unkempt hair and took a cigarette from Cameron. He said, "You once asked me where you could find a juggler named Andre Verlaix."

"Yes."

"I gave you his picture, dismissed him from my mind. Then a few days ago a friend of mine mentioned casually that he had seen Verlaix."

"Where?"

M. Lussac spread his hands. "Is the information of value?"

"It could be."

"How valuable?"

Cameron caught Lussac by the collar of his nightshirt and twisted it. When the face grew red, he released it. He stood back while Lussac coughed and rubbed his neck.

Cameron said, "Do you want to bargain?"

Lussac looked up, shock in his face. "It was never my intention. I want only to perform a service."

"Where's Verlaix?"

Lussac glanced around the room, looking for escape.

Cameron took the Beretta from his pocket.

Lussac stepped backward and said quickly. "Zurich."

"Where in Zurich?"

"I was not told. Verlaix was seen on the street."

"Which street?"

"Niederdorfstrasse."

"How did he look?"

"The same. He had not changed."

Cameron put away the Beretta, took out his billfold, and counted fifteen thousand francs onto the table. He said, "In case there might be hard feelings."

Lussac looked greedily at the money. "Of course not," he said. "You are truly generous."

Cameron laughed. "One more thing," he said.

"Yes?"

"Forget you ever saw me."

"Certainly, m'sieu."

"If others learn of our transaction, you will not live until autumn."

"*Eniendu.*" Lussac's face was gray. The mark of his collar circled his neck. "*Au revoir, m'sieu.*"

"*Au revoir,*" Cameron said. He unlocked the door, stepped out into the hallway. As he walked down the stairs, he could hear M. Lussac locking the door behind him.

He had reached the station too late to catch the Simplon or the Arlberg Express, so he boarded a local instead, and sitting all night in a third-class compartment he reached the Zurich Hauptbahnhof at dawn.

Cameron slept until noon, ate a heavy Swiss meal in the hotel restaurant, and walked to Niederdorfstrasse, passing the tall, pink-white Grossmunster church. Sitting on a bench in the warm sunlight, he took out the old picture of Andre Verlaix and looked at it again. He watched the passers-by carefully for an hour, then gave up and went to a cafe for beer and a sandwich.

A telephone directory gave him listings for seventeen booking agents. Sitting in the cafe's telephone booth, he called them all. None had heard of a French juggler named Verlaix. Cameron left the booth and walked along the Mythen Quai, looking at the blue water of the Zurichsee. Lussac could have lied, or his friend could have been mistaken about seeing Verlaix. And in three years a man could change his trade, learn a new one. And why should he retain the name, if he feared it enough to flee France?

Cameron watched one of the little white lake steamers casting off from the pier at Burkli-Platz, its red Swiss flag seeming to bisect the high Zurichberg in the distance. The sound of music floated across the lake. He felt discouraged now. To hell with the gold and everything connected with it except Phil's murderer. Last night Verrat had said Coudet was the killer. It could be true, or it could be the wild accusation of a badly frightened man.

Across the end of the lake was the Hotel Bellerive Cameron remembered being there as a boy with his father and mother. There had been big eiderdown beds, and hot chocolate and croquet on the broad lawn, and a concert orchestra in the domed dining room. The food had been good, and he decided to go there tonight for dinner. He would stay in Zurich another twenty-four hours, looking for Verlaix, before going back to Coudet and getting a few answers from him.

Walking back toward the center of town, he passed a wooded park at the end of the lake. The afternoon was warm, and Cameron sat down on the grass while he opened his collar. He spread his coat and leaned back against it, looking up at the high mare's-tail that hung over the Zurichsee. He closed his eyes, covered them with his forearm, and fell asleep.

The Bellerive restaurant produced an excellent rare beefsteak with browned potatoes and green beans. Dessert was heavy pudding washed down with a local wine. Cameron tried the coffee, but the chicory taste was too much for him, and he asked the waiter for his bill.

While he was paying it, Verlaix's picture fell out of his wallet. He started to put it back, then showed it to the waiter. He said, "Did you ever see this man before?"

In accented French, the waiter said, "I believe I have seen him."

"He is an entertainer. He used to call himself Verlaix." The waiter shook his head. "No. It is not the same man. The juggler I know is called Sardou." He picked up the silver change plate and began to walk away. Cameron caught his sleeve quickly. "Where is this Sardou?"

"Very near," the waiter said. "He performs each night in the ballroom."

"Here?"

The waiter nodded. "In the Bellerive. You may see his photograph in the foyer."

Cameron thanked the waiter, and walked quickly out of the restaurant. In the foyer he found a glass-covered display panel, advertising the Bellerive's entertainment: a balalaika artist, a Rumanian dance team, an Austrian acrobat, and finally, a juggler named Sardou.

Cameron did not need to compare the two photographs.

His heart pounding, he walked to the ballroom, took a table, and sat drinking kirsch, waiting for the performance of a juggler who called himself Sardou.

CHAPTER FOURTEEN

CAMERON drank kirsch while the balalaika played, while the dancers danced, while the acrobat levitated. In his mind he was back at the Cafe Adour, back at Le Carrousel. The entertainers merged into a gyrating montage until the crashing roll of a drum announced Herr Sardou, King of Jugglers.

He poured more kirsch into his glass and sat forward, peering through a haze of cigarette smoke at the lithe man in evening clothes who walked to the center of the floor and bowed to the audience. A woman assistant ran onto the floor briefly and threw an assortment of colored balls to Sardou. He caught them quickly and flicked them upward until the air was alive with motion and color. The orange-size balls popped energetically upward, bouncing from his forehead, his chin, his forearms, his biceps, his thighs and heels. Then Sardou began to settle slowly. He lowered himself on one leg until he was seated on the floor. Then he leaned backward until his shoulders were horizontal. Incredibly, the shower of colored balls had followed him down without losing their motion. His head moved quickly and precisely as a bird's; his arms jerked like whips. Then he began to sit up, to rise from the floor. When he was standing on his feet again, he caught the balls deftly, one at a time, and stuffed them into his pockets, until only one remained, bouncing rhythmically from the tip of his nose. The orchestra blared a crescendo, and the audience stamped the floor enthusiastically.

Sardou bowed, slipped out of his tailcoat, and handed it to the woman, who carried it off the floor into the shadows. From his trousers, Sardou drew out a silver baton and began turning it with the tips of his fingers. Cameron felt himself watching fixedly. The baton spun faster until it was a blur of silver, like a propeller in the sun. Then he was sitting in the bucket seat of a sag-winged C-47 flying back to France after London rest leave, looking out of the scratched window at the flare pots of Villacoublay below and the steel matting that covered newly filled shell holes, circling until the flight of fighter-bombers was airborne for Meaux...

Cameron shook his head quickly and looked down at the tablecloth. He picked up his kirsch glass and emptied it. The thin, biting taste of cherry pits stung his mouth. Their fumes seemed to fill his brain. He looked up and saw Sardou weaving three spinning batons through the air, the orchestra accentuating their rise and fall.

Cameron tried to visualize Sardou as Andre Verlaix, member of a Resistance group. He looked at the juggle's immobile face and realized how readily it would blend into any background. Sardou would have been a Resistance courier, darting swiftly through the shadows of an Orleans street, carrying his messages or leaving explosive envelopes in an SS maildrop. That would have been Sardou's role, and he was alive now only because his commonplace features defied accurate description.

Mme. Barjeval had said that even very good jugglers were finding postwar living hard. Sardou was an excellent juggler, and Cameron was sure that the Bellerive paid as well as any hotel in Switzerland. So far, Verlaix's luck had not deserted him, but Cameron wondered how long Verlaix would live if Renee or Victor or Astrel found out where he was.

The act ended in another five minutes, but Sardou was called back twice for encores. Cameron watched the juggler retire through the crowd, saw an exit door open to let him enter.

Cameron called for his check, paid it in Swiss francs, and rose from the table. The ballroom lights had gone on, and the dance orchestra was playing *"Mariandl"* for a group of well-fed Swiss dancers. He walked around the outside of the room and tried the exit door through which Sardou had left. The door opened slightly and a Swiss-German accent said, "What do you want?"

In bad German, Cameron said, "I want to see Herr Sardou."

"Herr Sardou has gone."

Cameron tried the door with the tip of his toe, but it was blocked solidly. He asked, "When will he return?"

"His next performance is at midnight."

Cameron took a calling card from his wallet. He wrote on it and handed it through the door. "Perhaps you will undertake to deliver this to Herr Sardou." He dropped two Swiss francs into the man's palm.

"Certainly. *Danke schon.*"

"*Bitte schon.*"

The door closed.

Cameron walked back to the main entrance and into the Hotel Bellerive lobby, sure that Sardou had not left the hotel. He was equally sure that Sardou had made himself as inaccessible as possible to people who wanted to see him.

Cameron put on his hat and folded his coat across his arm. He would go back to his room now and wait for the call that Sardou would be forced to make. He had written on the card, under his name and hotel: "A blind woman on the Rue Perronet told me you would know who killed Philip Thorne."

The doorman bent stiffly from the waist as Cameron walked down the steps to the driveway. Riding back along Bellerivestrasse, he watched the lights of a little lake steamer crossing from Burkli-Platz to the Zurichhorn.

You stand in your room smoking Swiss-made Philip Morris cigarettes, drinking Landtwing kirsch with chasers of Malessert, looking at the old-fashioned German phone beside your bed, waiting for it to ring, but hearing only the distant whistle of the night train for Basel.

A colored relief map of Zurich pressed under the glass bureau top had titles in five languages:

Zurich mit See und Alpen
Zurich avec le lac et les Alpes
Zurigo col lago e le Alpi
Zurich with Its Lake and Alps
Zurich met her meer en de Alpen

Cameron tilted the thin neck of the Malessert bottle and poured white wine into a water tumbler. Some of it spilled on the glass top, distorting the poly lingual titles, making the blue Zurichsee stand out as though it was a range of mountains. He looked at the lighted street below, thinking that the memory of James Joyce would always haunt Zurich. *The soul's incurable loneliness.* He thought of Joyce teaching languages at Berlitz so that he could eat until *Ulysses* was finished. Joyce, the rejected artist who swore himself to silence, exile, and cunning.

The telephone rang sharply, commandingly. Cameron clicked the tumbler against the glass bureau top and walked to the bed. He lifted the telephone.

A voice said, "Herr Cameron?"

"Sardou?"

"Ja," the voice said cautiously.

"Speak French," Cameron said, and heard a sound as though Sardou had caught his breath. "Where are you?"

"Hotel Bellerive."

"When can I see you?"

Cameron heard the sound of a muffled question. Then Sardou said, "After my next performance."

"Midnight?"

"A little later."

"In your dressing room?"

"No. We might be seen."

"Where?"

Conversation again. Then the voice asking, "When did you reach Zurich?"

"This morning."

"Were you followed?"

"I don't think so. I don't know."

In the background, Cameron could hear a woman's voice raised protestingly. Finally Sardou said, "How did you know M. Thorne?"

"We were friends. We grew up together."

"Where?"

"In France. In Lyon."

"Good," Sardou said. "Then you shared his secrets."

"I shared them."

"Stay in your room. I will come to you."

Cameron looked at his watch. It was nearly eleven. He said, "I'll expect you by twelve-thirty."

"Agreed." The phone went dead. Cameron replaced the receiver and poured himself another shot of kirsch. He drank it quickly, took the Beretta out of his pocket, checked the magazine, and put the pistol in his outside coat pocket.

An hour and a half to wait.

Cameron called the bell captain and asked for a copy of *Le Parisien*. When it arrived, he passed over the political news and read:

DRAME DE LA JALOUSIE A AUBERVILLIERS
*Un jeune chaudronnier
plonge un couteau
dans le ventre de son amie*

Cameron read the drab details of the Drama of Jealousy at Aubervilliers, then a plea for the necessity of heavy industrialization in France by *Le Parisien's envoye special* until his eyes were tired. He turned out the bed lamp and lay back against the pillow.

It was the ringing of the telephone that wakened him. He felt for it in the dark room, lifted the receiver, and turned on the light. "Yes," he said. "Cameron speaking."

Sardou's voice said, "I will be unable to keep our appointment as arranged."

"Stop listening to the little woman," Cameron said. "Meet me tonight, or I'll telephone Astrel."

Silence.

Cameron said, "If you're afraid of me, then don't come here. Meet me in some public place."

When Sardou finally spoke, he said, "Very well, m'sieu. The Hotel Central. In the bar."

"I'm on my way," Cameron said.

"How will I know you?"

"Look at the tables. When you see one on which two packages of cigarettes stand together, sit down."

"I shall come at once."

Cameron hung up, washed his face in the bathroom, and took the lift down to the lobby. Before he left, he bought two packages of American cigarettes at the tobacco stand.

He entered the Central Bar from the street. The lighting was dim, the room paneled in dark wood with heavy, Germanic carving. No more than a dozen Swiss sat at the small plastic-topped tables. Most of them were drinking beer. A barmaid wearing an embroidered Alpine dirndl stood talking with the bartender. Cameron sat near the door and ordered a glass of kirsch. He put the cigarette packages on the table in front of him. The revolving door reflected the yellow glow of the wall lights.

Cameron lighted a cigarette and watched the entrance.

Sardou did not appear for ten minutes. And he did not enter the bar from the street. He came through the hotel entrance slowly, looking at the patrons as he walked. When he saw Cameron, his eyes flickered to the tabletop, then he came forward more quickly, with something of assurance in his walk.

Cameron did not get up. He said, "Sit down, my friend. Join me in a glass of cherry brandy."

"I prefer whisky." Sardou pulled a chair from the table and sat across from Cameron. Even in the badly lighted room his face was pale. He looked like a man who lived in the stare of footlights, in badly ventilated dressing rooms.

Cameron gave him a cigarette and asked the waitress for whisky. He watched Sardou's eyes shifting from entrance to entrance, then back to the top of the table. "Were you followed?" he asked.

Sardou jumped. "I do not think so. Still, one must be careful."

Cameron nodded. "You're alive because you were careful," he said. "Philip Thorne was less careful than you. Someone got him when he was alone."

Sardou wiped perspiration from his lip. "I read it. M. Thorne's neck was broken."

Cameron leaned forward suddenly. "Were you there, Verlaix?"

Sardou leaned back quickly. "I? I have not left Zurich in three years."

"Can you prove it?"

"Yes," Sardou said defiantly. "If a witness is necessary, one will testify."

"Your girl friend?"

"My assistant."

"What if I don't believe her?"

Sardou's face became paler. His eyes darted from side to side. "What would you do?"

Cameron's hand clamped around Sardou's wrist. "I would treat you badly, Verlaix. Very badly indeed."

The waitress brought Sardou's whisky. Cameron released the juggler's wiry wrist. He said, "I don't want you. I don't even want the gold your brother had."

"What do you want?" Sardou asked hoarsely.

"A murderer. The man who killed Philip Thorne."

Sardou gulped his whisky. "It was not I," he said. "Do you think I would come to meet you if I had done it?"

Cameron shrugged. "You have strong hands," he said. "Strong arms. You could have done it."

"But I have not been in Paris."

Cameron lighted another cigarette. "We'll leave it that way for now," he said. "You were afraid of me tonight, Verlaix. You were afraid to be alone with me."

"My brother was killed," Sardou said. "M. Thorne is dead. Who can say who will be next?"

"If you know who killed Philip, I'll kill the man myself. That should end it."

Sardou stared at his empty glass. Cameron motioned toward the waitress. She brought over a bottle of whisky and left it on the table. Sardou filled his glass quickly, spilling a little on the table. He said, "I must think, m'sieu."

"How long?"

"Tomorrow."

"I've got a gun in my pocket," Cameron said. "I could shoot you in the belly and walk away. They'd never find me. If you stall me, I might try you for size."

"I swear I will not leave Zurich until I have talked with you. But then I will have to leave Switzerland. Perhaps even Europe."

"You frighten too easily."

"Does Astrel know where you are?"

Cameron shook his head.

"Coudet?"

"No."

"Mme. Barjeval?"

"No one knows."

Sardou sipped his whisky. "That is better," he said. "Now I am less afraid."

"Don't feel too happy. *I* know where you are."

A woman pushed through the hotel entrance. She stood in the doorway for a moment, looking around the room. When she saw Sardou she seemed to relax. Then she turned and went back through the doorway.

Sardou said, "My assistant."

"I recognized her."

"She waits for me. I told her to look for me in ten minutes. If I had not been here she would have given your name to the police." He stood up before Cameron could stop him. "I must go now. I am known here. We must meet at another place."

"Wherever you say."

"First, I must think, m'sieu. Then I must satisfy myself that all will be safe."

"I'll call you tomorrow."

Sardou held up his hand theatrically. "Do not do so. When the time is right, I will get in touch with you." He turned to look over his shoulder as the assistant came into the room again.

"Now you must excuse me, m'sieu. This has been a difficult evening. Tomorrow you will hear from me."

Cameron looked up at him. "Don't let yourself forget," he said. "You might be able to get away from me, but Astrel's police would bring you back."

Sardou's eyes opened wide for an instant, then his face became placid again with the fixed expression of the stage professional. He turned and went quickly to the end of the barroom. Taking the woman's arm, he walked out of the room with her.

Cameron sat at the table and finished his cigarette. Then he got up and walked out into the street. The night was cold and he shivered a little.

A locomotive clanged deafeningly into the station. A policeman paused under a street light and Cameron walked past him. Somewhere in the distance, he could hear the whistle of a steamer far out on the Zurichsee.

CHAPTER FIFTEEN

BY AFTERNOON he had grown to hate the sight of his room. Flies buzzed incessantly against the mirror, against the bureau where, last night, he had spilled kirsch and wine. His eyes pained a little; his throat had been dry since morning.

He decided to stay away from kirsch.

From the room he could see the Limmat River, hear the sound of the streetcars and busses. He opened the window, and looked at the high, wooded Dolder to the east. He remembered its warm swimming hall from his boyhood. He would have liked to spend this afternoon there, but instead he was shackled to his room. He turned away from the window and looked at the lattice-carved door. It seemed to lose color, harden into the blunt outlines of a cell door he had known for eighteen months. He closed his eyes and tried to think of something pleasant.

Or someone pleasant...like Mari.

Cameron sat at the heavily built writing desk and scrawled outlines on a note pad. Yes, it was pleasant to think of Mari, to remember how it had been with her at the beginning, to recall the unspoken understanding that had been theirs. Now that he could think about it without wincing, he knew that he had found with Mari what he had hoped to find with Marcelle. Yet there was a certain casualness, a hardness about Mari. He had seen the same thing emerge finally in his wife—a kind of resigned callousness that refused to distinguish right from wrong, true from false, trust from betrayal.

He knew that he had no right to include Mari in his thoughts, now or ever. But he could not help speculating on the way she would have come through, had he put her to a test...

And Marcelle?

He said the name aloud. He said it again. He was surprised to find that it evoked less than he had expected. Well, she was gone, too. Vanished in the night.

The soul's incurable loneliness....

He knew that he was lonely; sick to the bone with loneliness that he could counteract only momentarily with the emotional purge that went with brutality. Sometime that need for escape could smother him with its crushing demands, and he would regain consciousness to find that he had killed someone in an extraordinarily savage way.

He thought if there is a percentage of inversion within our makeup, then there is also a percentage of the animal that responds and enlarges to fill an emotional vacuum. If Verlaix turned out to be the killer of Philip Thorne, Cameron would not hesitate to kill him. *Lex talonis. Droit de la vengeance.* Justification was unnecessary. Yet in the act of killing would come an atavistic satisfaction extending beyond the simple needs of justice.

Cameron looked at his watch: after four o'clock. A train clanged out along the *Eisenbahn.* He looked through the window and saw it cross the Limmat, enter the Dielsdorf tunnel, and disappear. Another voyage begun; a departure made; an arrival to be awaited.

Since prison, his life had consisted of nothing but arrival and departure.

He looked at the telephone. Where was Verlaix? Why had he failed to telephone? Had Verlaix fled Zurich? Was he on a train going south, north, west, east, away from Zurich, fleeing the fear that had arrived in the night?

Cameron cursed. He should never have let Verlaix slip away from him last night. He should have followed him home, dragged him into an alley, and beaten the truth from him. If he had done so, Cameron would not be waiting in Zurich today. He would be back in Paris, probably; laying plans for the climax of his search. Instead, he was locked in a barren room waiting for the ring of a telephone, trying to avoid glancing at the door's carved parody of prison bars.

He felt that he must push the walls farther apart so that he could breathe.

He got up suddenly, slid the door bolt, and looked into the hallway. A linen maid walked by, humming to herself.

Cameron left the door ajar. He went to the closet, took out his valise, threw it on the bed, and opened it. Then he opened the bureau drawer and looked at his neatly folded shirts.

There had been two shirts in the drawer last evening, one with a laundry mark, one without. The marked shirt had been on top of the newer one.

Now their order was reversed.

Cameron kicked shut the door, bolted it, and walked back to the bed.

Someone had searched his room last night while he was with Verlaix.

Who?

Verlaix's woman?

Perhaps.

Someone from Paris?

More likely.

He wanted a drink, desperately, unreasonably.

The loneliness he had known had vanished; in its place had come clutching fear. He took the Beretta from his pocket and looked at it. His hands stroked the oily-smooth blue metal. Its coldness restored a sense of reality to his mind.

He did not want to be alone any longer. He wanted to be outside the room, walking down Stampfenbachstrasse, standing with crowds.

Cameron took the valise back to the closet. He took out his wallet, removed the Swiss bank notes and his calling cards. He pulled a small hair from his wrist, placed it between two of the cards, and inserted them in the wallet. Then he placed the wallet in his top bureau drawer.

He felt better now. The maid could have moved his shirts. The maid could pick up his wallet and search it for money. But a hotel maid or a thief would not bother with his calling cards. It was a way of determining his position, of finding out whether he was alone in Zurich.

He telephoned the Bellerive and asked for Sardou, but Sardou had not yet reached the hotel. He was not due here until eight-thirty. No, they could not say where Herr Sardou lived.

Cameron hung up. There was nothing he could do but wait. If Sardou did not call, he would go to the Bellerive tonight and wait for him to leave.

There was a knock on the door. Cameron started, then put his hand inside his coat pocket. He opened the door and stepped back tensely.

It was only the servant bringing Cameron's pressed suit.

Cameron watched the valet walk to the closet and hang up his suit. When he handed him four francs, he asked, "How many keys are there to this room?"

"Only one."

"And the housekeeper has a master key?"

The valet nodded.

"What happens if a guest neglects to return his key?"

"The lock is changed."

"Good," Cameron said.

"Bitte schon." The valet bowed, and Cameron walked to the door with him.

When the valet had disappeared down the hall, Cameron bent and looked carefully at the lock. He began to straighten up when a shaft of light illuminated something that clung to the keyhole orifice. Cameron lighted a match and looked at it closely.

The thing that had caught his attention, the thing he had looked for, was a scrap, a peeling of wax.

Cameron took it on the nail of his index finger, looked at it again, and wiped it off with his handkerchief.

Someone had made a key from a wax impression; enough wax had remained to scrape off when the key was inserted.

It had happened, Cameron was sure, last night.

He stepped back into his room, locked the door, and called the bar for a bottle of whisky.

As he lay on the bed, drinking slowly, he knew that in Zurich he was not alone.

By eight thirty, Sardou had not telephoned. Cameron had eaten dinner in the room, taken a sobering shower, and changed his suit.

He walked through the center of town, past the Grossmunster church, out onto the Seefeld Quai, near the Zurichhorn, killing time until Sardou's last performance.

There was a lighted pavilion in the park off Bellerivestrasse, with music of violins and a concertina. Cameron found a table under the trees, and drank brandy until midnight. Then he walked the rest of the way to the lighted porte-cochere of the Bellerive.

It was twelve-fifteen when he reached the service entrance behind the hotel. The barred door was brightly lighted by a single bulb. Fifty feet away there was a bench on the croquet lawn. Cameron stretched out on it and waited.

Waiters came and went. A chef stepped outside for a cigarette. A waitress and a bus boy disappeared into the shadows.

At one o'clock Cameron stood up and walked around the bench to stretch his muscles. The night was growing cold. He could see the lights of Zurich in the distance, the lighted quai that defined the Limmat River.

At one-fifteen Cameron left the croquet lawn and went into the Bellerive lobby. From a house phone he called Sardou's dressing room.

No one answered.

He tried again, then signaled a bellboy with a five-franc note.

"*Bitte?*"

"Herr Sardou. Has he left the hotel?"

"*Ja.* Directly after his midnight performance. I remember because I have never seen him leave the hotel through the lobby."

Cameron gave the boy the bank note. "Do you know where Herr Sardou lives?"

The bellboy shook his head.

"Could you find out?"

"It is not permitted. Perhaps if you asked the manager…"

Cameron went to the entrance and took a taxi back to the Borse.

The telephone wakened him. The glow of his wristwatch indicated four-thirty-five. He fumbled for the telephone automatically. A gasping voice said, "Come quickly, M. Cameron."

"Sardou?"

The voice breathed assent.

"Where are you?"

"In my room. Three-one-three Badenerstrasse."

"What's happened?"

The next words froze him. They were: "I am dying."

"Who was it?"

Sardou did not answer his question. He said, with difficulty, "Tonight I was watched. I feared to call you."

"Don't hang up," Cameron said. "Call a doctor. I'll be with you in five minutes."

"You may be too late," the voice said. "Too late…" It trailed off, and Cameron could hear the receiver fall against the floor.

He switched on the light, pulled on clothing, and when he could not find a taxi on the street, began running toward Badenerstrasse. Number 313 was beyond Langstrasse. His lungs felt like withered gourds by the time he had reached the building.

He stood in the entry, panting and trembling while he held a match and scanned the mail drops. A card in German script said: *"Sardou der Gaukler."*

Cameron ran up the stairs to the third floor. The hallway was dark, but he could hear moaning behind the nearest door. He pushed it inward and saw Sardou lying on the floor, the telephone by his outstretched hand. Cameron pushed the door shut behind him and locked it.

He walked toward Sardou.

Kneeling beside the man, he saw that he was wounded. Blood had spread out from his body, wetting the carpet. It was new blood, glistening in the dim light of the table lamp.

Cameron said, "What happened, Sardou?"

The man's head moved; he tried to look up at Cameron. His lips opened and closed. They said, "I am dying."

Cameron gripped his shoulders. "Hang on," he said. "Tell me who did it."

The juggler's eyes closed. He said in a whisper, "We were leaving tonight. Going to Livorno…should have gone before."

"Why didn't you call me?"

Sardou shook his head slowly, slackly. "Something you said. A name…" His back arched in pain. Blood flowed in a thin, spreading stream from the corner of his mouth. "Monceau," he said in a spasm. "My brother dead."

"What's Monceau?"

The juggler's arm flexed, rested on his forehead. "A park," his lips said. "Walked there…evenings."

The stain on the carpet spread toward Cameron's knee. He moved away from it. Sardou was not rational enough to follow his questions. Cameron would have to follow the dying man's words. He said, "What happened to your brother?"

"Betrayed. *The milice.*"

"Where did your brother keep the gold?"

Sardou's tongue licked his dry lips. "*Wasser. Wasser,*" he said.

Cameron got up, went into the back of the flat, filled a cup with water, and held it next to Sardou's lips.

Sardou tried to swallow, but the water deflected onto the carpet from the side of his mouth.

Cameron repeated, "The gold. Where was it kept?"

Sardou opened his eyes, stared at the ceiling. "The foundry."

"What happened to it?"

"Bombed," Sardou said, with an effort. "Destroyed."

"How did they catch your brother?"

The juggler's lips set themselves in a horrible grimace. "Astrel. Astrel told the *milice.*"

Cameron felt himself go limp. His throat was dry.

"And the gold?"

"Astrel," the dying man breathed. "Astrel," His eyes seemed to change, to focus on something a great distance away.

"Who came here tonight, Verlaix? Who was it?" Cameron gripped the man's body, raising it from the floor, but he might as well have shouted into a well. Sardou's muscles slackened, his breathing stopped. He died in Cameron's arms.

Cameron lowered the body to the carpet, turned it over, and looked at the dead man's chest.

Outlined on the juggler's evening shirt were three bullet holes.

Cameron stood up and walked into the bedroom for a blanket. He turned on the light and froze against the wall.

A woman lay on the bed; Sardou's assistant. Her waxy body wore a slip and stockings. Her right arm lay awkwardly under her body. Her mouth was open. Wide.

She had been shot in the throat.

Cameron turned off the light, feeling nauseated. He did not have enough strength to throw up. His stomach retched convulsively, but he fought the spasm and walked into the room where the juggler's body lay.

Then he heard a noise in the rear of the flat.

He pulled the Beretta from his pocket, flicked off the safety, and crept into the dark kitchen. The noise was closer now—plaintive, whimpering. It was from somewhere on the floor.

Cameron turned on the light and saw a baby dachshund standing in a cardboard box, its paws on the edge. The puppy yipped and wagged its tail.

Cameron began to laugh; slowly at first, then faster, until he knew that he was in the grip of hysteria. He staggered to the sink, turned on the faucet full force, and held his head under the rushing water until he coughed chokingly.

He wiped his head with a towel and blotted the collar and lapels of his suit. The puppy tried frantically to climb out of its box.

Cameron stooped down and lifted the little tan animal with one hand. He put the Beretta back into his pocket and carried the puppy into the other room...

As he opened the hall door, he could hear a metallic, questioning voice coming from the telephone receiver. The puppy began to whimper and lick Cameron's face. He stroked it comfortingly and closed the door behind him.

Walking back along Badenerstrasse in the grayness of dawn, he saw a milkman, bought a half-liter of fresh milk, and sat numbly in a doorway feeding the puppy while the sun beyond the Dolderwald lightened the high spire of St. Peter's Church.

CHAPTER SIXTEEN

YOU FLY in an Air France C-54 from Zurich's Dubendorf airport to Le Bourget in two hours, holding a tan *Teckel* puppy in your lap while the stewardess lets it lick drops of milk from her fingers.

You had packed so quickly that you had not bothered to check the lock of your door again or the position of the hair between your calling cards. Because what you would find would be without significance. You knew the answers now.

Andre Verlaix had been killed, together with a woman who once wore spangles and handed props to and carried coats for Sardou der Gaukler. His escape had been complete until you tracked him to Zurich, and now he was dead. He and a fleshy woman of forty-five who tried to keep him from meeting you, who knew the danger you represented. Cameron in Zurich had meant death for Verlaix.

Because you had been trailed.

It was not as though you had reached Zurich and found Verlaix dying of natural causes—say bad lungs or a weak heart. You found him, and that action had marked him for death. But now it was too early, too soon, to add together everything else. You knew that it would become clear now; a little clearer, because someone had been driven to kill the little juggler.

You looked at the puppy sleeping across your lap, her small pink belly quivering with the plane's vibration, and you wondered what prompted you to take her from Verlaix's flat. Was it a gesture of protection, a compelling need for companionship, or an automatic rejection of death? You were surfeited with death. It clung to you like a bad breath. Perhaps subconsciously you claimed the puppy to salvage something living from a scene of violent death.

After the taxi left Le Bourget he fell asleep and woke somewhere near the Gare de l'Est. The puppy was chewing his cuff. He stroked her silky ears and watched Paris roll by until he could see the dirty hulk of Notre Dame ahead. The taxi crossed the Seine at the Pont des Arts and turned right, and by the time he had lighted a cigarette they had stopped on the Quai. Cameron opened the door and got out, leaving his luggage inside.

"*Attendez,*" he said. "*Deux minutes.*"

"*Qui.*" The driver touched his cap. "I'll wait."

The Quai was lethargic in the warmth of mid-afternoon. A grizzled bookseller slept beside his stall. Cameron wiped his arm against his forehead and shifted the puppy to his other hand. He walked into the cool hallway of the apartment and up to the floor that had a silver nameplate set into the door.

He rang the chimes and waited.

After a while the door opened. A maid looked out, saw him, and started to close the door. Cameron pushed against it. The maid said anxiously, "Mlle. Mari is not here."

"Good," Cameron said. He handed her the puppy. "A present from Zurich."

"You have been in Zurich?"

"And points south." Cameron saw the puppy settle contentedly into the maid's cradled arms.

"But why do you bring this little dog?"

Cameron shrugged. "It's the only good thing that's happened to me since I left here. I want Mademoiselle to have it."

The maid lowered her head. "I understand, m'sieu. And now you leave Paris again?"

"Yes."

"Soon?"

"Very soon."

There was nothing else he could say. He turned and started to walk toward the stairs. Behind him the maid said, "You have been missed, m'sieu."

Going down the steps, he heard the door close behind him.

Another few blocks in the taxi, down the Boulevard Raspail to the Hotel Lotti, chosen because Americans who sought Left Bank flavor stayed there. One more American would not be noticed. He registered as Peter Caldwell.

In his room he undressed wearily and stretched out on the old, overstuffed brass bed. A few hours ago he had been in Zurich. He closed his eyes and remembered death in the flat above the Badenerstrasse. His fingerprints were there; he hoped that the murderer's were there, too. It was one thing to have discovered the facts of a case, but another to decide what to do with them. There was no one in Paris he could trust. No one.

Except Mari.

And Mari would not thank him for pressing unwanted confidences upon her.

But what about Phil?

Phil had said Mari knew people of influence. And what Cameron knew must be told to someone high up. A someone who could do what had to be done.

Cameron sat up on the edge of the bed, forced himself to walk to the writing table, and sat down again. He tore the letterhead from a piece of stationery, and on the blank sheet he wrote a letter to Mari.

In the morning he felt better. He ate a larger-than-Continental breakfast in his room, shaved, and took the Metro to Chevaleret. Walking back along the Boulevard de la Gare, he saw the intersection where the Rue Dunois began. There was a cafe nearby. He sat at a table where he could watch the entrance of the apartment building at Number 85. If Marcelle had not already left, she would be coming out before noon.

The coffee was bad, the waiter's conversation worse. Cameron bought a copy of *L'Aurore* and read of the mysterious double murder in Zurich. The dead man was known to have feared for his life; he had been preparing to leave Zurich when death had found him. Police, the report opined, would soon have the murderer at the bar of justice.

Cameron hoped so.

He stirred the brown, evil-looking coffee and called for another cup. The most that could be said for the refill was that its temperature was slightly higher.

Then over the rim of his cup he saw Marcelle come out of the arched entrance and go into the bakery next door. Cameron put some francs under his saucer and began crossing the street.

Marcelle came out of the bakery, carrying a paper bag, and went back into the apartment entrance. When Cameron walked past the conciergerie, he could hear the hurrying footsteps on the stairs above him. In the Thirteenth Arrondissement landlords do not trouble to carpet the stairs.

He reached her floor in time to see a hall door close. No one else was in sight.

Cameron walked silently to Marcelle's door and pushed it open. She stood beside a table, taking rolls out of the paper bag. Cameron said, "Good morning."

She turned quickly, and he could hear the sucking intake of her breath. "You!" she said. "Why are you here?"

"I have news for you." He walked toward her, saw her draw away from him. He said, "I haven't come to bother you, Marcelle. I've just come back from Zurich. A man was killed there. A man named Verlaix."

Her eyes opened wide. She looked over her shoulder at the closed bedroom door. She began moving toward it.

He said, "You don't need to run from me, Marcelle. I'm going. Only first I want you to know what I found out. In case something happens to me."

The bedroom door opened suddenly. A man stood there. A man half-dressed. A man almost bald. Holding a gun.

Coudet.

He said, "What you have to say concerns me also, M. Cameron. Say it quickly."

Cameron looked at Marcelle. He felt his lips tighten. He said, "I was wrong. You wouldn't really care. It wouldn't make any difference to you, Marcelle."

Coudet walked forward. He stood beside Marcelle. He said, "It makes a difference to me."

Cameron looked at him. "Go —— yourself," he said.

Coudet's face hardened. "There is a lady present," he said. "Kindly reserve such language for the *pissoirs.*"

Cameron laughed. "A lady?" He looked at Marcelle. "I've seen better ladies than this one walking the Rue Blondel."

"Swine," Coudet said. "You cannot call my wife a whore."

"Your *wife?*"

Coudet stepped forward, close to Cameron. "My wife," he hissed. "You were her lover but she is now my wife. We were married last week."

Cameron looked at her. He felt sick. He started to say, "I'm..." Then Coudet's pistol moved like a whip toward his head.

As he fell to the floor he could hear Marcelle's scream.

He was lying on something that pained him. He opened his eyes to a blaze of daylight, closed them quickly. His hands moved his body, and he could feel it settle to the sound of tumbling rocks.

He opened his eyes again and looked to one side. The rocks were black.

He lay on a pile of coal.

His head throbbed agonizingly. He sat up with an effort and coal cascaded down around him. His legs hurt. He closed his eyes until he was steadier, then stood up and half stumbled off the pile onto the ground.

He was in the rear of an apartment building. From somewhere came street noises. He walked vaguely toward them, saw an exit, and went through it. The conciergerie was ahead. Above him was the apartment of Marcelle and Victor Coudet.

Holding his head, he walked unsteadily to the street and found a taxi parked at the corner. Before the driver could protest, he got inside the cab, then held up a bank note to show that he could pay. As the taxi rolled away toward the Hotel Lotti, Cameron leaned forward and saw his face in the mirror.

He looked like a furnace stoker.

His body ached as though he had stoked the *Ile de France* across the Atlantic and back.

In his room, he stripped, sank back into a hot bath, and fell asleep. When he woke, the water was cold.

Night in Paris.

A summer night when all of Paris fills the streets; when the street lights burn brighter, when there is more laughter, when loneliness is a matter of choice.

Cameron did not want to be alone.

He walked across the Place de l'Opera, past the noisy *Pam-Pam*, to the lights of the Cafe de la Paix. Tunisian vendors displayed cheap brassware to patrons at tables. A Senegalese carried carpets across his arms, a turbaned native from Marrakech trundled leather hassocks from table to table.

Cameron sat at a table and ordered cognac and Vittel.

Drinking and smoking, he watched black-marketeers change money beside the news kiosk. Beside him, a man lighted an American cigarette, and from the sidewalk another man moved toward him. As the seated man struck a match, the standing man bent over him and said politely, "May I have a light?"

The seated man raised his arm toward the other's cigarette.

Suddenly there was a glint of steel, a quick, arresting movement, and a handcuff clicked around the wrist of the man with the match, who was no longer seated. He was standing, trying to jerk away from the man who had bent over him, but his wrist was manacled to the other's. The flic's free hand threw a folded overcoat onto their joined wrists, hiding the manacles; and the two men moved away from the table. As they reached the sidewalk, two others joined them, and in a moment all four were lost in the crowd.

Cameron finished his cognac, thinking that he had never seen an arrest carried out so perfectly.

Already a new patron was seating herself at the recently vacated table. Cameron looked at her while she adjusted the fur piece around her shoulders, then turned to watch the sidewalk crowds again.

Men walked past, arm in arm, wearing broad-shouldered polo coats with long wrap-around belts. Their Cuban heels grated against the pavements. Girls passed his table—alone, in couples and trios, their laughter artificially loud, their glances hungrily provocative.

Cameron ordered another cognac.

He lighted a cigarette, and the woman with the fur piece leaned toward him. She said, "May I have an American cigarette?"

Cameron half turned. He looked at her and pulled another cigarette from the package. Her long-nailed fingers extracted it, tapped the end expertly. She said, "Thank you, m'sieu. And now, please, a match."

Cameron lighted her cigarette. He said, "Anything else?"

The woman smiled. "A drink."

Cameron motioned toward a waiter.

She said, "Creme de menthe."

"Green?"

"No. White."

"Bring it," Cameron told the waiter. "Also another cognac."

The woman said, "Paris can be a lonely city at night."

"Paris can be anything."

"True, m'sieu. I was about to say that Paris is a state of mind. And that can be everything or nothing." She bent forward slightly and smiled. Her breasts seemed tremendous. Cameron wondered if they were real. He pulled a chair away from his table. Wordlessly the woman rose and sat beside him. She said, "Why are you here tonight?"

Cameron looked away from her. "I'm waiting."

"For a friend."

"No."

The waiter brought their drinks. She touched her glass to his. "To us," she said. "To the good fortune of our meeting."

Cameron drank his cognac and ordered another. A blind woman led by a shabby child walked slowly past. She whined a song, rattling a cardboard box. The child halted her at Cameron's table until he dropped some francs into the box. Pulling the blind woman's sleeve, the child led her away.

The woman beside him said, "You are kind, m'sieu."

"Sentimental, perhaps. Not kind."

"To her it is kindness."

Cameron put his arm around the woman's shoulders. She looked at him from the corners of her eyes. "You will go with me for an hour?"

Cameron nodded. "Is it far?"

"Only a few steps, m'sieu."

"A hotel?"

"Yes. Small and discreet."

Cameron paid the bill. As they walked down the Boulevard des Capucines he began to feel better. The woman clung to his arm until they were at the door of the room. Cameron paid the room fee, the *tarif en supplement*, and turned the key in the lock.

He sat on the bed, smoking, while the Spanish Jewess, undressed. Her brassiere was black lace, open around her dark nipples, and her swaying breasts were quite real.

CHAPTER SEVENTEEN

RAIN beat against his window at the Lotti. He raised himself on his elbows and looked out of the window at the smog mushrooming over Paris. His body was stiff. An abrasion on his wrist pained him—a souvenir of the coal pile and Victor Coudet. He started to think how badly he had bungled the last scene with Marcelle, then decided not to go over old ground again.

A morning paper had been pushed under his door. He got up and unfolded it. According to the lead story, a well-known Parisian criminal, Pierre le Fou, had been arrested at the Cafe de la Paix last night. The article listed the man's criminal record and said he had been caught while waiting for his mistress. His mistress, however, had informed the police, who quickly affected the capture of Pierre le Fou.

Cameron put *L'Aube* on the bed and went into the bathroom. As he waited for the shower water to warm he could smell a cloying, foreign perfume on his body. He thought briefly about the woman whose scent he had assimilated, and stepped into the shower.

He reached Astrel's office before the Inspector arrived. When he came, walking ponderously, breathing stertorously, Cameron stood up and said, "Congratulations, *mon inspecteur.*"

"Congratulations?"

"Of course. For the apprehension last evening of a pickpocket."

Astrel motioned Cameron into his office. He walked to the blinds and opened them. Gray morning light filtered into the musty room. "A pickpocket?"

"Certainly. Pierre le Fou."

Astrel sat at his desk. "I have not yet been informed."

Cameron sat across the desk from him. "I witnessed the capture."

"Was it well done?"

Cameron nodded. "Efficiently conducted. He lighted a cigarette. "Apparently your deputies are still capable performing certain tasks."

Astrel's eyes reduced themselves to slits. "You criticize the capabilities of my organization?"

"In part. Our friend Philip Thorne has been dead nearly a month. And still no one has been accused of the crime."

Astrel was motionless.

"Perhaps it is fortunate for you."

"Perhaps. But more fortunate for the murderer."

"Do you wish to make an accusation?"

"Yes."

"Whom?"

Cameron looked at the grilled windows behind Astrel. "Not yet," he said. "The man is clever. He must not be alarmed prematurely."

"Perhaps the police are the best judge of that."

"Perhaps. But since they have discovered nothing, and I have discovered everything, I shall continue the accretion of evidence."

Astrel shrugged. "You are an amateur," he said. "I advise you to withhold nothing from the proper authorities."

"Such is not my intention. The proper authorities will be fully informed."

Astrel toyed with his gold cigarette holder. He seemed to have lost interest in conversation. His teeth made a thin, sucking noise.

Cameron said, "The French police, however, will not carry the sole responsibility."

Astrel's head moved a little. His eyes flickered toward Cameron. "Who in addition?"

"The Swiss," Cameron said. "Yesterday the papers carried an account of Andre Verlaix's death."

Astrel's thick lips opened and closed. They formed one word. "Verlaix."

Cameron said, "Fortunately, he did not die at once."

Astrel leaned forward, pushing his belly against the desk. "He lived a time?"

"He lived. Long enough to talk with me."

"What did he say?"

Cameron laughed shortly. "He was incoherent."

Astrel's bulk relaxed against his chair. His mouth said, "Unfortunate."

"Was it not?" Cameron said. "His dying words would have made impressive evidence against the murderer." He stood up, placed his hands on the desk, and leaned forward slightly. "I have reached the conclusion that a relationship exists between these murders."

Astrel did not raise his head.

Cameron butted his cigarette against an ashtray. "Once the connection is established, the motive becomes apparent. Transparently clear."

Astrel said, "You are insane, M. Cameron. Grief has warped your mind. I have seen it happen before."

"Proof is not lacking."

"Proof against Victor Coudet?"

"No."

"He has been kept under surveillance. His actions have been unusual. Strange."

"He is a bridegroom."

"Precisely. Yet last night he entrained for Nice. Alone."

"Without Marcelle?"

Astrel nodded. "Perhaps Renee du Casse has sent for him."

Cameron felt his heart begin to pound. "Why would she summon Coudet?"

Astrel's hands spread themselves. "Once they were lovers—before Marcelle. Perhaps Renee is reluctant to lose to another woman—a younger woman."

"He is in love with his wife."

"Who can say?" Astrel breathed deeply. He inserted a cigarette into the gold holder, searched for a match until he found one. When he had lighted his cigarette he seemed to recover himself. "I need hardly elaborate on the fact that you have chosen to insert yourself into a dangerous milieu. I cannot guarantee your life."

Cameron laughed. "No one can. The grave awaits us all." He turned and began walking toward the door. "We must keep in more intimate contact, M. Astrel, lest the murderer escape justice. Lest the gold leave France."

Astrel did not reply.

Cameron opened the door. "We will share the responsibility," he said, and went into the corridor.

The afternoon flight to Nice was postponed until visibility at Le Bourget increased enough so that the Languedoc 161 could take off. From the air, Cameron could not see the earth until the plane dropped into the landing pattern at Nice. The last leg was over the Mediterranean, silver-blue in the late-afternoon sun. He could see the beaches below, the bathers, and cars moving like toys along the sea highway.

At the airport he rented a Citroen and drove rapidly to Menton. When he reached the Casino, evening had come, and the young moon was beginning to rise at the edge of the sea. Behind the Casino he found the place where he had been assaulted by Renee's gorillas. There was a lawn chair beside a tree, and Cameron sat in it, watching the blinds of Renee's office, waiting for her to turn on the light.

If Coudet were in Menton, he would be with Renee, and it was easier to find Renee than to look blindly for Coudet along the Cote. There was something he must tell Coudet. Victor had not cared to listen yesterday.

Coudet would listen tonight.

Cameron took the Beretta from his pocket, felt its assuring weight in his hand, and put it back into his pocket.

He looked at the dial of his wristwatch. Nearly eight-thirty. He wanted a cigarette badly.

He was thirsty and his body ached. He wondered what Mari would do about his letter.

Then a thin shaft of light knifed across the lawn. Someone was in Renee's office. He listened for a moment, crossed the grass quickly, and flattened himself against the stone of the building. Whoever was in the office was opening a drawer. There was no conversation.

He walked to the door, rapped urgently, and stood so that the light cut across his face. Footsteps walked toward the door. The blind was moved to one side. He could see the outline of Renee's head. He said, "This is Paul, Renee. Let me in."

A bolt slid open. The door moved inward. She said, "Why are you here?"

Cameron stepped inside the office, blinking at the light. "Victor Coudet."

"I have not seen him." She swept her skirts above her ankles, moved toward a divan. Cameron followed her, watched her recline gracefully against the rich fabric covering. He said, "Coudet left Paris last night on the Nice Express."

"Why do you wish to see him?"

"I'll tell him myself."

Renee's cat eyes looked upward. Behind them her mind was working rapidly. She said, "I am afraid I cannot assist you. If Victor left for Nice, he has not yet come here."

Cameron sat on an arm of the divan. He touched her hair with his fingers. Evenly he said, "You lie."

Something passed over her face making it suddenly hard. She said, "Verlaix is dead. Who killed him?"

"I'm not a detective. Ask Astrel."

She looked at him curiously. "Do you think he would tell me?"

Cameron shook his head. "Then why should I?"

"Was it Victor?"

Cameron stood up, walked to the desk. He picked up a jade paperweight, felt its cold slickness in his hand. He said, "I owe Marcelle something. She married Victor because he was in love with her. In spite of you, he's managed to love her for a long time."

"He is a fool."

Cameron laid down the paperweight and turned so that he could watch her. "I want to see Victor so that he can stay alive. So that Marcelle won't be a widow."

Renee went to a cupboard, poured herself a drink. Then she asked, "Did Marcelle send you here?"

"No."

"You have little reason to care what becomes of Victor."

"Only because of Marcelle."

Renee walked toward him. She said, "The gold is lost. Verlaix was the last link. Now nothing remains."

"But you'll settle for Victor."

Renee nodded.

"And I'll settle for the man who killed Philip."

Her hand touched the side of his face. "It may be your destiny," she said.

Cameron put his hand around her wrist. "You have a destiny, Renee. But not with Victor."

Lithely, she twisted out of his grasp. "It is not for you to decide. I can offer him everything he wants."

"Everything?"

Her face darkened. "We talk in circles. Victor is not in Menton. Your journey has been unnecessary."

Cameron walked toward the garden door. "I'll, find him," he said. "And you'll have seen him for the last time." He opened the door and stepped onto the grass. The door closed loudly behind him.

Cameron stood close to the building, listening. A drawer was opened, then slammed shut. He edged toward the window so that he could look inside through a gap in the blind.

Renee sat at her desk, writing rapidly. When she finished, she looked up and pressed a button on her desk. A guard opened the door inward, and a man walked past him into the office.

The man was Victor Coudet.

Cameron felt his throat tighten.

Renee stood up and motioned to the guard, who went out, closing the door.

She met Coudet in front of her desk, put her arms around his neck.

Coudet did not lower his head to kiss her. Instead, he grasped her wrists and drew her arms down to her sides.

Without moving, she said, "So it is true, then, that you married our little peasant."

"I married the woman I love." His face did not change.

Renee laughed bitterly. "How can you desire this child when you have known a woman's love?"

Coudet looked away from her. "Do you have only that to say? Is that why you sent for me?"

"Is that not enough?"

"I hoped for news of the gold."

She turned from him. "Verlaix is dead. The gold cannot be regained."

"Then I am glad." He began to walk away from her. "It has cursed all of us who touched it. Now, at last, I am free of it."

Her voice edged. "You mean to leave me?"

Coudet stopped. "Exactly. But first I must have something from you."

"What?"

"The check written by M. Thorne."

"Why should you want it?"

"Because you would not have obtained it except for Marcelle. It is the one thing that links her to our past. I must destroy it."

Renee's face moved like a rubber mask. It was not pleasant to see. "I do not have it."

Coudet took a pistol from the pocket of his jacket. "Give it to me."

"I destroyed it in the presence of M. Cameron."

Coudet laughed thinly and walked toward her, holding the gun. "Why would you do a thing like that?" He pressed the gun against her breast.

"Because of itself it was no longer useful. Its destruction purchased Cameron's assistance."

"Nothing can purchase a man like him."

"On the contrary; almost anything can purchase a man like M. Cameron."

Coudet shook his head. "You're wrong. Renee. You and the creatures you work for. So, in the end, you will lose."

She raised her hand, closed it around the pistol. "If you would point a gun at me, my love, then it is better that you kill me, too."

"Give me the check."

Her face held an odd, strained smile. Cameron saw the muscles of her forearm tighten. She pushed her hand against Coudet's trigger finger.

The gun exploded, jerking her backward. An expression of horror crossed Coudet's face. He watched her stagger and fall against the desk. He looked down slowly at the pistol in his hand.

Then he looked at the door. Someone was beating on it.

Coudet's darting eyes found the garden door. He ran toward it, reached it, and began to slip the bolt. Then the office door opened. The guard looked in, saw Renee's body, Coudet's frantic clawing at the bolt, and pulled a pistol from his pocket.

He shot from the hip. Twice.

The bullets ripped past Coudet and through the door, beside Cameron, streaking the dark wood with splinters of light. The door burst open, and Coudet half tripped on the doorsill as he rushed past Cameron. Footsteps pounded through the office. Cameron raised the Beretta, and when the guard's head was silhouetted against the doorframe, Cameron sapped him across the bulge of his skull. The guard gurgled something unintelligible, and dropped like a tackling dummy, his momentum carrying him forward so that he crumpled head down.

Cameron moved toward the door, kicking it shut. Even so, the clamor of excited voices rose steadily. For a brief instant, he thought of trying to overtake Coudet, substitute his gun for the one in the guard's clenched hand, but he knew that there was not enough time.

The guard could identify Coudet; no one else could.

Cameron went quickly to the guard's body, knelt, and lifted it around his shoulders. Then he walked to the sea wall, saw the waves breaking in the depths below, and pushed the guard's body off his shoulders. He heard the pistol clatter beyond the sea wall, but he did not wait for the heavy sound that would follow. Instead, he began running down a corridor of shadow toward the Citroen, keeping beyond the lights of the Casino.

When he reached the Citroen he started the engine and turned part way up the drive. People were running out of the Casino.

Someone stepped in front of the Citroen, waving at him to stop, but Cameron skidded past the man, and saw his hand slip off the doorsill.

He turned west on the dark sea highway, looked at the Citroen's petrol gauge. It registered almost full. From Nice, a road led to Grenoble, then to Lyon, Dijon, and Paris. If he drove all night— he'd need an open gas station in Lyon—he'd make Paris at dawn.

Behind him, headlights searched the highway. Cameron pressed down on the accelerator.

CHAPTER EIGHTEEN

HOLDING fear in your teeth like a bit, you run with it through the night toward a distant, sleeping city. It is a dream you have dreamed before, this flight and pursuit, this old and dreaded fleeing in the dark; only this time when you wake you will not be alone on a terrifying shore or lying on a prison cot. Instead, you will be in a city, surrounded and reassured by its people and its noises.

Dawn came at Fontainebleau. Sunlight at Choisy-le-Roi, and the sound overhead of a transatlantic Constellation dropping into the traffic pattern of Orly. Then the open-air markets of Villejuif, and a traffic circle past a vacant carrousel.

Bicyclists spinning around the Place d'Italie; then over through Montparnasse, and straight down the Boul' Miche to the Quai. He cut into the Rue St. Dominique and left the Citroen in the shadow of Ste Clotilde. The police would have it by noon.

As he walked, his thighs seemed numb, his feet dead weights. He tried to think of what he must do next, but his mind refused to fit the thoughts together in anything but an insane pattern. His body and his mind were painfully weary. Crossing the Rue de l'Universite he stumbled clumsily against the curb and fell to the cobbles. A policeman started to walk toward him, but Cameron picked himself up and forced his legs to walk at an even gait until he had turned and entered the Rue de Solferino. Ahead lay the Quai, beyond, the familiar, welcome expanse of the Tuileries. He rubbed his hand across his forehead, touched his throat. His thirst was strangling him. On the Quai was a drinking fountain. Sparrows dipped their bills into the collecting basin, flew through the little jet. Cameron began to run toward it and the birds, frightened, flew away. He braced his arms on the cool stone rim and plunged his face into the water.

He drank greedily, chokingly, until he could hold no more. Then he drew back, looked at the distorted reflection of his unshaven face, and ran his hands through his wet hair.

The water gave him new life.

He stepped back, turned, and looked at the gray facade of apartments along the Quai. The sun had risen enough to tint the sloping roofs and garret windows, cleansing them momentarily with its warm glow.

He walked away from the fountain and crossed the street to the sidewalk in front of the apartments. His eyes sought and found a number. He turned into the cool, shadowed hallway and climbed the stairs.

The silver plate still said "Mari." The button still brought the sound of chimes.

And footsteps came toward the door.

He waited until he heard the drop of the chain, and then he tried to smile. His cuffs and the lapels of his coat were wet from the fountain. He tried to smooth his hair again, and then the door opened.

At first his eyes saw only her face, small and bewildered, her hair done up with a ribbon. Then he looked at her shoulders and arms, at her hands held out toward him.

Her voice said, "Come in, Paul. Come quickly."

He tried to smile a smile he remembered, but the muscles seemed to have forgotten how. He said, "I need rest, Mari. Let me sleep here today, and then I'll go. You'll never be bothered with me again." He lurched against the door, and her arms steadied him inside. She locked and chained the door behind him.

As he walked through the apartment, he plucked at his tie, pulled off his coat. Mari took it and folded it over her arm. He started to turn the doorknob of the bedroom where he had slept before, but she pulled him away. "Not there," she said. "It is occupied."

Her words stabbed him. He said, "I can go somewhere else."

She shook her head. "Where can you go? You need rest now. My bed is empty." She drew him farther down the corridor into her room. The covers were thrown aside. Cameron pulled off his shoes and lay down. He felt her unbuttoning his shirt, loosening his belt, and then in his mind he was somewhere else, floating on a calm sea of bottomless waters. In the distance the shore receded until it was only a razor edge of blue between sea and sky.

He awoke to the sound of voices in the salon. Coming back from the distance where he had been, his mind collided unpleasantly with the present. Mari was arguing with a man, her lover, probably, protesting Cameron's arrival.

He struck the pillow in anguish.

The voices grew louder. He heard Mari say, "But I tell you I have not seen him."

A man's voice said, "The car he stole was found a few hours ago beside Ste Clothilde."

"Is it my responsibility that a man I may have known steals a car and abandons it in Paris? Thieves, swindlers—perhaps worse—listen to me nightly. My position would be ridiculous indeed if I were blamed for the crimes of my audience."

"Perhaps, mademoiselle. Yet this man was seen to enter this building."

"When?"

Cameron sucked in his breath.

"Three days ago."

"Then he was seen to leave within a few minutes. My maid answered the door and turned him away. Is it not so?"

The man didn't answer for a moment. Then he said, "It is as you say."

"Search elsewhere for this Cameron, but trouble me no further. Already I am late in meeting the Minister of Colonial Affairs."

"Of course, mademoiselle. You will understand that I come simply in the performance of my duty. I remain impersonal."

"Certainly. But do not again permit your duty to occasion such an incredible interrogation."

Footsteps. Walking through the salon. Not toward the corridor, but toward the entrance door. The voices grew muffled, indistinguishable. He heard the door close.

For a moment there was no sound. Then, quietly and rhythmically, like a hidden brooklet, came the sound of Mari crying. Cameron covered his face with his hands.

When he could stand it no longer, he threw aside the covers, opened the bedroom door, and walked into the salon. She lay, incredibly small and crumpled, on the divan. Cameron knelt quickly beside her and gathered her into his arms. He kissed her neck, her face wet with tears, and stroked her hair.

He said, "I don't know what they've told you, but my letter told the truth. Last night in Menton…"

Her fingers stopped his words. She said, "Once while you were gone, Astrel came to me. He said you were a man of violence, that because you were in love with Marcelle you made your wife's life miserable. Then when she met a man who was kind to her, you provoked him into a fight and crippled him."

Cameron looked at her. His face was rigid.

"Was Astrel right?"

Cameron shook his head. "He was wrong." He held her hands and put his lips beside her cheek. "Listen, my love, I came back from the war like any other guy who'd been shot at and lived. I didn't want to remember what it was like. I didn't want to try for fame or even success, and I made myself forget a girl I'd known and grown to idealize—Marcelle. When I went back to Ruth, I thought I'd have a chance to let my blood pressure drop back to normal. I thought I'd be able to sink back into a way of life that would let me live easily and peaceably with the woman I married. Only that wasn't good enough for Ruth. That wasn't what she had in mind at all. She told me that she hated the campus, hated faculty teas, but that didn't make her unique. While I was gone she'd fallen into a way of life that she couldn't forget. Even after I came back, she and Ralph couldn't keep their hands off each other. She was such an easy thing for him, such a familiar habit; he couldn't help gloating—even to me. Then in a split second he became the symbol of all the trickery, the swinishness, and the heartbreak I'd found in the war. If he hurt me unjustly, Mari, he's paid for it. But my revenge was expensive, too. I pay for it every morning when I wake and walk from my bed to the window." He felt her fingers touch his hair. "Do you understand?"

Her voice was so low he could hardly hear it. "I understand, Paul."

"She divorced me," he said. "She divorced me while I was in prison."

Her fingers touched the back of his neck, drew his lips close to hers. "And now we must forget all that because I love you."

He did not reply at once. He felt her heart beating against him, the smoothness of her cheek on his lips. Then he said, "I love you, Mari. I never should have left you." He turned his head and looked at the closed bedroom door. "What about that?" he asked. "How does he fit in?"

Her hand tightened on his. She sat up and pulled him to his feet. He followed her down the corridor, reluctant to face the issue.

She opened the door and said, "Come here."

He walked toward her, and when they were face to face he looked inside.

The bed was occupied.

On it, wrapped in a blue wool blanket, lay the little dachshund he had brought her. The puppy woke, crawled out onto the bedspread, and stretched herself.

Mari walked into the bedroom and caught the puppy in her arms. She said, "No one but your little dog has stayed here since you left," and brought the puppy to Cameron. He stroked the puppy's head, played absently with her ears. He felt that he needed a drink. A stiff one.

Walking out of the bedroom, he went to the bathroom and turned on the shower. Then he came out and stood in front of the billowing steam. He said, "I was saving Astrel for myself, but he's not worth dying for."

She ran her fingers through his hair. "I took your letter to the Minister as soon as I received it. Inspector Astrel has been watched constantly."

"Can they prove he was in Zurich?"

"They can prove he was not in Paris."

"That's something," Cameron said. "I guess you know Du Casse died last night."

"What part had she?"

"She called Phil out of the apartment that last night. Called him to a final meeting with Astrel. Verrat was probably there, too."

"But why did Astrel kill Philip?"

Cameron shrugged. "He may have suspected that Phil intended to take all the gold. Or he may have tried to force Phil to tell where it was." He put his arms around Mari. "I think Astrel is mad. Men like him always are."

"Then you will let the police take him?"

Cameron nodded. "I'll leave it to them." He patted the puppy's nose and closed the bathroom door. Then he stripped, rubbed the side of his grizzled face, and stepped into the shower.

It was late afternoon when he called Astrel. He stood in a phone booth, watching Mari play with the puppy, while the telephone rang in Astrel's office.

The voice that answered was not Astrel's. Cameron said, "Inspector Astrel, please."

"He is not here, m'sieu."

"Where may I reach him?"

The voice hesitated. "Who calls?"

"My name is Cameron. Paul Cameron."

"Ah," the voice said. "The Inspector left a message for you. He asks that you meet him in the rooms of M. Georges Verrat."

"What address?"

"He said you would know. Rue du Tage."

"Thank you." Cameron said. "I'll keep the appointment." He watched the puppy straining at her leash. "Don't bother to trace my call. This is a public phone, and I'm leaving now." He hung up and joined Mari on the sidewalk.

"Astrel is with Verrat."

"Why?"

"Verrat is valuable evidence. Against Astrel. The Inspector knows Georges is a homosexual. Georges would babble like a brook."

He felt her fingers tighten around his arm. She said, "Then Astrel may try to kill Verrat."

"We'll give him a chance."

"Then where shall we go now?"

"To the Rue Perronet," Cameron said. "To see a lady who remembers Phil."

"Marcelle?"

He shook his head. "Mme. Barjeval. I should have gone to her this morning."

"Of course," Mari said. "She must be told."

When they reached the Rue Perronet, Cameron opened the taxi door for Mari, and asked the driver to wait. They walked inside together and asked the conciere to announce them to Mme. Barjeval. The concierge shook her head and pointed to a wreath lying on a chair. The wreath was artificial. Its leaves were black. She said, "Mme. Barjeval was buried yesterday. Are you a nephew?"

"In a way," Cameron said. "I had something to tell her." He walked out of the dark hallway and helped Mari into the taxi. He did not speak until they were rounding the Etoile.

As they walked down the Rue du Tage, Cameron saw clusters of garishly costumed men and women, their faces striped with paint, feathers in their hair. Some of them were nearly naked. Mari saw him watching them and laughed. "Were you never a student?"

"Once."

"Then you know how one feels when school ends for the summer."

Cameron nodded.

"Each year the Sorbonne students parade through Paris, dressed in *motif*. This year—tonight—they celebrate as Indians. As Aztecs."

Cameron watched the band of Aztecs stoop and write on a shop window with soap.

Mari asked, "Is it not the same in America?"

Cameron laughed. "It is the same, but the month is different. In America it is October, and one dresses as a witch or a skeleton."

"Truly?"

Cameron kissed her. "Truly."

They walked into the hallway of Verrat's apartment building. Cameron knocked on the concierge's window.

"M. Verrat," he said.

"La Puce? He has gone. With a flic."

"I knew it would happen," Cameron said. "When did they leave?"

"An hour ago. Perhaps more. Do you make an official inquiry?"

Cameron walked back to the street with Mari. The sun had gone down and the bizarre Aztecs were crowding the sidewalks, laughing and shouting, walking grotesquely, shooting arrows at streetlights.

He guided Mari off the sidewalk and into the street, where they stopped a taxi. As they crossed the Seine he said, "The first Verlaix worked in a foundry before he was killed." He looked at Mari. "You know what they cast in foundries?"

"Machines," she said. "Statues."

Cameron lighted a cigarette and looked out of the window as the taxi crossed the Champs Elysees. "The Germans liked French statues," he said. "They liked them so well they took down the big ones and shipped them back to Germany for scrap metal."

"Yes."

He thought for a moment. "Suppose I worked in a foundry during the day and fought for the Resistance at night. Suppose the Maquis gave me a lot of gold to hide from the Germans, to keep until after the war was over." He chewed at his thumbnail. "I might melt it together and cast it as ingots, so that it could be buried, or if I were a little smarter, I might pour it into an old matrix and make a statue." He looked at Mari. Her eyes moved excitedly.

He said, "I'd dent it a little, paint it, let it weather, and then I'd get my brother to help me set it up some place where it would never be noticed."

Mari said, "Of course. Is that what happened to the gold?"

The taxi crossed the Faubourg St. Honore. "I don't know," he said, "but we can find out." The taxi slowed to make its way through a torchlight parade of Aztecs. "Verrat's missing all this," he said. "This would be a great night for his kind."

Knuckles rapped against the windows, grinning faces peered into the taxi. Torches were thrust forward and waved. In the distance a band was playing. A hunting horn blared drunkenly.

Cameron said, "We've never walked in a park, cherie. The Parc Monceau has statues. Lees begin there."

They entered the Parc from the Boulevard Courcelles, leaving behind them the frenetic noises of the fete. Only an occasional light flickered inside the park. Its trees and shrubbery deadened outside sound. As they walked along a gravel path, they saw a statue ahead on its tall pedestal. Cameron took a penknife from his pocket and scratched the statue's patina with the blade. The sound was harsh, resistant.

He shook his head. "Not this one. Maybe none of them."

Another statue loomed ahead. They reached it and Cameron dug at its leg with the point of his knife. He said, "The Verlaix brothers used to walk here in the evenings." He looked at Mari. "We have time, haven't we?"

"All the time in the world."

"What about the Cafe Adour?"

"Vincent will be angry."

Cameron took her arm, led her to another statue, and tested its metal. This one was bronze. Hollow. He tapped it with the knife handle and it rang slightly.

Mari picked up the puppy, and they walked deeper into the Pare Monceau. The night was dark; the moon had not yet risen. In the distance he could hear an occasional shout from the revelers.

Then came the faint sound of voices. Cameron began to walk faster. The voices were clearer now, argument active. The shrubbery was too high to see across; they had to continue down the path before turning into another. The voices became louder, several men talking at once. A light flashed upward.

A man spoke commandingly, authoritatively.

Astrel.

They were running now, running toward a light that flashed around a cleared semicircle. Four men stood near the base of a statue, a fifth lay on the ground. All four men were uniformed. The largest man was Astrel. A flashlight made the manacle around his wrist gleam like living fire. One of the uniformed men walked a few steps away and knelt beside the man on the ground. He turned the man's head so that he could see the face. He said, "His neck is broken."

Astrel laughed. "He attacked me. I was forced to defend myself. And so—La Puce is dead."

The officer to whom he was manacled said, "We watched you, Claude. You broke his neck. Deliberately."

"What difference does it make? A pederast is dead. You should congratulate your inspector, not manacle him."

The officer shook his head. "If Verrat were the first, Claude...but there was the American, and two in Zurich."

Astrel's voice changed. It was higher now. Wheedling. He said, "I am rich. Rich beyond your dreams. Let us forget this unpleasantness and share a life of wealth."

The policemen looked at one another. One of them began walking away. A whistle blew.

Astrel's voice became frantic. "Rich...gold enough for all of us. More than we can spend the rest of our lives."

An officer said, "Save your gold, Claude. You will need it for your trial."

Another officer asked, "Where is your gold, Claude? Tell us where it is. If you showed it to us, perhaps we might change our minds."

Astrel laughed. "You think to trick me, my friends, but I will not let you. No. You must release me now, and when I am free I will show you my gold."

Astrel's manacle partner spoke. "Is it far, Claude?"

"It is very near."

Cameron walked forward, into the circle of light. "Very near indeed," he said.

Astrel looked at Cameron and tried to run, but the policeman tripped him. He fell heavily beside the body of Verrat.

Cameron went to the statue and cut into it with his knife. He sliced off a paring of metal and held it under the ray of a flashlight. The weather side of the metal was dark, stained; but the inside was bright. Its surface glinted yellowly in the palm of his hand.

Astrel said something foul as he was dragged toward the statue. The policemen looked at the statue in silence.

Cameron walked to Astrel and held the knife blade against his throat. He said, "You wanted them to think I killed Philip Thorne. You thought you could arrange Verrat's death so I would be blamed for it. Then you would have shot me and called it self-defense." His hand shook a little, jarring the knife blade against Astrel's throat. He said, "If we were alone, this knife would drip with your blood."

A gendarme drew back Cameron's arm. "We must save this neck for a larger knife," he said. "Our orders were from the Minister himself."

When the patrol wagon had come and gone, when the ambulance collected its corpse and sirened back along the Boulevard Courcelles, Cameron and Mari walked away from the Parc Monceau. Ahead of them the sound of traffic grew. A rocket burst over the Place de la Concorde.

Once, as they walked back toward the heart of the city, they stopped in the shadow of a wall and kissed as though for each of them it were the first embrace.

When they moved on, they did not take the lighted Faubourg, for their way was lighted by the young moon rising over Paris.

THE END

THE MOURNING AFTER THE NIGHT BEFORE...

The first time Trex encountered the killer it was in the glare of headlights and the blood was dripping from the killer's hand. His boss had gotten the axe...literally. The second time Trex met the killer, he got a bullet through his arm. Then a studio writer was beaten to death with a fire poker...

Three people also had identical gunshot wounds. So by the third time Trex and the killer were ready to meet, it was obvious to him that he was being set up for the morgue. But this time Trex would meet the killer face to face with a leveled pistol. Provided, that is, that he could find out exactly who the killer was beforehand.

So less than thirty-six hours after almost running over the killer, Trex was staring down the barrel of the killer's gun. It was at that moment, he figured it all out...

POLICE LINEUP:

JOHN "TREX" TREXLER
He was a hard working assistant producer, moonlighting as a private eye…trying not to get himself and his gal killed.

VICTOR GAYLORD
This TV magnate played his greatest scene off camera—a love triangle turned murder mystery.

VALERIE WAYNE
She was a smart and beautiful actress who had an amazing set of pipes and a lot of moxie—and other plans, too…

BRYCE ELWIN
Another assistant producer at Raphael TV, he was a workaholic and a really helpful guy…too helpful.

MONA ELWIN
This popular TV star was quickly rising to the top. But the strain of it had her on sleeping pills—and a fear that she was going mad.

LOUISE GAYLORD
She seemed a bit frail on the surface, but while her husband was playing around, she attended to business.

HIGH HEEL HOMICIDE

By
FREDERICK C. DAVIS

ARMCHAIR FICTION
PO Box 4369, Medford, Oregon 97504

*For more information about Armchair Books and products, visit our
website at...*

www.armchairfiction.com

Or email us at...

armchairfiction@yahoo.com

CHAPTER ONE

THE FOLLOWING account—a good example of how fouled up you can get when you start messing around with murder—stands just as I wrote it, hour by hour, while it was happening.

If it seems a bit dizzy in spots, that's because the most important parts of it didn't make sense at the time.

For instance, take the way Victor Gaylord got himself murdered. Even granting that Gaylord was fairly sure to die a heel's death some cozy night, it seemed unnecessarily rough. I mean, we might easily imagine some lush babe shooting him or knifing him, or poutingly handing him a scotch well laced with cyanide, which would have been a ladylike way of doing it. But for some peculiar, private reason, this killer in high heels chose, instead, to kill him with a Boy Scout hatchet.

It was also tough to figure a sensible reason why this same man-killer should then go tripping daintily straight into the bright headlamp beams of a passing car. Having just hacked a guy's skull to splinters, a girl would naturally be a little nervous and in rather a hurry to get gone. If she had only waited at the gate for a few seconds, I would have rolled on past without seeing her at all.

She must have noticed the glare of my car coming, but nevertheless she went hurrying right out into the street, making herself as conspicuous as a ballerina in a spotlight. This was bad timing even for an inexperienced murderess.

However, that's the way I saw it happening. And that was only the beginning—just a taste of more giddy deadliness to come.

Here's the record, written in the thick of it, starting with:

Tuesday, April 1—
3:30 A.M.

Twenty minutes ago I arrived here at my apartment with a bullet wound in my upper left arm.

The blood and the hole had ruined my suit coat, which was also rain-soaked and smeared with mud. My shirt, one of those new nylon jobs, looked like a total loss also.

When I sloshed antiseptic onto the wound, it really burst into flame. Until it subsided, I hung onto the washbowl with my eyes clenched shut and called a certain young female murderer all the uncomplimentary names I could think of. Except her own. I didn't know who she was.

Then I wrapped bandage around it—awkwardly, because I could use only one hand. The flexing of the torn muscles started it to bleeding again. In exasperation, I held a towel against it, while I paced around the room wondering what to do.

By the time the blood had stopped seeping out again, I had decided that one thing I definitely did not want was to get myself fouled up in a murder case reeking with scandal. That meant I would conceal my gunshot wound from the police, and act as if I knew nothing at all about the murder.

This might be illegal, I realized, and also it might be dangerous—particularly if the police should somehow later learn about my part in it. In that event, I could anticipate a rough time making them understand why I had kept quiet.

This decided me that it would be a smart plan to make a written record of what I had seen and done, a record which I would keep entirely to myself, and not show to anyone else— unless it should become necessary for me to put it into the hands of the police...or my lawyer.

This, then, is a true, up-to-the-minute record of tonight's little bouquet of violence.

Let's take it back to two a.m. tonight, to the routine, daily act which dropped me smack into an ugly muddle of homicide—the simple act of going home from work.

The rain which is still falling now began soon after dinner last evening—dinner for me having consisted of one ham-on-rye and a quart of black coffee sent in to my desk. As I worked I could hear the rain rolling gently on the old shingle roof. Finally, at two a.m., I called it a night.

Until now, I hadn't realized I was entirely alone in that cavernous barn of a place out on Ashley Road. Since I was, I switched off the last light and latched the stage door behind me.

I hadn't brought a raincoat and I walked through the rain to my car without caring much. Mine was the only car left in the parking lot. Everyone else, even Allene Giles, my writer on the Moonbeam show, had given up and staggered homeward several hours ago.

I had an odd feeling, as if I had been abandoned in a dark, hollow world, like a character lost inside a television tube after the set had been turned off.

Sliding under the wheel, I sat for a moment looking wearily at the rambling structure of weather-scored wood wherein I spend my days and much of my nights cultivating ulcers. It should have stayed what it once was, a barn—but years ago it had been converted into a rustic summer playhouse. More recently it had been reconverted into a television rehearsal studio.

The sign across its front, *Raphael TV Productions, Inc.,* looked top-heavy on such an unpretentious building. It seemed tranquil enough now, sitting there in the fresh spring rain, surrounded by the soft country night; but early in the morning executives and technicians and glamorous actresses and yummy chorus girls would come crowding back in to turn it back into a place of fantastic turmoil again.

I tooled off toward my apartment feeling more than willing to hit the sack, after I'd had a few stiff nightcaps. I drove slowly; past the large, gardened homes of people obviously in the chips. This charming suburb, one of the choicest in Westchester, was the last place you might expect to find a plant manufacturing television musicals.

Why had it been chosen, then? Because of sheer lack of enough working space in New York, and also because it was handy to the telecast studios in Manhattan, but mostly because *Raphael TV's* top executives had their homes here. Very convenient for them, you see, although it had created a tough housing problem for several hundred others on *Raphael TV's* staff.

I had been lucky enough to find myself this one-room-and-bath over in the gas-pump-and-hamburger belt near the Boston Post Road. So, at a few minutes past two tonight, I was heading for it the shortest way—turning corners automatically, half asleep.

Then suddenly I wasn't half asleep any more, but awake and staring. Because that was when I saw death on spike heels come tripping out of Victor Gaylord's back gate, death with big, round, scared eyes.

She popped into sight through Gaylord's gate and headed straight across the street with her nylons twinkling in the shine of my headlights. She was wearing a black cape of the Dracula variety, but much shorter. She had the hood pulled over her head and, with one hand, was clenching it over the lower part of her face.

When I first glimpsed her I was not more than a hundred feet away; I had a perfectly clear view of her, and while I watched her for those few seconds, of course, I rolled even closer.

Then, when she was squarely in the middle of the street, she seemed to realize she had spotlighted herself. Instead of scramming out of there even faster, she stopped dead still. For several seconds she stood there gazing round-eyed straight toward me. My mind photographed her unforgettably.

Framed in the black of her cape's hood, her eyes were round and scared, really terrified. Her hand clenching the hood concealed her mouth. The cape had swung open, revealing that her dress—a bright red dress—was ripped.

She was wearing platform sandals, sandals with inch-thick soles, also red, and in her panic she teetered on her high heels. Her other hand was raised under the cape in a warding-off gesture, as if in instinctive fear that I might run her down.

One other detail put a chill into me. On her one visible hand were dark spots of something wet and sticky-looking. Somehow, I felt sure it was blood. Understand, that hand was not bleeding. The dark stuff was spattered over the whole hand and the wrist also. I sensed somehow that the blood was someone else's, that I was looking at the hand of a murderer.

For a few seconds she was as motionless as a manikin. Although I could see no feature of her face except her eyes I had an odd sense of recognition. Rather, I had the feeling that I *ought* to recognize this girl—that I had seen her somewhere before—but at the same time I could not place her.

Then she was running again. Sleek legs flashing in the bright beams of my headlamps, she flew to a car sitting parked on the left side of the street. She ran around to its far side ducked into it. Almost instantly the car was whirring away. Her take-off was so fast that I suspected she had left the engine idling.

She was alone in that car. She was driving it and driving it like a bat. It had already accelerated to at least forty before she switched on her headlights. At the first corner she whipped it into a screeching turn and jackrabbited out of sight.

I resisted an impulse to chase her. I was too tired to throw myself into the wild sort of chase she could lead me—it was too likely that I would wind myself around a telephone pole. Besides, I wouldn't know what to do with her if I caught her.

What she had left behind her, however, might be something else again. The place from which she had fled in such panic was the home of Victor Gaylord, president and head producer of *Raphael TV*, and my big boss.

I braked, swinging slowly to the curb. Not wishing to walk in on any brawls, I cut the switches and sat for several minutes listening.

A gal dashing out of Gaylord's back gate in the small hours of the morning was hardly a novelty. On any other night I would have shrugged it off. The thing that hooked me into it tonight was the blood I had seen on her hands.

The rain sprinkled on me as I left the car and went quietly to the gate. Except for this single opening, the rear of the Gaylord grounds was screened by a high, thick hedge. Just beyond sat Gaylord s guest house, a charming white cottage surrounded by gardened terraces. The main house, much larger, sitting beyond, was entirely dark. The only light was the soft glow fanning out from the cottage's open door.

I slowly approached that open door along a flagstone walk. Just outside it small red footprints were dissolving in the rain. Just over the sill, the footprints were clear-cut and red; they led me to the spot in front of the fireplace where Victor Gaylord lay dead, with the red Boy Scout hatchet lying beside him.

Oddly, my first reaction was one of relief. It was a selfish reaction because Gaylord had been about to stage a drastic shakeup at *Raphael TV*. It might have meant my job. There would be no shakeup now, not right away. Naturally I felt glad of that. Selfish no doubt, but human. Scores of others at *Raphael TV* would feel just as I did about it. In that sense, a killer had done us a favor.

I stepped back to peer around and became aware of the odor of burned cordite in the air. That was odd too. A gun had been fired in this room only a few minutes ago. A firearm added to the hatchet seemed superfluous indeed. There was no sign of a bullet wound on Gaylord's body, however—so far as I could see simply by bending over him—and there was no sign of the gun itself, either. I made a quick circle of the room and it stayed missing.

Now I began to feel that instinctive, prickly sensation of being watched. I listened, but there was no sound of a lurking presence, just the dripping of the rain. I went slowly to the door connecting with the room beyond.

It was empty now, although someone had evidently been here. Another woman. There was a small pair of pumps on the floor, a dress and a jacket trailing over the back of a chair.

This picture fascinated me. Gaylord appeared to have had not just one visitor tonight, but two. One of them had evidently been here in this room when the other came bursting into the cottage with a hatchet in her fist and murder in her jealous heart.

This left me with the beguiling question of what had become of the first one. To judge from appearances, she must have dashed out in terror, while the second babe was busy hacking the life out of Gaylord—dashed out minus her shoes, dress and coat.

It would be interesting to watch which of the girls around *Raphael TV* turned up with a cold tomorrow.

I was getting the jitters. The air reeked with the kind of rumors that would get smeared across every front page in the nation.

I stared at the telephone sitting within a few feet of Gaylord's body, recognizing that to report this to the police would be to drop myself into the thickest of it.

"Don't be a chump, Trexler," I said, half aloud. "Get out of here right now and play dumb."

Besides, I still had that crawly feeling that I was being watched.

"Out, Trexler," I insisted to myself. "On your way. Before somebody walks in on you."

Then, going to the door, I found the note. It lay there on an open leaf of an antique secretary. It was the gray-blue color used for *Raphael TV* memos. A closer look showed me that it was actually a sheet from one of our pads, with the printing cut off the top. It was a note written in flowing stylized handwriting and it said:

Tonight, darling—
Same place—
Same time—
Same reason too.

No salutation, no signature. On a note like that it would hardly be necessary. The woman who had written it had evidently had reason to believe that Gaylord would know just whom it was from.

It bothered me. There was a haunting quality about that handwriting, like the fleeing woman I had seen in the street. It seemed familiar, yet it wasn't. I felt I should know whose handwriting it was, yet I couldn't actually recognize it.

Somehow that note, so full of warmth and secrecy, stirred me up inside with an emotion I couldn't define. I couldn't explain it to myself then, and I can't explain even now, why I decided to slip that note into my pocket and take it away from there—but I did.

I have it here with me now. When I look at it I get a deep-down feeling that perhaps in some way this note is important to me personally.

I went to the door. My intention was to get back into my car, drive on home, have a couple of extra nightcaps and go to bed as if none of this had happened. So I stepped out onto the terrace—and that was when the house seemed to collapse on me.

Possibly it was a short length of pipe. It may have been a jack handle or some similar tool. It came slashing down out of the darkness at my side so fast that I didn't know what was happening until I found myself sprawling face down in mud—actually mud, a small plot of rain-soaked garden at the side of the terrace leading to the house.

The blow had glanced across my right ear hard enough to drop me but not quite hard enough to black me out. While I lay there stunned, something sharp and pointed pressed down between my shoulder blades. It felt like the point of a saber.

Actually it was a spike heel.

By twisting a little I could vaguely see a red platform sandal, a nylon leg, Little Miss Killer had circled back to the scene to watch me. Evidently she had decided I was the troublesome busybody type who had done a little too much snooping tonight.

Next, a loud, ear-splitting bang. A numb, pinching sensation sprang instantly into my left upper arm. That answered the question of what had become of the gun missing from the death room. The killer had taken it away with her. Just now she had given me a taste of warmed-over lead.

Too stunned and shocked even to roll over, I felt her sharp heel lifted from my spine and heard her running off. As she passed the open door of the cottage, I glimpsed her legs flashing again and her black cape flying. This time she raced off toward the front part of the Gaylord estate.

After a moment her car whirred away in the night.

I lay there in the rain wondering dizzily how come I was still alive. Either this babe was a damn poor shot, I decided, or else the wound in my arm was a warning. It seemed to say that unless I kept clammed up about tonight's little incident the next bullet would catch me closer to the ticker.

CHAPTER TWO

THAT BRINGS us up to now—4:45 A.M., Tuesday. Mostly I have been sitting here, pecking at this typewriter with only incidental help from my left hand. There is a towel wrapped over the bullet-cut, with a knotted necktie holding it in place. It hurts like hell and its stiffening up. I expect to have a sweet time acting as if it isn't there.

I keep wondering if Gaylord's body has been found as yet. All that chop-chopping and bang-banging in the guest cottage might have disturbed the neighbors.

Also, what about Louise, Gaylord's wife? Her room, separate from her husband's, is in the front of the big house, facing away from the cottage. Sooner or later somebody around there ought to be noticing the smell of murder.

I have spent more minutes studying that intimate little gray-blue note:

Tonight, darling—
Same place—

Same time—
Same reason too.

It still stirs me up. I still feel I should know who wrote those words. But I don't.

Pacing around the room again, I decided that this written record should be backed up by some sort of corroboration. As it stands, the police might choose to brush it off as an elaborate falsification, a fancy cover-up. They can point out that a lie written on paper is no truer than a spoken lie. They can say I've gone to a lot of pains to whitewash myself.

It's possible that I unwittingly left traces of myself back at the cottage where Gaylord was murdered—perhaps a footprint, or fingerprints. As an explanation of such evidence, this statement will draw a very fishy eye from the cops unless there are other circumstances or other statements to verify it.

So a few minutes ago I took up my phone and called Bryce Elwyn's home. Bryce is also an assistant producer at *Raphael TV*. We work together on the big Moonbeam Theatre show and share its major headaches.

He answered my ring immediately. Instead of sounding sleepy and resentful at being wakened, as I'd expected, he sounded normally awake and habitually worried.

"Bryce, this is Trex," I said. "Lord, you been working all night?"

"Not quite," he answered wearily. "My eyes gave out on me, so I turned in at a little past two." I knew that Bryce had taken home a truckload of scripts to read, more or less. "Set the alarm for four. I can tell you there is hardly any pastime more diverting than reading the book of a twenty-year-old musical comedy at four in the morning."

"Bryce," I began, and stopped.

In the background I heard a noise like, sobbing. It was faint, as if it were coming through a closed door. It was a sound of feminine anguish.

"Anything wrong there, Bryce?" I asked.

"Mona had a nightmare," Bryce answered impatiently. "TV is making a nervous wreck of her." It's well known that Mona Elwyn is one of the most popular dramatic stars in the new medium—that she is building up a fine new career in TV after having skidded out of the movies through a series of bad breaks.

Bryce added, "She won't let up, though, and these nightmares she's been having lately are getting to be a nightmare to me too."

"Sorry, Bryce."

"She woke up screaming her head off a few minutes ago. I've had a hell of a time quieting her. Sleeping pills don't seem to help her very much anymore." He added, as if fed up with that subject, "She'll be all right and back on the job tomorrow. What's on your mind, Trex?"

"I just had a peculiar telephone call," I said. "It's got me worried."

"Why?"

"It was about Gaylord. Somebody rang me a few minutes ago and said there's serious trouble over at the Gaylord place."

"Don't you know who it was calling?"

"No. It woke me up and I couldn't even tell whether it was a man or a woman. He or she said just that much, then hung up. I don't get it and I can't say I like it. You and I both know the way Gaylord has been asking for trouble for a long time."

"Sure he has." By now Bryce sounded plenty worried himself. "If anything serious has happened to Gaylord, it could kick up one hell of a nasty mess."

"That's why I'm calling you about it, Bryce," I said. "I don't want to get mixed up in it any more than I can help, naturally. I can't ignore that call, but on the other hand I want to protect myself. I thought it might be smart to tell somebody in advance what I intend to do about it."

"Why not simply tip off the cops?" As soon as Bryce asked it, he saw a good reason why not. "No, there might be good friends of ours involved."

"That's it. Now listen, Bryce. I'm going to get dressed and drive over to Gaylord's place. I'll take a look-see. Then I'll report to you again. I hope the call was somebody's cute idea of a practical joke. But if something is seriously wrong over there, then we can decide together what's best to do about it."

"O.K., Trex," Bryce agreed. "Better get rolling right away. I'll wait right here to hear from you again."

Before he hung up I heard again that same sobbing in the next room. Mona's nightmare seemed to be having a remarkably lasting after-effect. She'd better take it a little easier on this new career of hers, I thought, or else she'd fall apart soon.

I held the phone in my hands for a minute, feeling like half a heel. I had tried to sound convincing, and Bryce seemed to have taken my yarn at face value, in good faith. Still, I figured it couldn't hurt him. In helping me to account for myself, even falsely, he was helping to account for himself also.

I peeled the bloody towel off my wound, made sure it had stopped bleeding, then taped more gauze over it. I put on a fresh shirt and changed to a blue pin-stripe suit. My arm was surprisingly stiff; it wouldn't be easy to use it naturally.

Before leaving the apartment I stuffed the other suit and shirt, the messed-up ones I'd been wearing, into the laundry hamper. I cleaned stains off the washbowl, then stuffed the reddened towels out of sight also. The bath needed a better cleaning than this, but there wasn't time to do a proper job now.

I went down to the street where I had left my car locked. Driving at a normal speed, I retraced my usual course. When I reached the rear gate, I got out and looked across the grounds at the cottage. It looked exactly as I had first seen it, with soft light fanning out its open front door; but I was trying to act as if I had never seen it this way before.

I went in the gate, along the walk and across the terrace to the open door. I paused there, craning, behaving as if this was all new to me. Then I went inside and stood for a moment staring at Gaylord's corpse. Nothing seemed changed. Every detail seemed exactly as I had left it before.

Next I simply went back to my car, walking fast, and buzzed away.

Four or five minutes later I turned my car into the driveway of the house where the Elwyns are living.

The drive circles to a ranch-type dwelling, only one story high, surrounded by plenty of open space. Elwyn had rented it at a very reasonable figure from a friend of his, a radio writer, who had been called out to Hollywood to do a new show. It's so roomy inside for only the two of them that Bryce and Mona joke about rattling around in it—but it has plenty of privacy and comfort.

A light was burning in Bryce's study. It was the only light in the house until I rang the bell. The other lights flashed on, marking Bryce's progress to the door.

He looked out at me in surprise, having expected another phone call rather than a personal visit. My face warned him it was really serious. As he closed the door behind me I told him quietly.

"That call was the McCoy. Gaylord's been murdered."

Bryce is a man of reserve and self-control. He didn't start, or mouth exclamations, but just gazed at me gravely. The exceptionally long dressing gown he was wearing made him seem even thinner than usual. He looked tired almost to the point of illness, his eyes dull in the heavy plastic rims of his glasses.

"That's nice," he said finally. "That's going to provide a lot of jolly fun for all of us."

He led me down the pine-paneled hallway toward his study. Following him, I was reminded for no particular reason, that Mona's nightmare had occurred back in the rear wing. That part of the house was not entirely dark. Apparently she had quieted down. At any rate, the place was full of a predawn quiet when Bryce Elwyn led me into his study where scripts and musical scores were piled on tables and chairs.

He closed the door behind me and made a place for me to sit while we talked. He also poured two stiff shots of scotch from a decanter and passed one to me. For a moment I wasn't sure whether this was intended simply as a nerve-soother or whether he was about to propose a hearty toast to Gaylord's sudden death. Gaylord had been the kind of dog who would make the latter seem almost fitting and proper.

"I did what I told you I was going to do, Bryce," I went on. "That is, I parked in the street behind Gaylord's and looked in. There were lights burning in the cottage, with the door standing wide open, so I went in farther for a closer look. Gaylord was killed with a hatchet. I came right out again."

"Hatchet?" Bryce said, wincing.

I nodded. "It's lying there beside the body. Nobody need worry about Gaylord's coming back to life. He definitely won't. Neither need anybody feel surprise over the fact that a woman did it to him. She left a trail of bloody footprints across the floor when she left. To make it cozier, there wasn't just one woman there tonight. There were two at once."

Bryce's eyebrows arched over the rims of his glasses. "Two? How do you know?"

"Clothes left in the other room. Evidently the first doll was in there when the other suddenly barged in with her little hatchet. Apparently the first one scrammed fast while the second concentrated on murdering the rat. Then—"

Bryce broke in, startled. "Why, then the first one knows who the second one—the murderess—is!"

Of course that had to be true. For some reason this angle had escaped me until now, but it was solidly logical on the basis of the evidence as I had seen it. The identity of Gaylord's killer must be known to the other woman who had been present in the cottage.

"Where does that get her?" I wondered.

Bryce shrugged.

For another moment I mused over the question of what that other woman might do about it. The answer, offhand, was nothing. She might wish to accuse the killer, women being the jealous little minxes they are, but she couldn't do that without revealing herself.

On the other hand she could be rather sure that the killer, when caught, would vindictively blab out every juicy detail, certainly not omitting the babe in the room.

"Altogether a sweet situation," I went on to Bryce Elwyn. "Very probably we're acquainted with both the murderess and the witness to the murder."

Bryce agreed. "With *Raphael TV* crawling with luscious lasses these days, the chances are that both those babes are working for us."

"Beginning tomorrow every pretty face in the place will take on a new interest for me. It'll be fascinating to watch 'em," I said.

"Got any ideas as to who the two may be?"

I sampled the scotch before answering. "No. No idea at all about either of them. It might be any dame in the place. Also, the second one, the hatchet woman, might very well have been Louise Gaylord. She'd have a better reason to murder the heel than any of the others."

"I heard Louise is away."

"Where?"

"I think Chicago. I heard Gaylord mention it to Allene Giles this morning."

We sat staring at each other for a while, realizing how this thing could spread its poison. The virus would creep insidiously into the minds of husbands and boyfriends. On the other hand, my future and Bryce's, and that of scores of other executives in *Raphael TV*, would be definitely pleasanter, now that an exterminator had sweetened the air.

"All right," Bryce said. "We're in it already. What are we going to do about it?"

I sat silent. I wasn't thinking but listening. Slight creaking noises—perhaps the weight of feet shifting along the floorboards of the hall—seemed to hint that somebody was tuning in on this confab. It would have to be Mona. She could be awake and easing closer to the door of Bryce's study to eavesdrop. On the other hand, the noises might simply be the kind of noises that houses make of themselves in the quiet hours.

"We should tell the police, shouldn't we?" Bryce said.

I felt like a heel again, because I was holding out so much on him. I had described my second visit to the cottage, but not my first. I had not mentioned finding that note, much less that I had taken it away—removing evidence being a slightly illegal act. I was telling nobody that I had seen a very guilty-looking girl fleeing the scene of the murder—and I certainly intended to keep to myself the fact that I was carrying around a nasty bullet wound presented to me by that same hard-hitting babe. I greatly preferred to keep all this entirely under wraps, without making a slip that might give the cops a chance to pry it out into the open.

"Wait," I said. "Before sticking our necks out, let's find out where we stand. If we notify the police of a murder, they'll bear down on us to account for ourselves. That's not an easy thing to do in the middle of the night. For instance, I was working in my office, over at the studio, until two o'clock, and I was all alone at the last."

"I was working alone here too," Bryce said. "Mona can't back me up in that, either. She went to bed early, dosed up with scotch and barbiturates. I didn't happen to look in at her during the night, but I can say I did, and that can put her in the clear."

"Come to think of it, Bryce, we can vouch for each other fairly well. You phoned me several times, remember? Twice about stage cues in *Kill Me, Kate*. That second time, I remember, was just before two o'clock. That lets us place each other pretty definitely. From the looks of Gaylord's body I'd say he was dead before two, so—" I hesitated, then said. "Still, Bryce, I want to stay as clear of all this as I possibly can."

"You mean you'd rather not ask for trouble by notifying the police."

"Maybe I'm wrong but I'd rather not."

Bryce was silent. I could feel him picturing a dead man lying alone, neglected and undiscovered. He squirmed over it and went on thinking.

"This person who phoned you about trouble over at Gaylord's," he said. "Why did he or she do it? Why was that call made to you instead of to somebody else on the staff?"

"I don t know."

Bryce sat wordless again and I wondered uneasily if he suspected there had not actually been such a call. In the quiet I thought I heard again a creaky hint of Mona eavesdropping on us in the hallway. I felt a curious temptation to jerk the door open and catch her at it; but I sat still.

Bryce's decision, the one he was trying to make now about notifying the police, was important to me. If he agreed we had better keep quiet, then he would involve himself in a minor way that he would want to keep concealed too and this would force him to play along with me and back me up in case the going got rough.

"All right," he said abruptly. "Keeping quiet won't hurt anybody and it may help. Let's forget the little we know about it. We're going to have a tough day tomorrow I think so let's catch up on our sleep."

He rose decisively, scraping his chair back. If Mona had been prowling in the hallway, that sound would be enough to warn her off. Bryce went directly to his study door and snapped it open; and there was no sign that anyone had been lurking out there. No sign, that is, until I turned and the light happened to catch a dark, shiny mark on the hallway wall.

It was a fresh red smear left by a woman's hand wet with blood.

CHAPTER THREE

BIDDING Bryce good-bye at his front door, early this morning, I kept a straight face and made no mention of the mark I had seen on the wall. Driving away, I turned it upside down and sideways in my mind, looking at it from all angles.

I was sure it was Mona who had been eavesdropping on Bryce and me from the hall. It was her hand that had left a fresh smear of blood on the wall. But I couldn't make it add up to anything definite. Anyway, I decided, it was not my worry, but Bryce's—if he was aware of it.

I drove past Gaylord's place again on my way home, and regretted it. This time it was no longer a dark, quiet spot. More lights were blazing, several cars were parked along the curb and men were prowling around, some of them scanning the ground with flashlights—including the muddy garden spot into which Little Miss Killer's sap had spilled me.

I couldn't guess who had tipped the cops, but there they were, brother. They had taken over and were already hard at work.

Dawn was breaking when I got back to this apartment. I felt nervously unstrung and half dead from lack of sleep. Still, I took time to bring this record up to the minute before finally falling into bed.

Then sleep wouldn't come. I kept expecting a set of official knuckles to rap on my door. I kept worrying about those bloody clothes and towels crammed into my bathroom hamper. I tried to think of a way I could get rid of them so that they couldn't be traced back to me. When I finally got up again, still dead tired, the best I could do was to cram them down deeper in the hamper.

My arm was swollen, pulsing and fiery red. I was afraid it might become infected. That would be ducky. It would leave me with a choice of dying of blood poisoning or going to a doctor—who would be legally forced to report my wound to the police.

I flexed my arm painfully to limber it up, taped fresh bandage over the stain, got dressed and sized myself up in the mirror. I looked like something out of Skid Row. My face was gray and old. To me I looked exactly like a guy who had poked into a murder that was none of his business, then had spent the whole night trying to scramble back out of it.

After a drugstore breakfast—this time detouring around the Gaylord place—I drove out Ashley Road to *Raphael TV*. A noticeable tension hung over the place. The grapevine had spread the news of the murder early, and space was now at a premium in the parking lot.

Among the scores of cars were several costly land-yachts belonging to the big dough behind *Raphael TV*. There were also several more modest ones bearing the insignia of the police. The cops were here now, tireless, smarter than we knew, and boring in.

I stepped inside, sensed even tighter confusion. Even empty, this ex-barn, where once placid cows had peacefully chewed their hay, looked like something out of a futuristic horror movie.

Great banks of lights hung overhead, fat electric cables trailed around the floor like homeless boa constrictors. Microphones dangled like moss and those fantastic, top-heavy TV cameras stood about on their rubber-tired dollies. A street lamp stood here, the corner of a middle-class living room there, beside the front of a Western frontier saloon—all parts of sets. This morning it was packed with people trying to work with their minds on murder, speculating on the killer.

On one stage Dinah Coyle, our dance directress, was putting a row of pretties through their paces. In playsuits and swimsuits, their lovely long legs kicked in unison—reminding me, with a twinge, of a hatchet chopping.

On another stage Bryce Elwyn was attempting to direct a love scene between a fluttery soprano and a jittery tenor. I looked around for Mona Elwyn and didn't spot her, but did see Allene Giles, my writer, wandering aimlessly with two fists full of script, a cigarette pinched in her mouth, strictly against the rules. The atmosphere turned my own nerves on edge and the pain in my left arm began to grow sharper.

I climbed wooden stairs to what was formerly the playhouse balcony. The upper reaches of it had been made over into a group of offices for the executives. They were arranged in order of protocol, the big shots near the stair landing, the little shots over in the remote reaches.

The first doors were closed and men were talking behind them—the big brass conferring with the cops. Victor Gaylord's office was also closed. When I reached my own cubbyhole, down in the bass section, I was astonished to find it fastened also, from the inside.

A moment after I tried the knob, however, the bolt snapped out of its socket and the door was yanked open. I went in to find that Valerie Wayne had closeted herself alone here. She had been waiting for me in an increasing state of agitation. The air was fogged and a dozen rouge-stained butts lay crushed in my ashtray.

Valerie came to me on quick impulse, slid one arm around my neck and gave me a lingering kiss. Then, as suddenly, she pushed me away.

"Pardon the error," she said in her husky voice. "I don't usually do that to men who break dates with me."

It was true that I had been forced to break a dinner date with Val last night, due to pressure of work—and it really had been pressure of work. *High* pressure, at that. Among the many things I would greatly prefer not to do, breaking a date with Val stood at the top of the list.

She sat on the edge of my desk, eying me narrowly through the fumes of her cigarette, nervously swinging one neatly shod foot.

The many hundreds of thousands of men who have fallen in love with Valerie Wayne via TV really haven't seen anything yet, because they miss her coloring. Her reddish-blonde hair is cut short, in the new style, and on her it looks delicious.

As no customer of the Moonbeam Playhouse show needs to be told, she is attractive from that lovely haircut every inch of the way down to her toes. She is the most luscious woman I have ever known, and I have not the slightest inclination to try to find a more luscious one. I will gladly settle for Val any time.

Not that she is perfection itself. She drinks too much sometimes, smokes too much all the time, and is ridden by too much ambition. I often have it tough, persuading her to forget her career for a few minutes at a time.

As she sat there gazing at me with a calculating glint in her green eyes, and swinging one lovely leg, I said, "What's the idea, locking yourself in here?"

"I had to be the first to see you this morning, Trex, darling," she said quickly. "I've simply got to know what's going to come of all this. I *am* all set for Moonbeam straight through, aren't I, darling?"

I put on a wry smile, opened a window—using my right hand only—then turned to my chair, Val's voice is fully as lovely as the rest of her. She opens that lovely mouth of hers and up from her lovely throat comes lovely music. She has sung the lead in most of the Moonlight musicals so far, winning plenty of notice.

The show is growing rapidly in popularity. As late as yesterday's decision had been reached to give her star billing in the entire series, but so far the terms of her contract hadn't been fought out. What she was so upset about, of course, was her fear that the murder of Victor Gaylord might queer the deal.

"You'll have to wait for the answer to that one, Val," I said wearily. "At least until Gaylord's corpse cools off."

She crushed out her cigarette and immediately began fishing up a fresh one. "Vic wanted me there, darling," she reminded me unnecessarily. "It was just a question of—of working it out." She added hastily, "If I seem a little ghoulish this morning, it's only because a good chunk of my life depends on what comes next."

Yes. And a good chunk of coin, too—more than I could ever anticipate for myself. Val has it all dreamed out. In several more months the Moonbeam Musicals will sign off for the summer. By that time Val's popularity will enable her to keep busy on the straw hat circuit and cash in nicely.

Sooner or later, there'll be Hollywood, top money and even glossier fame. When this happens, incidentally, a little guy named Johnny Trexler will be left somewhere far back along the track, carrying a great big torch.

"Murder is a little upsetting to others, too, sweet," I reminded her. "Not even the big wheels here can guess so early how much Gaylord's death will change our plans. My own job was on the fence until this morning, and for all I know it may be still. So let's relax, Val. You don't really appreciate how cuddly you get when you relax."

She leaned forward and kissed me again. "You're right, Trex, darling. I *am* being a little previous. I really shouldn't fret so much. I know how much I can count on you—you'll get my contract through just as soon as you possibly can."

"Me?" I said in astonishment. "Gaylord handled all the contracts personally and now that he—"

"I know, darling, but somebody will move up to take his place, of course!" Val interrupted. "Everybody *knows* you're the man who deserves it."

"I deserve it, all right, my sweet," I said ironically. "But don't let yourself hope for it too much. They'll probably bring in somebody new over the heads of all the rest of us. You don t realize how much executive ability a man acquires when he buys a block of stock. I don't happen to own any *Raphael TV Common.* Do you?"

She shook her pretty head and, as we sat there gazing thoughtfully at each other, Allene Giles appeared in the door. Unlike Val, Allene is virtually unknown to the TV audience, although millions of viewers are entertained by her work every week. She is a writer and quite bitter about it.

Allene is bitter about the fact that writers' names are rarely noticed on the screen and writers' purses aren't fat. She is also bitter about the fact that she would rather be a writer than anything else. The total effect of all this had been to make her one tough babe to handle.

This morning her yellow hair was drawn back as sleekly and parted as meticulously as ever; her dress was as tidy as usual, and I had no doubt the seams of her nylons were ruler straight, as always. But she did have dark crescents under her eyes and she did look like a bad night.

She came to my desk with something black in her hands. She hesitated as if not knowing where to begin, then said, "Have those bright boys from headquarters gone to work on you yet, Trex?"

"Not yet, but they will."

Allene hesitated again. Her face would have been nicer without quite so much hardness in it. So would her heart. Perhaps she wasn't exactly cold, but only cynical.

Trying a new tack, she said, "They reached Louise at her brother's place in Chicago."

"I'd heard she'd gone there," I said.

Allene nodded. "Louise's brother was throwing a big party last night with Louise hostessing for him. She was right there in the middle of forty or fifty people until dawn. Couldn't I want a better alibi. Some women have all the luck."

"Such as having a ratty husband like Vic Gaylord bumped off for her," Val said cynically. "I'm sure she appreciates the favor somebody did her last night."

This trenchant remark reminded Allene of the black thing in her hands. With a quick, motion, she spread it over my desk. She did it so unexpectedly, shocked me so badly, that I jumped up and backed away.

The garment on my desk was a short, hip-length black cape with a cowl.

All three of us gazed at it in silence until I said, "Well, what about it?"

"Belongs in the wardrobe department," Allene explained. "We're due to use it in *Kill Me, Kate* night after next. Looks like we'll have to have it dry-cleaned first, though," She turned over part of it and pointed to a stain as big as a grapefruit surrounded by a lot of grape-sized stains and smaller. "I'm not sure," she added, "but that looks like blood."

We gazed at each other again. I instantly knew that this was the same cape I had seen worn by a killer fleeing from the murder scene last night. Allene and Val, both being bright girls, could at least suspect a connection. It clinched a point that Bryce and I had mentioned last night. There could be no doubt now that the murderer of Victor Gaylord was closely associated with *Raphael TV*.

"I don't know what the hell to do about this, Allene," I said, "except to turn it over to the cops. Do that, will you?"

She nodded, turned and went out with it. It struck me then that this was another of those senseless things that had begun turning up. Why should a woman take the trouble and the risk of snitching a garment from our wardrobe department to wear when visiting Gaylord either to kiss him or to kill him? Offhand I could see no point in it, except that maybe she had done it to keep the blood off her own clothes.

"Trex, darling," Val said, appearing to forget the bloodstained cape almost immediately. "When I sign that contract—"

"Val, darling, my sweet," I broke in, "for Pete's sake let up. Frankly, from my own selfish viewpoint it'll be fine with me if you never sign the contract. I have other things to worry about this morning, such as my own paltry future."

"But the salary Vic mentioned—"

"Val!" I blurted. "If you don't shut up about it, I'll put in a pitch for Mona Elwyn instead." That had the desired effect—hit her with dismay, because Val and Mona loved each other like a pair of competing prima donnas they were. "Tell you what, Val," I suggested, trying a little butter next. "Make a note of the main points you want in your contract and I'll take it up with the big brass as soon as the chance comes."

She got busy at once, using my desk pen to scribble on a memo pad. My nerves were jerky, my arm more painful. The noise in this place seemed worse than usual this morning—an orchestra tootling, the chorus girls' slippers slap-slapping, carpenters' hammers banging, the soprano trying to out-sing the tenor, technicians yelling at each other over the din.

Although Val is very pleasant to have around, I was actually glad when she dropped the note on my desk and slipped around for a good-bye hug.

"Sometimes I'm sure you're right, Trex, darling," she murmured. "I'd be happier, I know, if I'd just relax and settle down and let a big strong man take care of me. But somehow I just can't. Not yet, anyhow, darling."

She left me with one of her heart-stopping smiles. I picked up her note with the intention of chucking it into my file, unread.

But suddenly it was sticking to my fingers like flypaper and I was staring at it in cold shock.

Val's handwriting on the blue-gray bit of paper looked exactly like that on the endearing note I had filched from the scene of Vic Gaylord's murder.

CHAPTER FOUR

THE PRECEDING section of this record was a quickie, written partly in my office in longhand and partly here in my apartment during a hurried lunch hour.

After discovering the startling similarity between Val's script and that on the note, I locked myself inside my office and tried to pull my wits back together. It was a shock that really jolted me.

Instantly Val seemed to fit perfectly into the murder picture. Gaylord's romancing, Val's driving ambitions, her stormy emotions at times—all this was enough to turn my blood icy and leave me numb with heartsickness.

I came back here to my apartment at the very first chance for just one reason—to make a direct comparison between the two notes. I went straight from the door to the shelved book in which I had hidden the love message. One look cinched it. There was no possible doubt that Valerie Wayne's hand had written both.

I sat and stared at nothing, convinced that this murder case was answered then and there, once and for all. As I saw it, there had been two women present in the cottage for a few dramatic minutes at the time of Gaylord's death. It would have been small comfort to me to decide that Val was the one in the adjoining room. I knew she wasn't that one.

The abandoned shoes, dress and coat were not new, but also they were items of attire which I had never seen Val wear. So she wasn't the woman who belonged to those clothes, but the other one—the one with the hatchet in her hand.

That was it. So far as I was concerned, there was no need to take it any farther than that.

Then I began to wonder about the angles. Could Val have loved Gaylord so violently as all that, for instance, and at the same time showed affection toward me so consistently and apparently so genuinely? The answer to that one, and to other disturbing questions as well, is this: Val is a skilled experienced actress.

One other angle is even more disturbing. Maybe this was why Gaylord's murderer had shot me in the arm as a warning, instead of shutting me up permanently on the spot—because Val does care for me, in her way. But that puts an odd twist on it too. It seems to say that the murderess loved one man so much in one way that she killed him and loved another man so much in another way that she couldn't bear to kill him.

Without trying any farther than that to make sense of it, I went back to the studio with both notes in my pocket. The parking lot was as crowded as before, if not more so—there were a pack of newspaper photographers and reporters now prowling the place. The lunacy that is TV was still going on unabated inside. Conferences were continuing portentously behind closed doors. And in my office again, waiting for me, was Val.

I stopped short to peer at her. It was all so easily understandable. She was so attractive in every line, every posture, every gesture—and so definitely career-minded.

"You disappointed me again, Trex, darling," she said calmly. "I wanted you to take me to lunch. I felt the need of three or four extra-dry martinis—but they weren't as good without you there."

Her technique was perfect. A very clever girl, this Val. Ordinarily I would have burst into a glow, but today this gambit didn't win her even a smile. Unfortunately for her, too, it led directly into the subject uppermost in my mind.

"That makes two bad connections. Lunch today, dinner last night. May I ask, my sweet, how you spent your evening after I broke our date?"

Something in my manner warned her of stormy weather ahead. She slowly found herself a fresh cigarette and slowly lighted it, eying me. Instead of getting jittery she turned calmer and quieter than normal.

"I mixed myself a few highballs," she answered evenly, "decided to skip dinner, read a book for a while then went to bed early."

"So when the cops ask you to account for yourself at the time of Gaylord's murder, if they haven't already, you'll tell them that? You were alone at home and peacefully sleeping?"

"Just like millions of other people," Val added, her voice low. "I can't prove it, of course, any more than those millions of others can," Then she said, frowning prettily, "Trex, darling, I don t like the way you're looking at me."

"I don't like the way I'm seeing you," I said flatly. "How about this as proof—that you're lying?"

I placed the rendezvous message on my desk top. She frowned down at it, drawing a long pull on her cigarette. Then she gazed up at me, seeming puzzled.

"I don't get it, Trex."

"You wrote this note, Val."

Her answer startled me. I had expected a vehement outburst of denials. Instead, she shrugged and admitted, "Yes, I wrote it. What of it?"

"What of it?" I stared at her. "After making this little tryst with Gaylord last night, you kept it, didn't you—with a hatchet?

She smashed out her cigarette, seeming annoyed rather than indignant. Let's get this straight, Trex. This note I wrote has nothing at all to do with Gaylord or a hatchet or with anything else that happened last night."

It took a stiff effort to keep myself from snapping out: "*No? Then how come I found this note near Gaylord's dead body?*" That might have spilled me straight into the fire. I managed to hold it back and ask instead, "Then just what does it mean, Val?"

Suddenly she laughed, lightly, even delightedly. I was entertaining her—although I couldn't see how and I certainly didn't feel comical. But she laughed her beautiful laugh and then impulsively kissed the corner of my mouth.

"It was used as a prop in the Musical Romances show last week, Trex, darling—and you're being just too wonderfully silly about it!"

I didn't feel silly as yet, either. "As a prop?"

"Why, yes. The plot called for a secret rendezvous between the sweethearts in the play and a close-up shot showed my hand writing this note, Trex, darling, it's really sweet of you to be so deliciously jealous over it!"

"Look, Val," I said shortly. "With three different shows in production continually, a lot goes on around here that I don't have time to notice. I'm too busy to catch all our shows even when they're screened. If there was such a shot in the show you're talking about, it's definitely one I missed. Still, it's easy enough to check."

She was laughing again, feeling delightfully flattered. "Please do check, Trex, darling! It's one Bryce directed, remember?"

At that point I certainly had no choice but to push it through. I left my office and halfway down the stairs, with Val trailing me, chortling to herself, I spotted Bryce talking with Allene. I caught his eye, signaled him to come. I went back to my desk with Val to wait for him.

A moment later he came in, his shirtsleeves rolled up, looking worn. Allene trailed in with him, evidently not understanding that I hadn't wanted her to. But now that she was here, it didn't seem to matter.

I pointed to the note and asked Bryce, "Recognize it?"

"Why, yes," Bryce answered immediately. "We used it in a close-up on the Musical Romances show last week. Val wrote it. What about it?"

I sat heavily in my chair, gazing ruefully at Val. I felt like a good-sized heel and an even bigger jerk. I would never get finished with apologizing to Val. At the same time I was dizzy with a sense of relief to discover that I had committed such an unjust piece of foolishness.

Val, however, seemed less amused now. She was gazing at me with a peculiarly puzzled expression on her face.

"Nothing about it, Bryce," I heard myself answering him lamely. "Somebody used it to play a cute little practical joke on me, that's all. Funny how I can get so jealous about Val with so little reason."

Bryce and Allene grinned, but Val and I found it a strain to join them. I knew what was troubling Val. She was wondering why I had connected this note with Gaylord's murder—wondering where I had found it.

On my part, I found myself facing another of those angles that didn't quite make sense. I mean, why should one of Gaylord's playmates, in making a tryst with him, use a discarded prop note written by another woman? Just to tease him, maybe? A false lure dangled before a gluttonous fish? Yes, maybe.

"Bryce," I asked, "not that it's important, but can you remember what became of this note after it was used in last week's show?"

He shook his head. "You know how props get scattered around. I didn't give this one a thought. Hadn't seen it since, in fact, until just now. Somebody used it to rib you, Trex? Sometimes I think this place is too full of off-screen comedians."

A chilling thought hit me. Suppose some practical joker had decided it would be a great prank to slip this prop note inside an envelope and leave it on Gaylord's desk. This funny funny man would imagine Gaylord tantalized by the fact that the note was unsigned, then waiting for its amorous writer to keep a rendezvous with him—and wondering who she would turn out to be.

It would be more hilarious still if this same clown had slipped notes, forged with Gaylord's name, into the handbags or lockers or desks of three or four women who were suspected of being friendly with him, or who wouldn't mind being. In that case, this clever prankster could look on the results of his work this morning—murder liberally garnished with witch's brew.

"Well, let's keep this little incident quiet, anyway," I suggested. It struck me that this was the first time today— since coming to work—that I had seen Bryce. I also remembered that I still hadn't seen Mona around. "Mona's catching up with learning her part, isn't she?" I asked.

Bryce shook his head, looking troubled. "Mona's staying in bed this morning, feeling ill."

"Sorry to hear it, Bryce. Mona's been having it pretty rough lately hasn't she? What does the doctor say about her?"

"She wouldn't let me call the doctor this morning. It's just a hangover plus lack of sleep plus overwrought nerves, as usual. A little rest will put her back on her feet. Don't worry, Trex—she won't let us down."

I wasn't worrying so much about the show. Another actress could take it over on short notice. But I did feel uneasy about the way Mona was keeping herself out of sight today, and I kept remembering that smear of fresh blood on the wall where she'd spied on Bryce and me last night.

Now important noises came into the hallway. A door in the high-bracket section of our offices had opened, and several men were approaching. Two of them paused outside my door to exchange a few words in whispers.

One was Rexwell Barrett, the biggest wheel in *Raphael TV*—the back-slapping, haw-hawing type, but filthy rich. The second man was a stranger—a quiet-moving, sharp-eyed lad who looked exactly like a detective.

Barrett came breezing into my office in a surprisingly jovial mood, considering that one of his fellow hot-shots had been chopped down only a few hours ago. He greeted Val and Allene in what he imagined was a courtly manner, then greeted Bryce and me in the manner of a Major General loosening up to a couple of shavetails.

"Terrible confusion here today," he began in his unnecessarily loud voice. "Nobody's getting anything done. No use keeping it up. I have a little suggestion and I'd like to hear what you think of it."

Naturally he expected us all, in advance, to think yes.

"Let's close up shop for the rest of the day. Everybody come over to my place for a buffet supper and a swimming party. Plenty to eat and drink, plenty of chance to relax and get our bearings. My party entirely, of course. A pool party strictly—every lovely lady must bring her swim suit. Take the men's minds off less pleasant matters, haw-haw!"

While we assured him that this was a wonderfully kind and generous idea of his, and brilliant besides, I eyed the stranger who was waiting in the hallway. I got the impression that in his quiet way he was the mind behind this move.

"That's the way Vic would want it," Barrett boomed on. "No grieving, no long faces. Eat, drink and be merry." *For tomorrow we die?* No, I supposed not; he stopped with the merriment.

Turning to me, he added, "You and Bryce spread the word around, Trexler. Stress the fact that it's a swimming party, especially for all the girls. Nothing like sparkling water and freedom from too many clothes to relax the nerves. All right boys, take care of it."

With that, he raised one ham-like hand and gave me a jovial slap on the arm. It was an habitual farewell gesture of his, the kind you can easily get fed up on. Today it was damned near catastrophic—because that heavy hand slammed hard against my bullet wound.

For two frantic seconds. I was caught up in a whirl of desperately clashing impulses. Pain of blow-torch intensity paralyzing me. My mind was a runaway carousel, complete with flashing lights and bonging bells.

Only with a clenched-teeth effort did I keep myself from yelling out and smashing my fist into Barrett's face in retaliation. It was a fast trip through hell and when I arrived back in my office, shaken, I was amazed to find that no one seemed to have noticed my reaction.

Barrett was just then delivering a slap to Bryce's arm, exactly as he had mine, when cruising on out. The room was steadier for me now, but a new panic was forcing me to hold my breath, I was thinking, *"It's bleeding again!"*

I felt what seemed to be a warm trickle under the bandages. I could picture the blood streaming down, soaking my shirt and my coat sleeve. I could imagine people staring at my blood-soaked clothes, and myself making a crazy effort to explain it away.

But then, after half, a minute, I could go back to breathing again because it didn't seem to be bleeding after all. It had started, then stopped after only a few drops that wouldn't be noticed. If anybody there in the office saw me mumbling to myself at that moment, I was just offering up a short and fervent prayer of thanks.

CHAPTER FIVE

THE IDEA of the pool party was bringing out various reactions. Val seemed impatient with the notion of topping off a murder with merriment. Bryce simply began rolling his sleeves down, a gesture that said his day's work was done. But Allene—

She was standing back against the wall, her face suddenly deathly white. For a second her eyes were round with a kind of terror that I couldn't account for at all. Then she swallowed hard, pushed herself into motion and went hurrying out of the office.

We were a fine collection of nervous wrecks, all right, I thought.

I had noticed that Rexwell Barrett, after leaving us, had stopped to speak again to the quiet stranger in the hallway. Something was definitely cooking between them. Whatever it was, I had a hunch that Barrett had just handed me a song-and-dance and that in some way he was using me as a tool—and using me not entirely honestly, at that.

Although I had no real reason for resenting, still, perhaps because of that excruciating slap on my arm, it did start me on a slow bum. The next thing I knew I was out in the hallway, buttonholing that quiet-acting stranger.

"My name's John Trexler," I said.

He nodded, as if he already knew that. "Mine's Ray Ferry," he answered. "Detective, local force."

I went on bluntly, "This idea of the pool party is yours, isn't it?"

He smiled a little, studying me. He was really a likeable guy, not handsome, but decent-looking. The masculine type, with plenty of character in his face, although he was still young. Dogged, too. Tenacious and clever and tireless—somehow I could see those qualities in his clear blue eyes. Ray Ferry, I knew at once, was a man to watch out for in case you happened to be a murderer.

"Look here," I said. "Most of the people who work here are my friends. I'm not the type who enjoys putting over a fast one and I don't want them to think I am." Considering my actions last night this sounded ironic to me, but I went on, "I mean, I'm not quite willing to pull them into this pool party unless I know what's behind it."

Ferry's smile grew a little, quizzically. "Will you keep this confidential, Mr. Trexler?" At my nod he went on. "You see, we're just trying to work fast. The pool party is a way of saving us a lot of time. We could get the same results in other ways, but this way we'll get them quicker."

I shook my head, signifying that I didn't understand, and he went on, "We figure that the woman who killed Gaylord last night is wounded."

My arm gave an extra twinge. "How do you know that?"

"Well—this is the way we think it happened, Mr. Trexler. Gaylord was there in the living room of his guest cottage. Suddenly this woman burst in. One look at her warned Gaylord that she meant him no good. Probably she had the hatchet gripped in her fist. In self-protection he grabbed for his revolver. It was probably in a drawer of the desk and it took him a few seconds to get hold of it. Meanwhile the woman with the hatchet kept on coming at him, obviously intending to give him the business."

I let Ferry go on.

"Gaylord had time to fire one shot, at least. We doubt that he fired more than one, but that point is not important.

He did manage to pop one bullet at the woman as she came at him. It landed in the woodwork across the room.

"We've found the bullet hole, dug out the slug, identified the gun. It was fired from a .38. There's one legally registered in Gaylord's name—and missing. We put the slug through various chemical tests, which showed that the bullet passed through part of a human body before sinking into the wall."

If I looked astonished, my astonishment was entirely real. "In other words, Gaylord's shot at least nicked the woman who killed him—but you don't know just how badly?"

Ferry nodded. "That's exactly it, Mr. Trexler. As you can easily understand, this is an important fact in the case. We want to find a woman with a fresh bullet-wound somewhere on her body. As I said, we could corral all the more likely babes, line them up and have our police matron examine them all one by one, but that would waste a lot of time and be a big bother for everybody."

"But with bevies of girls frolicking about a pool in their little swim suits..." I took it up. "...you'll be able to sift out the little innocents in jig time."

He still smiled quietly. "And if a few women seem to prefer not to wear swim suits, or if a few don't show up at all, that very thing will make them especially interesting to us. We'll have to ask them to explain how come they're so modest."

I found myself smiling also. "I've got to admit it's a clever, practical idea, not to mention entertaining as well. The best thing about it is that the guilty woman can know it's a trap, but knowing it won't help her much. Every little dilly in the place can know all about it, in fact, and it will work perfectly just the same."

I added with a sense of relief, "I'll keep it quiet anyway, and I'll start spreading the invitations around the studio right now."

I went back into my office. Val was alone there now. She still looked puzzled, and I knew why. That note was still troubling her mind.

"You probably noticed," I said quickly, trying to switch her on to her favorite subject, "Barrett isn't falling all over himself in his eagerness to ask me to fill Gaylord's shoes here."

Val said softly, "Trex, darling, just where and when did you pick up that prop note?"

I looked at her hard. "I have a new thought about it, my sweet. Your explanation of that note sounded pretty solid at first, but actually it doesn't stand up. Unquestionable that note was used as a prop in a play. But that fact does not rule out the possibility that it may have been used again by, the woman who wrote it, to arrange a real meeting with Gaylord."

Val stood up straight, her eyes narrowed. "Really, Trex, I've had enough of this. You're going a little too far, and I don't like it."

"I like it even less than you do, precious. You thought it was a cute notion to pass Gaylord a note that was already scented with fictional romance, was that it? Then when you went to meet him—"

Suddenly I was sick of the whole subject. I shrugged at Val and said wearily, "The whole thing will be settled very shortly now, at Barrett's pool party. You'd better be there, sugar-pie. You'd better wear your newest and wispiest Bikini, too. Because the cops know that the woman who killed Gaylord was slightly wounded. They're looking for a little lovely having a small bullet hole in her pretty hide."

Then Val flared up. "Why, you! Swimming party! Why wait?" She kicked off her shoes.

"If you want to see a completely intact pelt, Trex, I'll prove to you right now that I own one!"

Much as I regretted the necessity, I did the only safe thing—I scrammed out of there fast, banged the door shut behind me and kept on heading away at top speed.

*   *   *

This part of this report will have to go fast. Our little mess of murder is now fouled up far worse than before. Something new has been added. Another corpse.

At this moment—Tuesday evening, 9 P.M., I am the only one who knows the killer has struck again. I have no idea how soon or how late the corpse will be found. The corpse doesn't care, I'm sure, that I have not yet notified the police.

But the police will definitely care when they learn that I have now held out on them twice. That's why I have stolen a few minutes from the evening's festivities to dodge back here and, for whatever it may be worth, bring this running account up to the minute.

I'm typing as fast as my fingers can poke the keys, in the hope that nobody will notice I'm not where I'm supposed to be.

Let's take it back only as far as the pool party at Barrett's and I wish I were there right now, with no second murder on my mind.

Even making allowances for its grim undertones—actually the occasion was a trap set to catch Gaylord's murderess—it was downright idyllic. Considering the short notice, Barrett really tossed off a little masterpiece of party-giving. It goes to show that having a mountain of dough had certain advantages.

Lanterns had been hung in the gardens and along the walks. Tables were heaped with the tastiest smorgasbord this side of Stockholm. Waiters in monkey jackets circulated continually with trays of any bacchic whim you might imagine. Even more stimulating was the fact that all the little pretties present had fallen nicely into the spirit of the occasion. Their little swimsuits vied with each other's in not-thereness, and the pool was a dream of loveliness.

The award for the lightest-weight Bikini, had there been such a trophy, would have been won hands down by Miss Valerie Wayne. Val had evidently decided I meant it when suggested she take the test seriously. She had outdone herself, had scorned to add to her costume even with shoes or a flower in her hair. She wore only that wisp of a suit and absolutely nothing else. The detectives present could feel no doubt whatever that she was entirely unscratched from head to toe.

What's more, none of the other lovelies sported any bandages, either. All of them were clad in a little fabric and a lot epidermis, thus proving their complete innocence. It can put down as an absolute and incontrovertible fact that there wasn't one little bullet hole in the lot of them.

As lusciously as Val had presented herself to the challenge however, her eyes remained ice when she looked at me. I felt like four kinds of a heel for ever having doubted her—my doubts having been obviously absolutely groundless. I thought she might give me a break even so, but no; she was an unbelievably desirable woman who gazed at me with frigid scorn. Also, she kept giving me trouble by walking away when I went after her, and getting herself lost inside a beaming crowd of junior executives.

Detective Ray Ferry obviously felt that he had really pulled off an admirable idea here. I'm sure he never worked on a murder case he enjoyed more. He did not neglect his duties in any way in satisfying himself as to the innocence of every little chick. With a beatific expression, he checked off each name on a long list.

I watched the cars streaming in and the honeys frolicking in the pool and tried vainly to win a half-way warm glance from Val. All the time the back of my mind was worrying about that list of names with which Ferry had been provided.

It included the name of every woman who worked for *Raphael TV*, of course, and no doubt others as well. At every opportunity I snitched a look over his shoulder, to see who hadn't shown up yet. With the help of four quick scotch-on-rocks, I began worrying about Allene Giles.

Allene was conspicuously absent. So was Mona Elwyn, for that matter—Mona, at whom I hadn't had so much as one look since Gaylord's murder. If Mona didn't show up, it could be put down to a temper tantrum or a load of rye or another slug of sleeping pills or even to just plain perversity. Allene, however, was a very solid doll. She had talent, she could take a lot of toil, she knew what the score was—and I did not want to lose her as a dependable worker.

Yet I kept remembering that expression of stark terror that had appeared on her face this afternoon, there in my office. Why? Had she realized instantly that the pool party was a trap set to nail a murderess, realized instantly that she wouldn't dare come?

I began running a fever over Allene's absence. Ferry was getting too thoughtful about it, too. The party was well under way now, there were only a few women who hadn't shown, and the case was rapidly boiling down to them as the chief suspects in the murder. I decided suddenly to check on

Allene on my own, so I wormed my way into the house and found a phone.

Allene's number didn't answer.

As I turned away, my host and big boss, Rexwell Barrett came at me. Deliberately I turned so that he couldn't take another swing at my wound. I still felt the punishment of his last friendly swat on my arm. He did it again, but luckily landed this time on my shoulder.

"We have a duty tonight, Trexler," he suggested. "Louise Gaylord arrived back home from Chicago this afternoon. The police have been talking to her—being too damned stuffy about it, if you ask me—keeping her friends away. However, I am going over to the Gaylord home to see Louise very shortly and I thought it would be a thoughtful gesture if you and Elwyn came with me."

"Of course," I agreed. "Just let me know when you're ready to leave."

Bryce Elwyn had arrived late—and alone. Ferry had been getting his help in checking the gals against their names on the list of guests. More worried than ever, I buttonholed Bryce the first chance I found, and asked, "Have you seen Allene?"

"No—and Ferry's getting interested in her."

"And where's Mona?"

"I don't know where the hell Mona is," Bryce answered, looking badly worn and harassed. "When I got home I found she'd gone without leaving a message. I haven't been able to locate her. She's done that before. But I don't understand about Allene. Allene definitely said she would be here."

With my nerves rubbed ragged by the strain of last night, that was all the suspense I could take. I found my car and followed a driveway to a gate near the servants' quarters. With so many people coming and going and milling around, I think I eased away without being especially noticed. I headed straight for the place, not far from here, where Allene had found herself a one-room, ground-floor apartment with a private entrance.

The door was unlocked. I went in and found her in almost the same position that I had found Gaylord—lying in front of the fireplace. She was wearing a bathrobe twisted around her. The murderer evidently hadn't planned in advance to kill Allene—this time the hand of death had not used a bright new Boy Scout hatchet, but, instead, a poker from the hearth.

I can tell it a little more calmly now, but it came then with a jolt that really rocked me back on my heels. I could hardly register the fact that Allene had been so brutally killed. Only a short time ago, too—the blood was still wet.

She had really planned to come to the pool party. There on the bed lay the dress she had selected to wear, and beside it a sleek, sun-yellow swimsuit.

And there was an important point about Allene—she had had no bullet wound.

CHAPTER SIX

PLENTY has happened since that last short report on the murder of Allene Giles. It's hard to believe, in fact, that I began writing this account less than twenty-four hours ago. When I began it I thought it would remain a comparatively brief statement. Instead, it has kept building up on me and last night was no let-up.

After completing that short section above, I drove back to Barrett's estate, where the festivities were gathering momentum. I eased through the service entrance, left my car in a dark spot and returned to mingle with the happy crowd around the pool, while pretending I had been there all along.

The first character I met was, of course, Ray Ferry, who eyed me as if I had taken on a new interest for him.

This was my opportunity to come clean and tell him what I had found in Allene's apartment. I was afraid that once he began questioning me it might grow to be too rough for my twitching nerves. I gazed at Ferry poker-faced and swallowed, first, a lump, and second, a martini.

Val Wayne, having proved her point beyond all possible question, had gotten back into her party clothes. This time she actually noticed me—gave me a curious glance. It was welcome, except that what it signified was not good. She knew I had slipped away from the party.

Next came the big wheel, Rexwell Barrett, rolling importantly along. "Been looking for you, Trexler!" he boomed. "We're leaving now. Come along."

He already had Bryce Elwyn in tow. The three of us went to a car that was waiting for us, complete with liveried chauffeur, in the driveway. Climbing in, we found that the party no longer consisted of three, but of four. Detective Ray Ferry had decided to join us.

"I say, Ferry," Barrett protested. "Aren't you detective fellows going to let up on Louise soon? Aren't you making it a bit hard on her?"

Ferry gave him a sidewise glance and answered quietly. "Murder is almost always hard on people, Mr. Barrett— especially the victim."

Barrett fell heavily silent. Ferry pointedly scanned his long guest list with all the check-marks on it. That was an opening for me to ask, "Well, you know now who stayed away. What's the score?"

"There are not many girls," Ferry said. "To begin with, Dinah Coyle."

"Girl?" I said. "Dinah's pushing fifty. She's our dance director. If she wanted to kill a, guy, she wouldn't need a hatchet. She'd take him by the ankles and pound him against the floor."

Still quietly, Ferry added, "Mona Elwyn."

"My wife," Bryce informed him. "I haven't seen her since this convivial little wake was announced. I doubt if she's even heard about it yet."

Ferry nodded and added, "Allene Giles." Nobody commented, so he added, "And a few others. Checking on the will be easy and quick. The party certainly boiled 'em down fast."

Barrett grunted. I was thinking uneasily about Allen trying to figure an angle. I remembered something Val ha said to me about Allene.

"It's true Allene would rather be a writer than any thing else. But that doesn't mean she'll go on taking the chump's end of the deal. Allene can produce or cast or direct. She can even go up higher than that, into the really big jobs in TV. That's exactly where she's heading, too. Also, she knows exactly what it may take to get her there, so she's playing it plenty cagey."

All right. Let's also say that sort of thing has been done before. But in Allene's case, then she would definitely not endanger her future with *Raphael TV* by murdering one of its top execs in jealous pique. So that left one other possibility—that Allene was the other woman who had been there in the cottage at the moment of murder, the woman who had left hastily, with the secret of the killer's identity.

With Ferry at my side, this was a chance to feel out this angle even before he had learned about Allene's sudden death. There had been a lot of news about the Gaylord murder in the evening papers.

The abandoned clothes had now been mentioned in public, so I could safely ask about them.

"Among the few women left on your list—I mean those who didn't show up at the party—are there any who might fit the clothes left in the cottage?"

Ferry smiled slowly, not too happily. "We know who fits those clothes," he answered.

I stared at him, thinking that this was fast work. "You actually know the identity of the second woman who was there in the cottage at the time of the murder?"

He answered cryptically, "I said we know who fits those clothes. It's not quite the same thing."

Puzzled, I asked, "The gal's name is a deep, dark, official secret, no doubt?"

Ferry shrugged. "Not exactly, I'll let you in on it." Then he added, deadpan, "Those clothes were custom-tailored for Miss Lois Garth-Smith."

I went on staring at him in disbelief. The Garth-Smiths are one of the most socially elevated families in this choice suburb in Westchester. So far as I knew, their daughter Lois had never had any association whatever with *Raphael TV*, and I had never heard her mentioned in connection with Gaylord.

"The shoes also belonged to Miss Garth-Smith," Ferry went on. "She had an exceptionally tiny foot—a three-and-a-half A.

Rexwell Barrett, who knew the Garth-Smith family, was making indignant noises.

"You may recall reading about Miss Garth-Smith in the papers recently," Ferry said. "She died last week."

As news it couldn't have been more stupefying.

"Miss Garth-Smith died in a fire in her home. She made the mistake of falling asleep while smoking in bed. The blaze was discovered by a servant, in time to prevent much damage to the house, but by then the girl was asphyxiated."

Dead a week ago!

"Following her funeral, her clothing was being aired on clothes-lines in the rear of the Garth-Smith place. That was one day late last week. A few pieces were stolen, among them the shoes, the coat and the dress later found in the cottage with Gaylord's body."

I heard myself saying, "Some of the little chorus girls who work for us don't make out too well. Their pay is far from lush and some of them have the expense of commuting out here."

Ferry gave me an acrid glance. "Back there at the party, I was looking for something besides a wound. I was also looking them over for size. A sort of Cinderella operation without actual use of the shoe. Also, I've been asking questions around. Well, I haven't yet found a girl who is small enough to wear Lois Garth-Smith's dress and shoes."

I shook my head dizzily. "So there wasn't any other woman in Gaylord's cottage when the murderess busted in on him."

"That's right," Ferry said.

"I must be caving in," I groaned. "I hear what we're saying but I can't make it mean anything."

Ferry handed out one more bit of information. "Those clothes were a plant—put there by a killer who is really very tricky worker."

A plant? A woman had planted another woman's clothes in Gaylord's bedroom just to give herself an excuse for chopping him up with a hatchet? It seemed hardly necessary. If there was any sense in it at all, in fact, I just couldn't find it.

Again I found myself wondering numbly about Allene. It hadn't been Allene for the reason that there hadn't been any woman there at all. It hadn't been Allene who killed Gaylord, either. So how had Allene gotten herself fatally tangled up in all this, and why was she dead?

I couldn't even begin to guess.

Barrett's big car had just turned into the Gaylord driveway. Two cops blocked it. Ferry held a brief conference with them while Bryce and I looked around. More cops were patrolling the rear grounds. They were there to discourage the morbidly curious public from tearing pickets off the fence or uprooting prize rosebushes as souvenirs.

We went to the front entrance of this fine Colonial mansion.

Our ring was answered by a detective. We were escorted into a living room that was a model of charm, comfort and color. Louise Gaylord, the murdered man's widow, came to us graciously, with one patrician hand extended in welcome.

As we exchanged the usual expressions of grief and sympathy I could not help admiring Louise's poise. Obviously she was badly shaken but she had complete control of herself. The only signs of agitation in her came when, once or twice, she looked slowly all around the room and then shuddered slightly. Always before she had shown great pride in her home; but now murder seemed to have done something ugly to it.

"I can't stay here tonight," she said suddenly, in her tired voice. She was strikingly dark. She carried herself beautifully. Sometimes when I admired her I thought of finely bred horses and sleek greyhounds. Being far from a fool, she knew her husband's kind, and she had taken plenty of cruelty from him, but she had held up straight and fine under it. I couldn't help thinking how fortunate it was that she had been hundreds of miles away when murder had struck down a heel who had so richly deserved it.

"I couldn't rest here tonight," she went on, "with policemen moving around the place all night, and horrible people ready to peer in the windows at the first opportunity. If only I could be alone where none of this could reach me—"

Rexwell Barrett began chivalrously, "Mrs. Gaylord, may I—?" and stopped. Suddenly he realized, red-faced, that he could not offer her his hospitality, not with the place swarming with merry revelers.

Bryce Elwyn took it up. He had said almost nothing since leaving the party, and he looked tired beyond words, but he made his offer sincerely. "Come to our place, Louise. We have plenty of room and it's perfectly quiet there. Mona loves you and will like taking care of you tonight. Nobody will know you're there, I promise."

"Thank you, Bryce," Louise said, smiling. "I can't think of any place I would rather be tonight."

She still had the packed bag she had brought with her from Chicago. Under quiet strain, she simply went about doing what she had decided to do. We all went back to Barrett's car and in a few minutes we were rolling on our way.

Nobody said much. Louise remained dry-eyed and perfectly poised every minute of the trip, I couldn't speak for Barrett, but Louise was certainly in better shape than either Bryce or I was.

Lights were shining inside the Elwyn place. Bryce said in a mutter, "Well, thank heaven, Mona seems to be home again." He opened the way for us and we went into the living room, Mona was there and, of all things, quietly reading a book. Moreover, she was entirely sober and on her good behavior.

Seeing Louise, she gave out a half-glad, half-grieving cry, rushed to Louise and hugged her hard. They chattered at each other, while Bryce explained that Louise would spend the night here. This went on until a quiet descended—a tenseness that came of the discovery that Ray Ferry was gazing searchingly at Mona Elwyn.

"Who is this guy?" Mona asked of Bryce. "What's the matter with him?"

"His name is Ferry and he's a detective, Mona," Bryce told her. "He probably wants to know why you didn't show up at the party."

"Party?" Mona answered impatiently. "What party?"

"You hadn't heard?" Ferry asked smoothly. "Or did you decide you'd rather not come?"

"You mind your own business," Mona said with forthright unreasonableness. "I'll go to parties when I feel like it. As it happened, I didn't even know about this one—and even if I *had* known. I wouldn't have been interested."

Ferry persisted quietly, "Why did you stay away, Mrs. Elwyn?"

Mona faced him with her fine chin lifted. She was darker than Louise, and taller, and full of nerves. Her face, once beautiful, had become lined and strained, but it was still photogenic. Whenever she registered an emotion, she registered it full scale, and at the moment she was burning with annoyance at Ferry.

"I'd heard Louise was back from Chicago and of course I wanted to see her. I drove over to her place but those dumb gumshoes of yours wouldn't even let me in the gate. I waited in the car a long while, thinking Louise might come out, but she didn't. So finally I came home and tried to get her on the phone but all I got was busy signals and more moronic gumshoes." Mona's raven-black eyes flashed. "Next question?"

Ferry did the smart thing. "No hurry, Mrs. Elwyn. Tomorrow will do, or the next day. Good night, now."

He withdrew—too quietly, I thought. Mona immediately began urging Bryce to mix up a round of drinks. Barrett demurred, insisting that he must get back to his guests.

Since I had left my car at the party, I had small choice but to go with him. I bid Mona and Louise and Bryce good night, and with Barrett and Ferry, both silent. I cruised back to that fairyland where the crowd around the pool was still making merry.

Barrett went pompously into the great house while Ferry began making the rounds of the other detectives present. I looked for Val, but didn't find her. Snagging a double scotch off a passing tray, I gathered a handful of canapés and found myself a quiet shadow. The little sandwiches and the big scotch were all gone, when I heard a quiet approach in the dark. It materialized in front of me in a shape that could be nobody's but Val's.

She had a glass in one hand and a cigarette in the other. She came close, said softly, "Have I been a little rough on you, Trex, darling?"

"Not very," I said. "At least, you stopped short of murder."

"Poor boy," Val murmured.

She tossed her cigarette away. It disappeared in the darkness in a comet-like arc. She brought her lips to mine and kept them there. Her free hand slid up my left arm and she stiffened as her fingers ran over the lump of bandages. Suddenly she was squeezing my wound—*hard.*

At that moment Miss Valerie Wayne, captivating television star, came within a hair of losing all her pearly teeth down her lovely throat. I wrenched myself back with a gasp and managed to keep my knuckles out of her face, realizing that with that nimble mind of hers, Val had reasoned there was only one place where I could have found that unsigned love message—the scene of the murder.

"Let's not play quite so rough any more, Trex," she whispered. "After all, we have so many mutual interests— and we *do* have to think of our future, don't we, darling?"

Then she hurried off.

CHAPTER SEVEN

AT THAT point, when I had written that far, an interruption came—a knock on my door. I sat frozen, hands lifted, in front of this typewriter, cold sweat popping out of my forehead. Not having much choice, I forced myself to get up and let the cops in.

Only, it wasn't the cops, but Val.

She came in slowly and curiously, dressed as I had last seen her. Evidently she had been spending some wakeful hours in her own feminine scheming. Back there at Barrett's castle she had left me hanging on that last cryptic remark of hers—"We *do* have to think of our future, don't we, darling?"—and I had let it ride at that.

Here she was again, with something more on her mind—and I knew she hadn't come to bake a cake.

"What are you typing so industriously at this hour of the morning, Trex?" she inquired lightly. "A long love letter to me?"

She went straight to my typewriter for a look. Like many starry-eyed women, however, Val is very far-sighted. She hadn't brought her reading glasses along, so the words I had last written were merely a blur.

I offered her no explanation. She went to the table where a tray of the makings sat, and she used them to make. Then she sank into a chair, crossed her lovely legs and gazed at me through the smoke of a fresh cigarette.

"Well?" she said. "You've had time to think it over now. Strictly business, Trex."

"What are you talking about?" I said.

She smiled beautifully. "Well, Vic Gaylord was a wild spender, so there's not much left for Louise except the house and his insurance—and his shares in *Raphael TV*. They're enough to give her a pretty solid voice in what goes there."

"What's Louise got to do with me?"

"The man who marries her will become a power in *Raphael TV*, thanks to those shares. Won't *you*, darling?"

"Just a minute," I said. "Me marry Louise? The notion has never popped into my head—or into Louise's either, I'm sure. Not that she isn't a thoroughly desirable woman, but for Pete's sake, Val haven't you sort of picked up a hint by now that you're the gal I want to marry?"

Val's smile faded and she shrugged. "But you're also the lad who plays the angles, Trex. We all have to do it in this crazy back-stabbing racket. Not all of us would go as far as murder, though. If you felt you had to push it that far, why—?"

She shrugged again, cynically. "Anyhow, I'm counting on you to put across a nice, plushy contract for me, Trex, darling."

"Are you nuts? I'm not even half-sure of my own job at this point, let alone—"

"Please, Trex. It was easy for you. All you had to do was rig up some fake evidence at Gaylord's cottage and leave him dead there. Soon you'll marry Louise and move into a soft spot in the top brackets of *Raphael TV*. I don't approve of murder, darling, but you seem to have a fairly good chance of getting away with this one. I couldn't bear to turn you in for murder, so I really haven't much choice but to cash in on it with you."

I stared at her. "Val, you're wrong," I said heavily. "I didn't murder Gaylord. The cops believe he was knocked off by a woman, remember?""

"It was you who went at him with your little hatchet," she insisted. "That's when he shot you in the arm, isn't it?"

I was getting plenty sore at Val for forcing me to defend myself with a confession. "A woman did it, Val," I insisted. "That's what the cops think—and I happen to know they're right."

"Do you really?"

"Yes, I saw her. I was driving past the rear gate of Gaylord's place when she came popping right out into the shine of my headlights."

Val laughed lightly. "Careless little dear, wasn't she?"

"I know it sounds cockeyed, but I can't help that. I saw it happen in just the way I'm telling you now. I watched Gaylord's murderess go looping off in her car. Then I went into the cottage and found him dead. I also found that love note you'd written—as a prop or otherwise."

"And you carried it away to protect my good name," Val said. "Why, Trex, darling, I'm touched."

I decided that if she went on laughing at me like that I would presently put both my hands on her pretty neck and wring it. "Then I left. I didn't know the murderess had sneaked back to watch what I was doing. She must have been afraid that I'd recognized her, although I really hadn't. Anyway, when I stepped out of the door onto the terrace she slugged me down."

"Then she tried to silence you by shooting you in the arm." Val was giggling over her drink. "Come, now, Trex. Hadn't you better think up a more likely—?"

"Val!" I broke in heatedly. "I don't know why she shot me through the arm instead of through the head or through the heart. All I'm sure of—and I'm sure of this much—is that the arm is where she shot me. How else can you explain that wound, my pet?"

"Easily. As I said before, it was Gaylord who shot you," Then Val added, "How do you like that medicine, Trex? It's the very same brand you spooned out to me this morning. Ugly tasting stuff, isn't it?"

Yes. She was handing it right back to me. She was just as mistaken about me as I had been mistaken about her also. I felt I had less than a chance of convincing her of it. I think she actually believed I was guilty of murder. I decided, all right, let her. I was too burned up and too disgusted to care much about defending myself further.

During this sweetly charitable conversation I had turned to the phone at intervals to call Bryce Elwyn's number. My mind was nagged by worries about the late Allene Giles. Perhaps her dead body was still waiting to be found. I hadn't yet had a chance to brief Bryce on that. But Bryce's number wasn't answering.

I rose and said sourly, "Thanks for covering me, Val. Naturally I won't forget the favor when I become one of the big wheels of *Raphael TV*—but you may have to wait as long as next week."

I went out. My car was parked at the curb and when I reached it Val was close behind me. As I turned to face her, she asked, "Where are you going, Trex?"

"Nowhere much," I told her. "Just out to commit a couple more murders. I'm a little behind in my quota for tonight." Suddenly sickened by the childishness of these cracks, I added;

"Val, let me alone. Go on home."

I slid under the wheel of my car. Val hustled to plump herself into the seat beside me. I stared at her hopelessly. I might yell my head off at her, I knew, and still she would stay right there. I might heave her bodily out of my car and she would follow me in her own. So I did the wisest thing a man can do when up against a woman in Val's frame of mind— saved my breath.

Not speaking, I angled through streets full of pre-dawn darkness. Presently I turned into the driveway of Bryce's place. The sprawling L-shaped ranch house was all dark except for one window, that of Bryce's study, off in the wing.

The guy was punishing himself too hard, I felt. Despite the strain we were all under—nerve-racking even when it wasn't topped off by a murder—he had evidently been working through the night again. A very silly way to kill yourself, I thought...by producing TV shows.

I braked at the front of the house and Val came with me to the entrance. After ringing the bell we waited. Nobody came. I sensed Val tightening up; she turned her head to listen. The night seemed utterly quiet until I focused my ears, carefully, and then I caught the same sound that had interested Val—low, quick voices.

Inside the house or out? We couldn't tell. They were just the fast whispers of two people speaking together urgently.

Val, never one to stand on ceremony, made a quick grab at the knob of the front door. It was unlocked; it opened at her first thrust. She breezed right in, that alert, audacious mind of hers having fastened on something. I couldn't guess what it was, so far, but she wasn't letting it go.

She stopped in the center of the living room, in a position, allowing her to gaze down the long hallway of the main wing of the house—at a series of doors.

The whispers had stopped, but now there were the sounds of quick motions. Val moved again, fast. She went down the hall on tiptoe, stopped suddenly again, then turned and pushed one of these doors wide open. She went even farther—stepped into the room and snapped the wall switch.

I stopped behind her in amazement. This was Louise Gaylord's room for the night. Louise lay there in bed, her lovely dark hair splashed across a pastel blue pillow. She did not stir under the glare of the ceiling light, or respond to the noise of our sudden entrance. I began to get sore at Val for busting in on an overtired woman, like this—until Val's finger pointed at the window.

It was half open. The screen was unhooked and hanging loose. From outside came, faintly, the sound of running feet.

Val moved again with electrical speed. She whirled about and flew back out the front entrance. My tired brain was finally catching on, so I headed in the opposite direction, fast—down the hallway to a rear door. I stood in the dark listening; but now the night was silent, the running footfalls gone.

I looked around and saw nothing in the faint shine of the night except the light gleaming from the window of Bryce's study. I wondered why he hadn't answered the bell, but mostly I stood there numbly trying to grasp the fact of Louise's nocturnal visitor.

She was only pretending to be asleep now, of course; there had been somebody in that room with her who'd left fast at our approach—and to me he was a totally unexpected and amazing character.

Presently Val came hustling quietly across the grass. She paused beside me, breathing fast, and asked, "I didn't spot anybody. Did you?"

I shook my head. "Might have skipped out the back way, to a car parked down the road. Anyway, some guy seemed to know where to find Louise tonight. I wonder how."

"Well, who *did* know?" Val asked eagerly.

"Rexwell Barrett and a detective named Ferry," I answered ironically. "Nobody else that I know of. Her whereabouts were supposed to be kept under wraps, so she wouldn't be hounded by reporters and such disturbers of the peace."

"She knows how to use a phone, doesn't she?" Val said quietly. "There could be a certain person she felt she wanted to talk to—someone she hadn't seen since her return from

Chicago. So she waited until Mona and Bryce had retired, then she made a call to suggest a private little conference here." Val gave me a significant glance. "Interesting, don't you think, Trex?"

"To me, especially," I said. "At least it shows you that if there is another guy in Louise's life—I'm not him. I doubt if there is one, anyhow. But it can wait, I'm worried about Bryce. Why hasn't he noticed we're here? The way he's been overworking himself, he could drop dead at any minute."

I cut across the patio to the study window. The bamboo blind was down, but through the cracks I could make out Bryce seated at his desk. Val dogged me, as I turned to the rear door of the smaller wing.

It was also unlocked—people who drink a lot have a tendency to forget such things as putting out the cat and locking the door, I'd found—so Val and I eased in.

CHAPTER EIGHT

WE QUIETLY opened the door of Bryce's study and found him at his desk with his head down on his arms. Scripts were pile around him. His thick-rimmed glasses lay aside. His posture was that of a completely exhausted man.

After drinking with Louise and Mona in the living room, Bryce had evidently tried to bolster himself with more drinks here, in order to get himself through a night's work. His collar was open and his shirt-sleeves were rolled up, but he hadn't lasted very long. Near one of his limp hands was tall glass still a quarter full of straight scotch.

Val and I looked a silent question at each other: *Shall we put him to bed?* I shook my head. Better not to disturb the poor guy, I thought. Before long he'd probably wake up and take care of himself. So I reached to his desk-lamp snapped it off, and we went out quietly, leaving him in the peculiarly pearly darkness that means dawn is not far away.

Now that I was well launched on a snooping tour through the Elwyn household, I felt there was one more bit of prying I must do. Without explaining to Val, I went along the dark hallway to the door of Mona's room. The distance from this door, to that bloody spot on the wall beside the door of Bryce's study, was about twenty feet. I listened for a moment with my hand on the knob, then looked in.

The blind was down, the room black; Mona was just a shapeless form on the bed. Her breathing was slow, heavy, deep. I sensed that, unlike Louise, she wasn't faking. On top of the drinks she had had, she had probably taken her usual dose of sleeping pills—for her, a highly dangerous habit. I stepped in quietly, Val close behind, crossed to the bedside table and pressed the switch.

The light fell across the bed. Mona lay like the dead, unnoticing. She was curled up under a blanket, the strain gone out of her face in sleep. She looked almost beautiful again, like the Mona who had once enjoyed a promising career in the movies. She was lying on her right side. Irresistibly my hand went out to the blanket and I slowly drew it down.

It was there. On her left upper arm, in almost the same position as my own wound. Bandages spotted with dried stains, swollen flesh, reddened skin. I did not need to look farther to be certain that the dressing concealed a bullet slash exactly as old as my own.

Val saw it and gasped. She stepped back, pale, shocked. Val and Mona had never been good friends—on the set they were venomous rivals—but I'm sure Val would never have gone so far as to wish to see a murder pinned on Mona.

Gazing at this staggering evidence, I thought back. Was it Mona I had seen rushing from Gaylord's cottage? I still could not feel sure. There was nothing in the picture to show that it hadn't been Mona, and the wound in her arm seemed to be proof enough, I could picture her then rushing back home, terrified at what she had done, made hysterical by the pain and the danger inherent in that injury.

"A nightmare," Bryce had explained to me on the phone—covering up for her, of course. Then, when I had come to the house with the news of Gaylord's murder, she had crept close to the study door to eavesdrop, and a few trickling drops on her fingers had marked the wall.

Well, I told myself, it all fits again, even to the fact that Mona had been unaccounted for at the time of Allene Giles' death.

Mona stirred a little as Val and I stared down at her. I turned then to Mona's clothes closet. It was a large one, but it was packed with dresses and suits and skirts and coats, I poked and tugged until I found a bright red one, then pulled the dress loose. Detaching it from the rod, I brought it closer to the light. A little groan came from Val as she bent over it, and I felt a surge of heartsickness.

The skirt of the dress was ripped and it was spattered with dark spots that had to be blood—Gaylord's blood.

I turned back to look for the red platform sandals, Mona had dozens of pairs of shoes of all kinds in racks and piled on the floor. The red sandals I had seen a murderess wearing were not there—but the dress was more than enough.

It was hard to understand why Mona had been so careless as to put the bloodstained dress back in her closet—the very first place the cops would look. But then, she had hardly been in condition for straight thinking since the murder.

We were startled by a motion on the bed; Mona stirred out of her lethargy. She pushed herself up, blinking at us, then stared at the dress Val was holding. A sound of confusion and despair came from her throat. She pushed herself to a sitting position, her hands clenching the edge of the bed.

"Whadda ya doin' here?" she said thickly. "Where'd you get that?"

"Out of your closet, Mona," I said. "Just now."

She shook her dark head. Wakefulness was coming back to her rapidly now, pushed by fear. "It's not mine," she said next. "Never saw that dress before." She closed her eyes and blurted, "I don't understand what's happening to me! It's horrible—and I can't understand it."

"Nightmares, Mona?" I asked wryly.

She opened her eyes again, wide. "No. That wasn't true. Bryce told you that to cover up what really happened. He didn't really believe what I told him, but he thought we'd better keep quiet about it. He didn't want to tell anybody else until he got it straight from me. That's what he kept saying, 'Don't hold out on me, Mona, tell me the truth.' I was telling him the truth, but he wouldn't believe me."

I was watching Mona closely. Like Val, she was an actress of experience and skill. Being married to one wouldn't necessarily make it easier to tell when she was coming clean or when she was putting over a fast one.

Even Val was listening to Mona now with an alert, searching light in her eyes.

"Tell us, Mona," Val urged her quietly. "Tell it to us just the way you told it to Bryce."

She gazed at us with appealing eyes. "All right. This is how it was. It was last night, the night Vic Gaylord was killed," She swallowed. "Bryce was in his study, in the middle of a long night's work. I'd gone to bed early. I was right here, right in this bed, asleep. Then I began hearing a sound. It was a scratching at the window. It woke me up and I looked and—I guess I was pretty bleary—but I saw it. There in the dark…" She pointed. "…a hand scratching at the screen."

She looked around the room next, as if thirsty for a drink, but neither Val nor I moved.

"First just that hand in the dark, and then a voice," she went on. "A voice speaking my name. It said, 'Mona, Mona, please. Help me, Mona. Mona, come out, help me.' I was scared. Didn't know whose voice it might be, but it had to be somebody who knew me, somebody who'd turn to me in an emergency. 'Please, Mona, come out, help me.'

"Well, I was woozy from sleeping pills, or maybe I wouldn't have gone out. Wobbly on my pins too. But I went hustling out the back door, the closest way—and as soon as I set foot outside I got grabbed."

Mona shuddered and hugged herself. "Grabbed and knocked to the ground. Face down. I was held there and then a gun was fired," She touched the bandages on her upper left arm. "That's where the bullet hit me. Then I was suddenly alone. It was all over, except that I went right into a fine, full blown fit of hysterics."

"As who wouldn't?" Val said, showing Mona a surprising degree of sympathy.

"Bryce came bursting out and picked me up. He took care of the wound, said it wasn't anything to worry about. But I couldn't make him understand what had happened. He just couldn't believe I'd been shot right outside our back door for no apparent reason."

"But he must have heard the report," I said.

"He couldn't help hearing it," Mona agreed. "He came out right away. After I told him what had happened, he went out and stared around at the ground as if looking for proof. He said he couldn't find a thing, kept saying he couldn't understand it."

It occurred to me abruptly that, on my part, I was unable to prove my own story. I had been lying on the rain-softened soil of a garden when I was shot. The bullet had undoubtedly driven deep down in the ground. Maybe it could be recovered, maybe it couldn't. If not, there would be nothing to back up my story. The same thing applied to Mona—if she was telling the truth.

"Bryce said that calling in the police wouldn't do any good, and he didn't want that kind of trouble. He said we should keep quiet and try to find out on our own what it meant. Well..." Mona smiled ruefully. "...we found out."

I tried to put myself in Bryce's shoes, pictured myself hearing a gunshot on my doorstep in the middle of the night and then finding my wife punctured in the arm and explaining it with a tale which made no sense. I went on to imagine myself, in Bryce's place, next hearing the news of Gaylord's murder, then having it topped off by the additional news that Gaylord's murderess was marked by a bullet wound.

By that time I would feel justified in doubting wifie's story a little more, I would be wondering what to do about it and I would be looking for an opening to drink myself to death.

Mona was staring at me. "Don't you see what it *really* means? Somebody's framing me!"

To myself, I remarked that that's what they all say, sister, I told myself that this was the answer, this was it, there couldn't be any more.

Mona said with a groan, "You don't believe me either!"

Val, wordlessly thoughtful, left it to me to answer that one.

"I don't know what to believe, Mona," I said. "In the past two days and two nights I've had so little sleep that I can't think any more. This was none of my business to begin with, except as it might affect my friends—and I shouldn't have been snooping in here tonight, either, except that in some oblique way I was trying to help.

"Instead, I seem to have fouled it up even worse. I'm sorry, Mona, sincerely sorry for you and Bryce both—and all I can say now is that if there is any way in the world that I can help you, you can count on me to do it."

"That goes for me, too, Mona," Val said.

She murmured, "Thanks," and it was a sound of hopelessness. She fell back on the bed and stared at the ceiling. "Just send a bunch of posies to my funeral after they've fried me, kids," she added, her voice shaking. "Never mind anything else. It would be waste motion."

I stood there holding the red dress up in one hand and pulling at it with the other. For the first time I saw the rip in the left sleeve—the bullet-tear, in the same position as the wound in Mona's arm. With a gesture of regret, I dropped the dress on the bed beside Mona. After that there seemed to be nothing more to say and nothing to do but for us to leave quietly.

Val and I went out the back way. We walked to my car, got in and sat there. I looked at the house and thought of Louise pretending sleep. Bryce passed out from overwork and drink, and Mona practically as good as nailed for murder, and I thought that we were leaving a really fine mess behind us.

Then Val said, surprisingly, "Mona didn't kill him."

I jerked and stared at her. "How do you know?"

"I just *know* Mona didn't kill Vic Gaylord," Val insisted.

"Womanly intuition, hey?" I said sourly. "Very solid stuff, that. Just tell it to the judge and he'll let Mona right off with an apology."

"It's better than that," Val asserted softly. "I see it now. I see the whole thing perfectly clearly."

"Smart girl," I said with weary cynicism. "I don't see a thing. Would you mind spelling it out for me?"

Val stared off into the dawn without answering.

"All right, don't," I muttered. "At this point I am too bushed to care who killed anybody. To me, at this moment, Victor Gaylord seems as far off as Garfield."

I started driving. I drove and turned corners and drove some more. All the while Val sat there with her thoughts humming inside her beautiful head and somehow her silence—so sphinx-like, so eternal, so feminine—threw a chill into me.

CHAPTER NINE

THIS ENTRY written at 5:45 A.M., Wednesday morning, will have to be another quickie. In a few minutes Val and I are going to leave this apartment. I feel there's a fair possibility that I may never see it again—at least not without a steel cuff on my wrist. It wouldn't surprise me too much to find myself writing the last of this record in a snug little cubbyhole in the clink.

When Val and I came in here, not many minutes ago, we found a tired, sober-eyed guy named Ray Ferry waiting for me.

I had just driven Val back from the Elwyns'. Her car was here. I said, "I don't know why the hell I'm suggesting this. But come on up and have a nightcap."

Still thoughtfully silent, Val had come on up, I opened the door for her and we stopped short. Because there in my living room, sitting beside a drink he had mixed for himself, was Detective Ferry in person.

Instantly my thoughts and fears began pin-wheeling. Those bloody clothes in my laundry hamper—had he found them? This record, which I had tucked out of sight inside a magazine between takes—had he found it and read it? Would he ask me to account for myself tonight? There were so many lovely possibilities that I began to feel tried, convicted and sentenced already.

"Come in, Pal," I said to him sourly. "Come right in and have a drink."

Ferry didn't smile. He didn't apologize either. He just said, "Your door was open."

All right. Val had left my door open when hustling out after me, on our way to the Elwyns'. Other doors had been left open tonight and I had taken advantage of a few of them myself. But I still didn't like wondering how long Ferry had been here in my apartment and how much snooping around he had done. That grave look on his face didn't make me feel any happier about it, either.

He put his drink down, stood up and said, "O.K., Trexler, start giving out."

"With what?"

"I understand you can give me certain inside information about the woman who murdered Gaylord."

"You understand that from where?"

"From somebody on the phone. From one of those muffled voices that sometimes rings up a cop and drops a hot tip. This one sounded level. I came right over. So give out, Trexler—about murder."

I didn't get it, couldn't figure why anyone should phone such a tip to Ferry, couldn't figure who it might have been. I was sure of two things about it, however. First, I would not finger any friend of mine. Second, my wisest play was to stay clammed up.

So I shook my head and said, "Sorry, Ferry, but I have nothing to give out about either of them."

Ferry pounced on those last words like a hungry fox hitting a drowsy rabbit. " 'Either of them?' *Either of what?*"

I groaned inwardly again. *That does it, brother!* I had tipped my mitt that time, but good. Because I had unwittingly revealed my knowledge of two murders. The way Ferry had jumped me for that, it meant either that they still didn't know Allene Giles was dead, or, if they did know, then they hadn't given out the news.

Ferry asked sharply, his eyes glinting, "Just what did you mean by that, Trexler?"

"Why," I heard myself muttering. "I meant that I can't give you any inside information about either Gaylord or his murderess."

Ferry shook his head. I wasn't fooling him. He knew it was a revealing slip of the tongue. He instantly grasped its possible meaning. He turned so grim that I, on my part, felt sure that Allene Giles' dead body had not been found. Ferry stood there, peering at me and knowing he faced the job of finding another corpse about which I already knew.

A cruder cop would have begun roughing me up then and there. Ferry was too smart to risk weakening his own case with such tactics. First he had to make sure.

What he needed to clinch it was not more witless babbling from me, but a murder victim. He wasn't a guy to waste time throwing his weight around, either. Abruptly he brushed past me to the door.

"I've been ringing doorbells all night," he said, stopping there. "Those women on my list; you know, the ones who didn't show at the party. From one of them I didn't get an answer. Allene Giles, her name is, I figured she had probably flown the coop, but now I think I'll go back and try her door again."

Val was staring at me.

"Stick around, Trexler," Ferry added. "Understand what I mean?"

We understood each other, all right. I listened to him running down the stairs and knew he would be back soon; and when he came back I could tell myself, *"Trex, kid, this is all there is for you—you've had it."*

Val blurted, "Trex, darling, you look sick."

"Who, me?" I snapped at her. "Why, I never felt better in my life."

Looking hard at her, I told myself that this gal knew something solid. In some way she had it all figured out. This smart cookie had come up with the answer ahead of me. I didn't know how she had done it, but she had. Right now was the time for me to go to work and get it out of her.

But before I could even start, the phone rang.

I fumbled for it and heard a breathy voice saying, "Trex? This is Louise."

I said wryly, "Up early today, aren't you, Louise?"

Val came closer to the phone as Louise went on.

"Is Val still with you?"

"Ah? How did you know—?"

"Of course I know that you and Val were here at the Elwyns' place tonight," Louise broke in quickly. "I know you noticed something—well, something questionable. That's why I'm phoning, I want to explain."

"Go ahead," I said.

"Not over the phone, Trex!" she blurted. "I want to see you and Val personally—and as soon as possible. Will you both meet me in Vic's office as soon as you can get there?"

"Why in Vic's office?"

"Because Vic once told me that in case anything happened to him, I should look in a certain section of his personal file in his office. He said I'd find something very important there. I haven't had a chance before to look, and I want to get there before the crowd starts mobbing in—but I haven't a key. You have one, haven't you, Trex?"

"Yes. All right, Louise. I'm hardly conscious due to lack of sleep, but I'll try to keep from falling on my face first. When you see Val leading a zombie around, that'll be me."

"Right away, Trex," Louise urged. "I'll leave in Mona's car just as fast as I can get dressed. See you there."

The connection clicked off. For a few seconds I hung onto the phone feeling that there was something wrong, with that call, something tricky about it. In some subtle way, I sensed that this murder case was coming to a head now. A killer is still on the prowl and anything can happen. That's why I have taken time to bring this record up to the minute again—just in case.

Val and I are leaving right now for the studio of *Raphael TV*.

CHAPTER TEN

IT'S ALL over. It ended suddenly, yesterday morning, at the *Raphael TV* studio. It wound up with a bang, and corpse No.3 was a very near miss. But there won't be any more murders now. Not in this case.

Immediately after finishing the previous installment of this record, I drove Val out Ashley Road to the studio—neither of us suspecting then that we were heading straight into the big blow-up.

It was a little past dawn when we arrived, but still murky, with a promise of more rain. It wasn't the first time I had arrived for work at the studio this early in the morning. More than once I had found Bryce Elwyn already there. This morning, however, mine was the first car in the parking lot and I unlocked the door on vast, silent darkness.

I snapped switches and bulbs sprang to life among the mad hodge-podge of the stages. More switches lighted the stairs and the hallway in the balcony. I paused at the door of

Victor Gaylord's office, found it locked—by the police, of course—and decided to wait for Louise to arrive before trying to open it. I felt as leaden as the humor of a TV comedian as I escorted Val into my own office.

She had been silent the whole way, with her busy brain buzzing. Now she sat at my desk and went on being wordlessly thoughtful. I rummaged around, found a bottle half full of dark rum, poured a shot into a glass for Val and four or five shots into a bigger glass for me. Then I eyed my beautiful song-warbling girlfriend with the Sherlock Holmes mind and I asked myself, *"Trexler, if this chick can figure it out, why can't you?"*

So, half-dead as I was, I began trying, while we waited for Louise. After trying for half a minute I said the hell with it.

"The only way I can see it," I informed Val, "is Mona."

She sipped her rum.

"'Mona did some planning in advance," I went on. "She wanted to set the scene there in a way that would mislead the cops. She saw a chance to steal some clothes out of somebody's back yard, so she did, and left them in Gaylord's cottage as a teaser. She chose a weapon that would be impossible to trace—there being millions of Boy Scout hatchets in the world, and you don't even have to be a Scout in order to acquire one."

I paused there, puzzled, realizing that this, though it was valid, didn't explain the hatchet completely. There must be more of a reason than that behind the choice. Was it just because violent women seem to have an affinity for hatchets? No; that couldn't be it either. There was something else, some other way of accounting for the choice of a hatchet, but I was too tired to think of it.

"Mona," I mumbled again. "She hasn't a prayer of beating this little murder rap."

"Stop being silly, Trex, darling," Val said impatiently. "I told you, Mona did not kill Vic Gaylord."

"Convince me," I said skeptically. "Go ahead; try to prove it to me."

Val fished up a cigarette and talked while nervously lighting it. "Mona told the truth about that dress. It's not hers. It came out of our wardrobe department, the same as the black cape."

"Sure of that, are you?"

"Yes," Val said flatly. "It was worn in a show week before last by an adagio dancer. The dress got torn like that during the dance, I saw that number on the set at my apartment— and so did you, darling."

It came back to me then. On the screen the dress had looked gray, since we aren't televising color yet. But now that Val had mentioned it, I did remember the tear.

"So answer me this, my fine, groggy lad," Val went on. "Why should Mona wear a prop cape and an adagio dancer's torn dress when dropping in on Vic?"

"Why would any other woman do it, for that matter?" I retorted, "To disguise herself, of course."

"Who from?" Val countered. "Not from Vic. She couldn't, at that close range, and anyway, Vic would stop mattering as soon as he died. So who else would she expect to have, to fool?"

"Anybody who might happen to see her." I wagged my head, again realizing somehow that this must be only a partial answer. "You're being very bright this morning, sugar, but all this celebration of yours doesn't prove anything. I was there—I saw the gal wearing that outfit—and you can't argue with that."

Val crushed her cigarette with quick, tense motions. "It couldn't have been Mona you saw. Why should Mona kill Gaylord anyhow? Because she was jealous of him? That's silly. I've never seen a sign of it and neither have you, Trex. The fact is, Gaylord's death was a bad blow to Mona professionally, a bad upset."

"How?"

"Allene told me about a conference she got wind of last week. A meeting of the top brass of *Raphael TV*. All the big shots there felt that Mona should be dropped next option-time because she was getting to be too unreliable. All of them, that is, except Gaylord. He felt she would snap out of it in time.

"He wanted a chance to talk it over with her first and they deferred to his judgment. Gaylord alone was keeping Mona in and she knew it. She would *never* have killed the man who was helping her in her come-back."

I heard myself muttering, "Why doesn't somebody tell me what goes on around here? All right, you've sold me—"

I stuck to the subject. "So Mona isn't the dame who did the murdering. That means she was right when she said she's been framed. So that means, further, that her story about how she got shot must be true."

Then I blurted, "Hey, wait a minute! Suddenly it's beginning to make sense."

Val didn't comment, didn't even seem to be listening to me. "The real killer has been scrambling like crazy since the murder," I went on quickly, "because of the fact that Gaylord shot and wounded her!"

Val frowned at me, as if wishing I'd shut up.

"I mean this," I persisted. "The killer's plan was simply to walk in, hack Gaylord to death, then leave. She could then frame Mona, since her plan included that, simply by slipping the bloody dress into Mona's closet. Other circumstances, such as Mona's lack of an alibi, would help to pin it on her. That was the original scheme—a straight kill and double-cross. But when Gaylord shot and wounded the killer, it brought an unexpected complication into the picture."

Val said, "Don't you think it's taking Louise too long to get here?"

"The murderess, being smart, knew that the police these days have a lot of slick scientific tricks up their sleeve, in eluding tricks with blood traces and bullets. But that wasn't all. There was also the plain fact that the red dress now had a bullet hole in the left sleeve. This made it necessary for Mona to have a bullet-wound in her left arm, in the same location, because otherwise the frame would not fit.

"This forced the murderess to take the time and trouble to shoot Mona in the arm in an apparently fantastic, unprovable way. That is, she wasn't shot indoors, where the slug would lodge in the floor or a wall—it was done outside so the slug would then be lost in the ground."

"You talk too much, darling," Val said shortly.

So I stopped there for a moment to wonder why the killer had shot me also, in the very same way. I had become so fascinated in all this that I had wakened a little and I was still holding the glass full of rum in my fist, untasted.

. "So you're right," I went on. "Mona is innocent but caught in a mean bad frame. Besides this, you seem to feel just as sure of who is really guilty."

She rose suddenly and began pacing around behind the desk. "I'm in a fine fix, Trex. This could mean a whale of a lot to me. What I know is worth so much that it could buy me anything I might want from this outfit—any contract, any job. It's what I've worked like hell to get and now I've got it within my grasp."

"All yours," I said quietly, "just for keeping clammed up about the identity of the murderess. Fame and fortune based on a little ladylike blackmail. Very fine, very noble."

She turned on me. "Damn it, Trex, you know I couldn't do it at the cost of seeing this thing pinned on Mona. You know Mona and I have never been pals. But I could never stand by and let her take the rap for this, no matter how big it might pay off—I couldn't."

"That's better, Val," I said. "So what are you going to do about it?"

She grew quiet. "I'm going to figure the angles, like a lad I know named Trexler. I mean, as long as Mona stays in circulation, I won't have any reason for sounding off. Will I, Trex?"

"Honey, you don't dare. Getting fancy with a killer is a very good way to get yourself dead. Just letting her know you've tagged her could be fatal." I added. "You'd better take a lesson from Allene. She tried it—and died of it."

Val gasped and stared, *"Allene?"*

"Ferry has found her body by now. I found it earlier this evening. In some way she had learned the killer's identity too."

"But how, Trex? *How?"*

"I don't know how. I think that in some way the realization struck her right here in this office. Maybe it was something said or done that the rest of us didn't even notice. I saw her face a second afterward and it was deathly white; she seemed terrified. That must have been when she suddenly knew. But I still don't know how."

Then from below, from the tangled and gloom-filled depths of the studio, there came the noise of a latch clicking, then a door being shaken by a hand on the knob.

"That must be Louise," Val said quickly. "Didn't you leave the latch open for her?"

"I thought I did, but at this point—"

"I'll let her in."

Val hurried out first and along the hallway. I followed but slowly, the drink still untasted in my hand, my mind still rummaging among my private accumulation of facts and guesses. Some of the things that hadn't made sense before had taken on solid meanings now—for example, the significance of the gunshot wounds. But one thing that was still only half explained was the choice of a hatchet as the weapon of murder.

Silence. That must be part of the answer too. A weapon with a long reach—longer than a knife or an icepick, for example, far more effective than either of them too and faster—and silent. It must have been especially important in some way for the killer to want to do the job as quietly as possible.

And the way she had run right out into the beams of my headlights—that was still a puzzler.

Then I startled myself by coming up with a bright thought, a really spectacular thought, considering my condition. Suppose this killer is different from all other killers in one special way. Another killer might naturally wish to disappear without a trace after doing the job, but suppose this killer *wanted to be seen!*

I was moving automatically, like a sleepwalker, following Val down the stairs with the untasted drink in.my hand.

That supposition started clearing up the picture fast. It showed why the silence of the hatchet was important. Actually Gaylord had fired a shot, but it had not aroused the neighbors—a lucky break for the killer.

The important thing was that the murder should not be discovered immediately, or too soon—because the killer wanted to wait there.

The killer wanted to wait for an opportunity to be seen fleeing the scene!

The killer had waited until a car came along—cars being scarce in that neighborhood at that small hour of the morning.

The first to come along—it was mine—gave the killer the desired chance of being seen. I remembered that surprisingly fast getaway, as if the motor of the waiting car had been left idling. To me it had seemed like an accidental encounter, but every move of it had been in advance.

Why? So that I, an eye-witness, could supply the police with a completely misleading picture—a false picture that would conceal the real murderer's identity and help to nail the frame around Mona Elwyn.

By this time Val and I had reached the bottom of the stairs and were moving toward the door. She was a few steps in front of me when she grasped the knob and pulled the door open. Then, in that instant, the picture I had just been examining in my mind sprang into life again.

She was there again—just outside the door now—the same unforgettable figure that I had first seen running through the beams of my headlights!

CHAPTER ELEVEN

VAL GASPED, shrinking back, and I stared in paralyzed consternation. Again she was wearing a black, hip-length cape with the hood drawn over her head, with one hand clasping it over the lower part of her face so that only her widened eyes showed.

Under that she was wearing some sort of garish dress—not red, this time, but a ghastly green twinkling with sequins. Her legs gleamed in nylons and she was teetering again on those same platform-soled, spike-heeled red sandals.

She had a revolver gripped in her fist—Gaylord's gun, I knew instinctively—and she was pushing it straight at Val.

She fired twice, swiftly. I saw Val's body jerk with the impact of the bullets. The force of them knocked her back against me. She groaned with shock and her breathing went jerky. For a fraction of a second the killer paused to make sure that the bullets had hit her. Then the gun lifted a little again to signal that more bullets were coming, that Val was meant to die then and there.

My response was crazy, instinctive and ineffectual—except that it sent the next two bullets wild. I simply dashed out my glass, sent rum flying. Not much of it landed, but at least it forced the killer to duck aside and that motion sent the next bullets wide of Val.

She was sliding down against me. I was making a groping effort to hold her up—and then that hideous figure in the cape hurled the gun. It came whizzing from that deadly hand straight at my face. I ducked, but not fast enough. The steel slammed over my left eye and I went down backward, hard, with Val sprawled over my legs.

When the world stopped rocking there was no sound. If the killer had come in a car, it was gone again now. I hadn't half a thought of giving chase anyhow.

"Val—Val!"

I got my legs out from under her—she was a limp, dead weight—and twisted myself around. Two of the bullets had hit her. She could die of those wounds—one under the collarbone and one by the ribs—unless she got help fast.

Somehow I had enough sense to leave her right there where she had fallen. I scrambled up the stairs, into the nearest open office and used the phone. I called for an ambulance, making very clear exactly where it should come. Then, as I started down the stairs again, I heard a car pulling into the parking lot, closely followed by a second.

I was bending over Val, checking her pulse, when the door opened. Not until then did I notice that the vision in my left eye was dancing fantastically. That was the eye the hurled gun had very narrowly missed. Several seconds passed before I could recognize the man who came in. It was Ray Ferry.

He stared down at me, hard-faced, saying nothing.

"I know how it looks," I snapped out at him. "It looks like I'm the guy who killed Gaylord, then Val found it out and I just now tried to shut her up. There's Gaylord's gun on the floor to back up your theory. Only that's not how it is." Then I added in what sounded like a snarl.

"If you touch her before the ambulance gets here. I'll cut you down to size!"

Ferry just nodded. His face stayed rock-hard and he kept staring at me. Then the door opened again and this time it was Bryce Elywn who came in. He stopped short, staring down at Val. Then he hurried over for a closer look. His face turned ashen, he closed his eyes and turned away and for a second I thought he was going to be sick on the floor.

"This is going to be too bad for a killer," I heard myself saying next. "Because Val isn't dead. And she's not going to die. She's going to live to tell what she knows." Then, feeling dizzily amazed at myself, I heard my voice saying, "But we won't have to wait that long. Let's finish it up right here and now."

Ferry stepped closer. Bryce turned back, his eyes watery behind his glasses, his face expressing utter weariness.

"Louise isn't really coming," I said. "That phone call of hers was just an invitation to Val and me to walk into a trap and get carried out dead. I know now when it became necessary to kill us. Louise was awake, of course, when we left your place this morning—awake and watching us. Val sat beside me in my car and said right out loud that she knew the answer, "and Louise heard it, which meant more killings to be done."

Ferry asked suddenly, "Where is she now?"

I shrugged. "Still back at the Elwyns', I suppose. That doesn't matter. Louise hasn't committed any murders, at least not personally. She was a party to the plan of course but they weren't her hands that got bloody."

Part of me was listening for the first bong of the approaching ambulance. No sign of it so far.

"Val's getting shot up seems to have made me a bright boy all of a sudden," I went on bitterly. "I can even figure out how Allene tumbled to the truth. A few minutes ago I couldn't, but now I can."

Bryce gazed at me with his shoulders drooping, his eyes dull.

"There in my office yesterday morning, Allene was standing back against the wall. You were standing in front of her, Bryce, at my desk. Barrett had come in, the hail fellow, the back-slapper. He whacked my arm, here, over my wound. I almost blacked out with pain and I was terrified that it would start bleeding. He did exactly the same thing to you, Bryce—same arm, same spot.

"A second later Allene, behind you, was looking deathly pale and scared. Because, just before you rolled your shirt-sleeve down, she saw the blood trickling down to your elbow. My wound hadn't bled, but yours had, and you didn't cover it quite fast enough to keep Allene from seeing the fresh running blood."

I stepped forward, one hand raised for a blow, and said, "Shall we try it again, Bryce, just to show Ferry how it works?"

Bryce's fist smashed at me. He attempted to whirl away and bumped headlong into Ferry moving up. I dove in from the side. For half a minute it was a crazy struggle between the three of us. Ferry and I between us forced him to the floor. Then we pulled at his coat and his shirt and bared it— the bandaged wound on his upper, left arm, in exactly the same position as Mona's and mine.

But it was something else that really clinched it. While Bryce lay pinned to the floor, I lifted his feet and pulled up his pant-leg. He was wearing a pair of full-length smoke-colored nylon stockings.

Somewhere down the road an ambulance bell was bonging. Val, still huddling on the floor, had begun to sob. I went to her and bent low. She hooked one arm around my neck.

"Take me away from this, Trex, darling," she choked out. "Please marry me, Trex. Please make me be a quiet little homebody. Please, Trex."

I thought to myself that this gal was plenty delirious, all right.

When Ferry staged that scene again, under the same conditions, it was a pretty ghastly thing.

He put my car down the block in the street behind Gaylord's. Dark it was, headlights on. Then he stood Bryce Elwyn in the headlight beams, just as I had first seen him. Black cape—at least a dozen more was in the wardroom room—adagio dancer's torn dress, nylons again and those red sandals we'd found in the trunk of his car. Now we could see his feet straining the straps and bulging over the platform soles—but those thick soles left small prints regardless.

It was so easy to check back now and see how Bryce had planned it in advance. The dead girl's clothes stolen from the line, for example. The other stuff filched from the wardrobe department of *Raphael TV* because he was too large to wear one of Mona's dresses, which, of course, he would have preferred to do.

Sending Louise to Chicago, also, so she would have a perfect alibi. Planning it so that Louise's husband and Bryce's wife were both eliminated, thereby bringing Louise and Bryce together in a fine, enduring union based on murder and a double-cross.

The timing also. That night, when he had phoned me at the studio just before two A.M., he had called from Gaylord's cottage, even then in costume. Unwittingly, during that call, I had said I would leave in a few more minutes, and that had been his cue to get set to stage his carefully planned scene of the fleeing murderess.

Easy to see now, also, why Louise chose to go into seclusion at the Elwyns'. It was Bryce talking to her when Val and I barged in, forcing him out a window, then over into his study, where he had convincingly faked a picture of a sleeping, exhausted man.

As to why he had shot me, as well as Mona—that was in case the cops learned that the killer was a man.

"I'd like to mention," Ferry said as we finished that demonstration in the dark street behind Gaylord's, "that nobody actually phoned me a hot tip that you knew the murderer's name. That was just a way I took to pry you open. It paid off, too." He grinned, then grew sober and added, "Don't ever do this again, Trexler."

"Brother," I assured him, "that's for sure!"

Then I went over to the hospital where Val was doing beautifully and looking beautiful too.

"I can't believe it," I said. "Such a luscious woman with such a pretty voice and such a fine brain, too. Very smart about figuring out things such as careers and murders. You haven't told me how you doped out the murder thing?"

"I guess being a woman helped some," Val answered. "See, it went like this. It seemed to be a crime of jealousy, but that appearance was faked. So it had to be a practical murder, one done for gain.

"The gain had to come through Louise's shares in *Raphael TV*. That inevitably meant a man. Since it wasn't you, it had to be some other man in about your position, such as Bryce. And since it was Bryce's wife who was being framed, the whole thing became very clear."

"It seems too simple now," I said. "One other thing. This is something you mentioned the other morning. Now's your chance to take it back. You were all shot up when you said it, and out of your head, so I won't hold you to it. About marrying me, I mean."

Val smiled enchantingly and said, "But Trex, darling, I've always been a woman of my word and I love you very much for bringing me to my senses. If you'll just lean over this way a little, I'll prove it."

As I mentioned at the beginning, when you start messing around with murder it can lead to the darnedest things.

THE END

If you've enjoyed this book, you will not want to miss these terrific titles...

ARMCHAIR SCI-FI & MYSTERY CLASSICS, $12.95 each

C-40 **MODEL FOR MURDER**
by Stephen Marlowe

C-41 **PRELUDE TO MURDER**
by Sterling Noel

C-42 **DEAD WEIGHT**
by Frank Kane

C-43 **A DAME CALLED MURDER**
by Milton Ozaki

C-44 **THE GREATEST ADVENTURE**
by John Taine

C-45 **THE EXILE OF TIME**
by Ray Cummings

C-46 **STORM OVER WARLOCK**
by Andre Norton

C-47 **MAN OF MANY MINDS**
by E. Everett Evans

C-48 **THE GODS OF MARS**
by Edgar Rice Burroughs

C-49 **BRIGANDS OF THE MOON**
by Ray Cummings

C-50 **SPACE HOUNDS OF IPC**
by E. E. "Doc" Smith

C-51 **THE LANI PEOPLE**
J. F. Bone

C-52 **THE MOON POOL**
by A. Merritt

C-53 **IN THE DAYS OF THE COMET**
by H. G. Wells

C-54 **TRIPLANETARY**
C. C. Doc Smith

If you've enjoyed this book, you will not want to miss these terrific titles…